PORCUPINES

PORCUPINES

a novel

FRAN FABRICZKI

FIG TREE
an imprint of
PENGUIN BOOKS

FIG TREE

UK | USA | Canada | Ireland | Australia
India | New Zealand | South Africa

Fig Tree is part of the Penguin Random House group of companies
whose addresses can be found at global.penguinrandomhouse.com

Penguin Random House UK,
One Embassy Gardens, 8 Viaduct Gardens, London SW11 7BW

penguin.co.uk

First published in the United States of America by Summit Books,
an imprint of Simon & Schuster, LLC 2026
First published in Great Britain by Fig Tree 2026
001

Copyright © Franciska Fabriczki, 2026

The moral right of the author has been asserted

Penguin Random House values and supports copyright.
Copyright fuels creativity, encourages diverse voices, promotes freedom
of expression and supports a vibrant culture. Thank you for purchasing
an authorized edition of this book and for respecting intellectual property
laws by not reproducing, scanning or distributing any part of it by any
means without permission. You are supporting authors and enabling
Penguin Random House to continue to publish books for everyone.
No part of this book may be used or reproduced in any manner for the
purpose of training artificial intelligence technologies or systems. In accordance
with Article 4(3) of the DSM Directive 2019/790, Penguin Random House
expressly reserves this work from the text and data mining exception

Printed and bound in Great Britain by Clays Ltd, Elcograf S.p.A.

The authorized representative in the EEA is Penguin Random House Ireland,
Morrison Chambers, 32 Nassau Street, Dublin D02 YH68

A CIP catalogue record for this book is available from the British Library

HARDBACK ISBN: 978–0–241–74167–2
TRADE PAPERBACK ISBN: 978–0–241–74168–9

Penguin Random House is committed to a sustainable future
for our business, our readers and our planet. This book is made from
Forest Stewardship Council® certified paper.

*To my mom, for believing I could,
and to Adam, for asking me to prove it.*

If this is the best of all possible worlds, what then are the others?

VOLTAIRE, *Candide*

There's been a load of compromisin'
On the road to my horizon.

GLEN CAMPBELL, "Rhinestone Cowboy"

PART I

Los Angeles, 1996

WHAT MILA'S MOTHER TELLS HER ON THE FIRST DAY OF SCHOOL is different from what other mothers of children at Mount Washington Elementary School are saying at the very same time to their very own six-year-old children. This is almost certainly a fact. But it is not for Mila to know the difference. That will come later: at bars while forming new intimacies over tepid beer; at her therapist's office, divulging childhood stories with little prompting; or perhaps in self-serious short stories sagging with the weight of too many metaphors. For now, though, she is unaware of any oddity in her mother's behaviour. Sonia leans down and holds Mila's shoulders as though afraid she might fall backwards from the burden of her backpack (a not entirely unfounded fear—children's backpacks never do seem proportionate to their small frames).

She looks Mila in the eye and says, "Now, remember, Mila, we live about a five-minute drive away, your mother works at an office, and you're not Russian, your mother just liked the sound of your name."

Mila nods vigorously—a model pupil, for now, at least.

"Any follow-up questions, then what do we say?"

"Mind your own business."

"That's right."

Sonia straightens up and takes out a mirror from the little purse hanging on her shoulder. She refreshes her lipstick with a satisfied smack and kisses Mila's left cheek, leaving a perfectly formed imprint of herself on the child.

"Off you go," she says to Mila with a wink, turning her towards the flat, terra-cotta bungalows of the school.

And so begins Mila's instruction—or indoctrination, perhaps—in the American way of life. Soon she will be made aware of the market economy of the playground, where her measly Lunchables will provide paltry currency; she will realise the income inequality inherent in one's possession or lack of crayons that smell of fruits; and, most important, she will come to understand that her place in the pecking order of this society in miniature was long decided by the mothers and fathers who dropped off their children at the gate and eyed Sonia with suspicion as she made her way to her car trailing the scent of lemongrass and foreignness.

Budapest, 1989

THE FIRST TIME IT OCCURRED TO SZONJA TO GO TO THE UNITED States, tears streamed down her face while George H. W. Bush made a speech. It was July, and she was watching him on a small grey television set in her parents' living room in the suburbs of Budapest.

"What in the world is so funny?" her father asked her, but Szonja's breaths were coming in small hiccoughs as her shoulders shook—she tried to subdue her mirth, but it was proving to be obstinate. She knew he would work himself up into a sullen anger if she continued for long—her father did have a sense of humour, but it was mostly revealed in the moments immediately following his own witticisms—and yet she couldn't help it.

The president of the United States had just arrived in Budapest and come straight to Kossuth Square to speak in front of a crowd that had awaited him patiently in the rain, their reward being the first glimpse of the American man. For him, this was a flyover visit, hastily tacked onto a more important one to Poland; for them, it was a sign of change, a little shard of light bouncing off a single sequin that made up the glittering West. For Szonja, it was the evening's entertainment on a humid summer night, her only options being a half-hearted outing with friends or stewing in the quiet frustration of her parents' waning marriage.

Szonja's father was a retired diplomat, something she would eventually learn not to mention to new acquaintances—it created some confusion. The word *diplomat* arouses ideas of a glamourous cosmopolitanism in the minds of people outside the Eastern Bloc, and no amount of insistence that a diplomat in socialist Hungary could be an ordinary government position, underpaid and tedious like any other, will disabuse them of the notion. It was true that the Imre children were rich in education and experience, having lived in five different countries within fifteen years, but it was also true that when they returned home to Budapest, the money saved from a government salary over these years amounted only to a small deposit on a two-bed flat in the suburbs. Which is where Szonja still resided at the age of eighteen, recently released from the clutches of an indifferent high-school education, working odd jobs and saving up for a revolving door of life-changing schemes, all yet to be actualised.

On the screen Bush had just taken the podium after fifteen minutes of homilies by the Hungarian head of state, Brunó Straub. The American president dismissed an umbrella politely placed over his head and, with apparent disdain for all the bureaucrats standing around him, barked out, "Is anybody gonna translate this?" His attitude—so incongruous with the respectful officiousness surrounding him—was enough to set off Szonja's laughter, but then, as though he were in the closing scene of one of his country's great movies, he tore up the large white index cards of his speech and promised to speak only from the heart. The crowd cheered while, out of sight, some poor translator fumbled with his own notes, unprepared for this show of spontaneity. Bush called over to him, off-screen: "Tear that thing up!" Szonja's English was good enough to understand the president's slow, chewy American words, and the crowd could at least understand his Hollywood gestures—oh, but that poor, underpaid translator. He began to chase the president's sentences like a clumsy echo.

"You've been out here in the rain for too long, but Barbara and I feel the warmth of this welcome."

"*Nevertheless the feeling of the warm—*"

"And the rain doesn't make a darn bit of difference. We feel at home right here in this great capital."

"*The rain doesn't stop at all, in the love and the wel—*"

"And I salute the leaders of Hungary, and I salute the reforms and the change that is taking place in this wonderful country."

"*I say hello to all the leaders, hello to all the people, and hello to all the reforms that are—*"

"And I want you to know that I am here as president of the United States because we have in our country a special affection and feeling for the people of Hungary."

"*The reason I come here as president is that I have separate warm feelings—*"

"So thank you very much for this welcome, you'll have to listen to me again tomorrow, I'm sure at some dryer time and place."

"*Thank you for your welcome and I hope tomorrow you will hear of a dryer place—*"

"Thank you. God bless you, and God bless your great country!"

By the end of it, Szonja's mother had the giggles as well, though hers were more timid and as respectful as giggles could be.

"Don't know what you two find so funny about this—for better or worse, it's a historic moment, you'll be glad to have witnessed it someday."

"Oh, I'm perfectly happy to have witnessed it already," Szonja said, flipping through a magazine lying between her legs on the floor. She tried to keep the tone light, careful not to prompt one of her father's increasingly frequent bouts of quiet discontent, which, though muted, somehow still managed to fill the whole room. Mr. Imre had the diplomat's habit of reticence; he would rarely give voice to his grievances, but privately he viewed with increasing discomfort his country turning, little by little, from all that he had been told to believe and uphold his entire life. There was a bitterness even to his silences now.

And then there were other, more private resentments. As she looked up at her parents, it occurred to Szonja how deftly the both of them skirted around what was on all of their minds—this vision from the West must surely have reminded them of Rina. Had she, after five years spent in America, adopted their outsized gestures? When her sister spoke English, was it with their voice, projected above all others? Did she share their president's "special affection" for this forgotten chip off the Eastern Bloc?

Before Rina set her heart on marriage that heart belonged to something else entirely—something with a lot more synthesisers and simple chord progressions. At least that's how Szonja saw it when she remembered their nights spent under the spell of the Pet Shop Boys, Boy George, George Michael (the word association between these artists was incidental yet somehow made their enjoyment feel inevitable). Side by side, they strained to hear the tinny sound of Rina's secondhand cassette player and wrote out the lyrics in a notebook for closer scrutiny.

Szonja and Rina hadn't always been friends as well as sisters—there was a six-year gap between them, which, depending on their respective ages, meant that they had either everything or nothing in common. When Rina was six and Szonja was a baby, one had newly joined the choir at school while the other was testing out her vocal cords in an entirely different way. When Rina was thirteen and Szonja was seven, they played together nicely, but only a few months later, puberty hit, and Szonja was left to hold up both sides of her dolls' conversation (this particular skill would remain useful later on in life, when assaulted with tedious company). At twenty and fourteen, during the mild spring of their first months stationed in Washington, DC, they both briefly had the right combination of patience, enjoyment of popular music and interest in each other to spend hours in their shared bedroom talking and listening to their collection of tapes.

Now, as Szonja prepared to visit her sister in America, this was the place her thoughts lingered, despite the letters and occasional phone calls that had detailed moves, jobs, the birth of two daughters—a whole new image of her sister over the past five years—because it was the last time they had been close, sure, but also because it was the first time Szonja became conscious of her sister having a specific, distinct personality—one that was not simply defined as part of their family quartet, but in all the ways she stood in relief against them. Rina was studious, unlike Szonja; she was passionate, unlike their mother; and she was compassionate, unlike their father. And the more that Szonja had seen her sister as something separate from herself, the more she had wanted to join her on the other side of that difference—in her interests, her manners, her choice of words. And briefly, it seemed, Rina did not mind her mimicry.

Yet, like all their other fleeting moments of alliance, this was sure to end—Szonja had seen the signs when Rina met Aron, a young man more sombre and studious than Rina herself who had bent Rina's interests just enough to be a branch out of reach for Szonja.

In the end it was Szonja who had stopped searching for Rina's company, leaving her to long walks and murmured discussions with this boy they knew little of. It was always easier to be the one who left—she had learned this at the age of seven, sitting among a cluster of plastic friends, talking to herself.

Los Angeles, 2001

Between the Taco Fiesta and the Winchell's Donut House at the far end of the Albertsons parking lot sits Mateo and his fruit cart. The modest locale doesn't fool anyone—he is a master of the blades, slipping the skin off mangoes, slicing them up so fast that not a drop of their sweet juice leaves the flesh before it can make it to his customers.

"Con chile y limón, por favor."

Mateo smiles without looking up—there's no need to ask for it, but Sonia likes to practise her Spanish. It feels closer to her mother tongue than English, all the syllables sounded out without mystery. She asks for a bag of sliced, salted cucumbers as well, and she eats them slowly with a plastic fork as she sits sideways in the driver's seat of the car, legs dangling towards the warm pavement.

Sonia worries that this might be her favourite part of the week, sitting here after her grocery shopping, before school pickup. She loves the store too. It's bright and spacious and she could spend hours leaning over her cart, looking up and down the infinite, colourful rows of shelves. There is something sturdy about it all, something that makes her think the world is bountiful, and she's destined to take her share. And then, afterwards, there's Mateo: his smile, his mangoes, chile y limón.

The sound of Sonia's cell phone—one note at a time cutting through the air—interrupts their quietude. It's Mila's school, asking Sonia to come in.

Under the vivid midafternoon sun Sonia glides into the school parking lot. She can immediately spot her daughter—little frame perched on the thin slab of the curb, her legs pretzeled in front of her. She is looking resolutely ahead, a small sign of petulance Sonia has come to recognise in her of late. Mr. Alvarez, the vice principal, is hovering nearby, neither close enough nor far enough for comfort. He is the one who called Sonia into school a full hour before the kids are normally out.

"Here we go," she says, sliding the station wagon between faded white paint, rolling her shoulders back and putting on a smile. As soon as Mila spots her, she gathers her little chopstick legs, makes for her mother and burrows into her midsection so that Sonia is immobilised.

"Rough day, Milosh?"

She tries to swivel the both of them back towards the car, but Mr. Alvarez calls out to her. "Just a moment, Ms. Imre!"

Despite the balmy ninety-six-degree weather, Mr. Alvarez is dressed as though he imagines himself to be teaching at a New England boarding school (in fact, he is currently accruing delay charges at Blockbuster for his late return of *Dead Poets Society*—$8.97 and counting) rather than a public school in the suburbs of Northeast Los Angeles. All three-piece suit and polished loafers, checked tie in brown hues.

"I must inform you of a little situation in Mila's class today," he begins, his mournful brown eyes glancing at Sonia from under heavy lids.

"You mean the reason my daughter is currently digging her way into my side?" she says, smiling sweetly. "Honey, go wait in the car, would you? I'll be right there."

After Mila is safely in the Buick, Mr. Alvarez clears his throat. "As you know, the children in the lower grades are preparing for the annual father-daughter picnic." He looks at Sonia apologetically, but Sonia meets his gaze with an amused lift of the eyebrows. "Yes, well, it seems that Mila was reluctant to take part in the preparations. The children were making some artwork today: paintings, collages, macaroni portraits, that sort of thing."

Poor Mr. Alvarez—to be possessed of a PhD in education and still have to use the term *macaroni portrait* on a regular basis.

"In short, it seems one of Mila's classmates . . . er . . . pondered the question of Mila's parentage aloud in class."

"What a lovely, curious child."

"Yes, well, it seems Mila's answer was—and these are her words, of course—well, what she told her class was, in short, something along the lines of 'My mother says my father was a good time.'"

It is probably true—Sonia has a vague memory of making such an offhand comment. If the Los Angeles sun does not make Mr. Alvarez regret his sartorial decisions today, this conversation certainly does—sweat is prickling at his starched white collar.

"I see," she says with as much dignity as anyone can be expected to muster. "Still, I'm not sure what this has to do with my daughter being sent home early."

"As you can imagine, Mrs. Flores was somewhat flustered by the . . . um . . . implications of the statement."

"Yes, well, I've met Mr. Flores . . ."

Mr. Alvarez makes a curious noise then—"Ha-ah"—as though

he is letting out a laugh in one breath and reeling it back in with the next.

"Mrs. Flores did her best to manage the situation. Of course, there are many single parents at Mount Washington Elementary School, and we don't want to exclude anyone from class activities," he says, slipping into the register of a flimsy guidance councillor pamphlet. "She told Mila to make her portrait of someone she considered a father figure. And now, this is very flattering, of course, but it seems she chose to make a portrait of me."

Mr. Alvarez rifles through a folder replete with images of various men. A few paintings are quite accomplished; the ones rendered in complex carbohydrates less so. He finally presents Sonia with a piece of card stock—on it a clumsy but unmistakable replica of Mr. Alvarez collaged from the cut-up pieces of a colourful magazine. Underneath, in block letters that look vaguely like a ransom note, it reads *My Daddy*. He looks at Sonia uncertainly, as if to contemplate the possibility of this—never mind that the sum total of words exchanged between them has only recently doubled with their current conversation.

"Oh, I'm sorry," she says, taking the picture from him. "Did that make you uncomfortable?"

"Well, that part, really, is absolutely fine, and it's actually quite normal for a child her age to see someone on the pedagogical staff as a sort of father figure, but I'm afraid it went a little further than that."

Sonia looks over at the car, where Mila is now swaying her head gently to some music they can't hear. "Did she ask you for pocket money?"

"Excuse me?"

"Nothing, just a little joke."

Mr. Alvarez pulls a little at the shirtsleeves under his suit jacket.

"The thing is, once she had made the portrait, she seemed very convinced that this was in fact . . . a fact."

"That you are her . . . ?" Sonia looks at the portrait and can't help but smile. "Daddy? Dr. Alvarez—"

"Please, Mr. Alvarez is fine," he says with a proud little smile that somewhat negates the request.

"Mr. Alvarez, I know you must meet a lot of delusional parents every day. Parents who think their kid is going to be on the Olympic team for trampolining, first violinist in the Berlin Philharmonic, or, you know, best at something or other they had once wanted to be good at themselves. But trust me when I say my daughter has a decent amount of intelligence. At least, enough to prevent her from believing that the vice principal at her school is actually her father."

"Oh, I'm sure she's a very smart girl, as of course are you . . ."

"A smart girl?"

"An intelligent human, I mean. Both very intelligent, I'm sure. It's just that, during the lunch break, Mila told some of her classmates that I *am* in fact her father. She spun quite a story."

Sonia tries to hide her surprise at this piece of information and gives silent thanks for the oversized sunglasses that hide most of her face. Sure, Mila has a healthy imagination, but Sonia has also known her daughter to have an outsized sense of integrity; she often expresses discomfort at Sonia's somewhat elastic handling of the factual, which, all in all, makes this an unlikely scenario. "Well, imagination is encouraged, is it not? You said it yourself, she told a story."

"Yes, but—"

"Great, so she's followed her teacher's advice, she's made her portrait, she's participated in class activities, she's socialised in her breaks, and on top of that, she's practised her storytelling skills.

Seems to me you all are doing a beautiful job here at Mount Washington, and Mila is doing wonderfully."

"Well, thank you—"

"Now, if you don't mind, I'm going to use this little extra time you've so kindly gifted us and beat the afternoon traffic. You have yourself a terrific day, Mr. Alvarez."

There are not many rules between Sonia and Mila in their household of two. However, Mila knows there are a few questions it is best not to ask her mother, among them *Why do you smoke?* and variations thereof, such as *When will you quit smoking?* as well as comments that imply a question or remonstrance; for instance, *Megan's dad says smoking makes your teeth fall out. What's for dinner?* is equally important to avoid unless Mila wants to be reminded that she is a big girl who can toast her own Bagel Bites.

She has also been careful to avoid the question of their cultural heritage, ever since her mother sent her into school on International Food Day with a container of rice and peas—*rizibizi*, it was called back home, Sonia had said, but the reduplicative rhyme did little to mask the fact that rice and peas are hardly a Hungarian specialty or even vaguely Eastern European. When Mila's third-grade teacher probed the topic, with her hand uncertainly clasped on the Tupperware container and its lacklustre, culturally unspecific contents, Sonia had looked Mrs. Harmon in the eye, put a hand to her chest and said, "That's offensive," with a menacing kind of deliberation. No one went near the subject again, not even Mila.

The most important question to avoid, though, is undoubtedly *Who is my father?*. Variations on that theme are equally unwelcome:

PORCUPINES

Where is my father?, *Does every child come from two parents?*, *Kelly says I look a lot like Mr. Zapata*, et cetera.

But apart from these, it must be stated that Sonia will answer almost any question with an admirable amount of composure—she reminds Mila constantly that she can ask her anything, and when no particular questions are forthcoming, she provides her own and then answers them at length herself, a Socratic monologue on topics ranging from why unscented lotion is the best (it doesn't mingle with your perfume) to how contraception works (it's never too early to be informed).

With all this in mind, Sonia is fairly certain that the child in her back seat mournfully staring out of the window as though she were in a music video is making a statement. Sonia would have it out with her, but beside her in the passenger seat, holding a leather case between knees that knock against the glove compartment, is Simon, Mila's violin teacher, whom they've picked up along the way. Simon is a teenage prodigy who has agreed to give Mila lessons at the pool, straight after her swim practice, doing his homework by the changing rooms as he waits, so that Sonia doesn't have to suffer freeway traffic in another direction. Every Tuesday, Mila stands at the bottom of the empty bleachers, still dripping water onto the hot concrete, telescopic music stand and gangly violin teacher before her, while the older kids go through their drills in the pool. The two of them sometimes remind Sonia of the musicians on the *Titanic*, playing with studied indifference while water sloshes all around them. Mila's coach tried to ask them to leave once, but Sonia pretended not to speak English, a charade she has since forgotten to keep up, but WASPy politeness thankfully prevents further questioning.

Simon's stomach grumbles, and he sneaks a look at Sonia

hopefully. She hands him a bag from Winchell's, glances at Mila in the rearview mirror and turns up the radio.

The fallacy isn't unique to their relationship but it is no less true that Sonia believes she knows what is going on in her daughter's life. Some days she is consumed by the weight of all the knowledge: of permission slips, of appointments, of hurt feelings and of favourite songs. However, unbeknownst to Sonia, a little wedge of mystery inserted itself into their lives two days, four hours and thirteen minutes ago, when Mila started the computer languishing in a corner of their living room.

As the dial tone gasped and spluttered in its effort to connect their desktop computer with the World Wide Web, Mila absently munched on a tuna sandwich—not the most auspicious moment to begin with, but you never know what kind of sandwich you'll be holding when life decides to take a turn, and something had to fill the interminable waiting time. Their old secondhand desktop had seemed bewildered when they'd installed AOL on it a couple of years ago—like an old dog whose owner suddenly decided to dress it up in a knitted sweater, it froze in confusion and blinked in incomprehension, for things had been comfortable the way they were before.

Sonia had signed up for and then unsubscribed from a slew of newsletters, and Mila entertained herself for an afternoon looking up the biographies of her favourite monarchs. (As well as being a member of the orchestra, she was head of the school's history club, a regular contributor to its poetry anthology and treasurer of the student council.) But after this initial burst of excitement, they mostly disregarded the wonders of the internet. That is, until

PORCUPINES

Mila signed on that day in search of information on the Russian composer Dmitry Shostakovich and found instead Sonia's personal email account. Now, Mila was old enough to have some vague understanding of the concept of privacy—certainly she understood the use of the term when she wanted to sulk in her room behind closed doors—but that understanding was outmatched by a budding sense of curiosity about her mother, especially the parts of her mother's life that weren't readily shared with her. Which was why she found her hand, almost of its own accord, clicking through Sonia's inbox.

Sonia's early emails would paint a bleak portrait of her life, as anyone's early emails certainly would, but in among the eBay purchases and PTA newsletters, Mila found something she did not realise she'd been looking for.

The email was from a man named Anthony. Mila considered briefly whether he was some adult version of a pen pal. Her class had been encouraged in the third grade to practise their handwriting by trading letters with their sister school in Zanesville, Ohio—this had led to a few desultory exchanges between Mila and a boy called Quentin who collected rocks but did not, on the whole, seem to be worth the effort. (Quentin himself rather enjoyed their back-and-forth and felt the loss of a sympathetic ear keenly—it wouldn't be for another couple of years that he found someone who took even a passing interest in amateur geology.) Anthony's letters (much like Quentin's) were lengthy, and although Mila did not fully understand certain turns of phrase, she took away a few salient points from her reading: This man lived in San Francisco, he'd known her mother before Mila was born and there was almost certainly something between them. So, really, it was about time her mother start coughing up some answers.

When Sonia finds that Mila's defiant expression is still resolutely in place after an hour of swimming and an hour practising scales under the rafters—two things that, despite sounding like the antithesis of a good time to Sonia, do tend to cheer her daughter up—she decides to change tack.

"How about a drive-through tour?"

Mila wants to hold on to her sulk, really roll around in it—she's only recently discovered the joys of self-pity, and she's testing the bounds of its indulgence. Yet all the exercise—of both her body and mind—has made her hungry, so she relents. "Just the sides?"

"*All* the sides."

Like many traditions, the drive-through tour comes from a combination of necessity and unanticipated enjoyment. In Sonia and Mila's case, it started when they were still living in Eagle Rock and Sonia worked downtown, as a way to make an otherwise boring commute more interesting and trick their stomachs into satedness. They drove right through the middle of Los Angeles, past a carnival of fast-food signs on stilts, stopped at drive-throughs and ordered only the cheapest sides. They would ask for extra condiments, which no self-respecting American fast-food chain would deny them, and the array of bright, colourful packets created a sense of cheerfulness and plenty.

Today, they stop at Jack in the Box first, where they get curly fries that are too hot and will be just about edible by the time they get the rest; then they stop at the Taco Bell on Colorado Boulevard, where they get a cheese roll-up each; at the Carl's Jr. for jalapeño poppers; and finally, in the homestretch, they see the FRESH sign on the Krispy Kreme drive-through illuminated, so they stop for a single glazed doughnut each.

Sonia doesn't drive towards home, though—it takes Mila a few seconds to realise they're going in the wrong direction, but she doesn't say anything. They drive up a sloping road that passes right over the Wiltingdon Golf Club. Sonia pulls over at a dirt turn-out and backs the car up so that when they sit in the trunk, they can see over the little hillock, down to the toy soldier–size golfers. Mila looks uncertainly at the men and women below them, gauging whether they can see her as well as she can see them.

"What are you doing?" she asks her mother as Sonia opens up the bags and spreads the food around them. "I don't think we're allowed to be here."

"Don't be embarrassed by your mother, Mila—remember, the worse I act, the better people will think of you. They'll say, 'Wow, how did that smart, well-adjusted young lady come from that?'"

Mila considers this. "Or they'll think I'm adopted."

"Hey, either way works. But I have to say, you've inherited my disproportionately small forehead, so unless micro-bangs come back into fashion, nature's gonna give you away."

Mila takes her hair and brushes it in front of her face, flattening it against her forehead.

"Yes, my other suggestion was going to be the Cousin Itt look, but you're one step ahead of me." Sonia worries that her voice betrays a forced cheerfulness, but she is relieved when a fraction of a smile breaks across Mila's face as she begins to unfold the wax paper of her cheese roll-up.

Below them, the light thwack of golf balls lends a rhythm to the silence; the manicured landscape of the course is a gentle pattern, the literal definition of easy on the eyes. Sonia takes a breath and thinks, *I have fed her, and I have loved her*, and for now, that feels like enough.

For some time, they sit in silence at their tailgate for two, both wanting to ask the other something, but neither wanting to disturb the equanimity of the moment—many an important discussion has gone to the conversational graveyard in such a manner. And yet people continue the grand tradition of assumptions and misconstrued subtext when a simple question would clarify. But what fun would life be if you didn't create your own hurdles?

Los Angeles, 1989

Los Angeles was literally brighter than anywhere Szonja had ever been—the light beamed down and burst through the streets, through the sprawling, flat landscape, and when she closed her eyes it lit up the veins in her eyelids like an X-ray. Beneath the palm trees, squat buildings bore advertisements and signs—always hustling, shifting, shucking. The city had never known the words *elegance* or *restraint*; never seen a flat surface it didn't want to use for some commercial enticement. As first impressions go, Los Angeles struck Szonja as (a) sunny and (b) litigious—1-800-SUE-HIM, 1-800-CLAIM-IT, 1-800-THEY'LL-PAY-FOR-SERVING-YOU-TOO-HOT-COFFEE. The advertisements on benches and billboards were accompanied by images of either aggrieved-looking middle-aged women with expressions that seemed to indicate a toothache or tanned smiling men with unnervingly straight teeth. (Whichever way you sliced it, teeth seemed to be a crucial element of the American way of life.) All of it crude and graceless, and yet, as they floated along the concrete river in her sister's Subaru, winding their way from LAX, the seats warmed by the unceasing heat, tires taut, rolling smoothly over pavement, it all lulled Szonja into a sense of overwhelming contentment.

Perhaps it also contributed to her serenity that she no longer had to listen to her parents' sighs as they moved around their apartment in Budapest. It had been years since she had seen her parents united in such a way, although she would have preferred their moment of concord to be about something other than their dissatisfaction with her. Of course, even in this brief harmony, their sighs had different meanings—her mother's delicate suspiration said *Don't leave me alone with him*, while her father's intermittent groans said *Just like your sister*.

But Szonja had assured them that she would be back in three months, ready to take up her spot in the university course they'd chosen for her (finance and accounting), with her English improved, her nieces met and her mind broadened by the experience. No one in their family had visited Rina yet, even though their mother dearly wanted to now that barriers to travel were crumbling along with the Berlin Wall. Her husband would not consent to the trip, but when Mrs. Imre spoke to Rina on the phone, what she'd said instead was that it was too expensive and difficult to arrange. Their father still resented Rina's departure, but what *he* said instead was that he did not care for air travel. In this way no one knew exactly what the other was thinking, and no one went to America. Until now.

"Aron's very excited to see you," Rina said as they waited at a light, the lack of motion alerting them both to their lack of conversation. Their first embrace at the airport had felt natural, elemental even, but since then they had lapsed into a shy quietude. "He wanted to come too, but he's at home with the girls."

Szonja didn't know her sister's husband well, despite his heavy presence in their lives five years ago—all she knew was that his family had come to the US on an earlier wave of immigration, before '56, before the war even, so he spoke Hungarian with an accent and he kept Jewish traditions more seriously than their own family (which in itself was a hurdle of minor proportions). She remembered vaguely that Rina had seemed enthralled by this and assumed that her own feelings about him—that he was dull and rigid—were due to the fact that when she had met him, at the age of twelve, she had thought most adults around her dull and rigid. Whether this had softened the blow of Rina's departure at the time was hard to say—Szonja had been too caught up in the casual self-absorption of a preteen to indulge in feelings of loss. Those came later.

Her father's parting words to her as he had dropped her off at the airport were rather more cryptic than moving: "Remember, everyone in America is part of some cult," he said. "Including your sister, even if she calls it religion." But Szonja had no patience for any more dissuasion, so she simply kissed him and told him to take care of her mother.

But soon, she and Rina would arrive at the single-storey family home on Glenville Street, and Szonja would be surprised to find that her brother-in-law was not just "more religious," as her sister had put it in her letters, but specifically an Orthodox Jew, the kind who believed in prophets and prayer; the kind who celebrated holidays she'd never heard of and feared censure from a vengeful God if he didn't observe those holidays the way that God prescribed. The kind of man who delighted in his heritage, one they at once shared and yet shared not at all.

Soon she would find herself at his dinner table listening to the unfamiliar rhythms of his rapid-fire prayer, followed by a disquisition on the history of Jews in Los Angeles. Then she would be chided gently for turning on a small desk lamp in the living room (it being a Friday) and sent to sleep on a mattress between the beds of her two nieces.

But for now, she squeezed Rina's hands as they parked, feeling the dry skin on them without thinking much about it, the jet lag and the heat leaving fuzzy imprints on her mind.

Szonja awoke on her first night in America at 3:43 a.m., her eyelids heavy, her body sticky and yet oddly alert.

She left her nieces' room, careful not to wake them, and quietly made her way around the house—there had been no time for a tour the night before, but now, with a little light already filtering through the papery shades, she could see for herself where Rina spent her days. Her sister's house was arranged over a single floor—a squat little thing that nevertheless gave the impression of rambling spaciousness. She looked around the living room, which had two plump leather sofas arranged in an L shape and a large vitrine in dark walnut that held a variety of ornate silver objects—cups, plates, candelabras—as well as leather-bound books with Hebrew lettering. Szonja wanted to reach in and touch the gold embossing on their spines, to feel the grooves of the unfamiliar letters on her fingertips, but she knew the vitrine would protest loudly as she opened it, and she couldn't be sure how lightly the rest of the house slept.

In the kitchen she found the cupboards and the refrigerator replete with unfamiliar foods—they had an air of care and organisation even though they were so full, they could barely be closed. Little snippets of masking tape had been fastened to some of the cupboards, and Szonja recognised her sister's neat handwriting on them in black marker.

As she closed the door of one cupboard full of breakfast cereals arranged by size and colour, Szonja was startled by one of her nieces, Hannah.

"Hello there," Szonja said, in English.

Hannah only stared at her disapprovingly—a little disgruntled housewife in miniature, copying facial expressions she must have seen on her mother. Then, relenting, Hannah took one of the boxes of cereal, climbed onto the countertop, hitching herself from a lower cupboard's handle, and took down two bowls. She shook the cereal into the bowls, then, holding a jug of milk in two hands, sloshed milk unsteadily over them.

Hannah picked up her bowl and Szonja followed suit, then trailed the little girl into the living room and sat down on the carpet in front of the television with her. Sitting side by side, they watched cartoons, the volume set resolutely to zero (when it came to the rules of the Sabbath, Hannah still had a few years of credibly feigned ignorance ahead of her). Even though she was mostly disregarded by her niece, Szonja felt comforted by the synchronous clatter of their spoons at the bottoms of the bowls, the warm blue glow of the screen on their arms.

Szonja woke again hours later, slumped against one of the leather couches with a light blanket thrown over her legs. The bowl she had eaten from was nowhere in sight; only the milky residue at the roof of her mouth indicated that she had not dreamt it.

Rina stepped softly into the room. "Are you awake?" she asked, in Hungarian—Szonja could hear the edges of their language softened and rounded by her habitual English.

"I think I've gone past sleep and wakefulness—this is some other state entirely."

Rina sat down next to her on the floor, her legs bound together by her skirt, like the fin of a mermaid. She brushed some strands of salty hair from Szonja's face the way their mother used to when they woke in the middle of the night.

"Will you come to synagogue with us?" Rina asked simply, as though this were something they had always done, and although Szonja couldn't imagine even making it out the door, she was also curious and longing to be near Rina in this unfamiliar place.

The children were ready to go before Szonja, and when she found them all politely waiting for her in the foyer, she felt like she was one of the kids—another body for Rina and Aron to herd out the door. They walked outside, and Szonja started towards the car, but Hannah poked her in the thigh, then clasped her left hand with a little exasperated sigh and led her down the driveway towards the sidewalk.

They wound their way through streets of little squat houses with little front yards until they reached the main road—at the very same time several other families were also winding their way towards West Pico Boulevard, like Pac-Man and the ghosts in their maze, going to one of a dozen synagogues lined up close to one another.

Szonja had had in mind the classical architecture of home when she imagined what her sister's place of worship might look like; what she found instead was much the same as every other building in Los Angeles: flat concrete painted a shade of beige, steel block capitals announcing what was to be found inside. On the sidewalk outside the building a grubby-looking man held a Styrofoam cup in his hand, methodically stirring in packets of white sugar two at a time until the coffee must have achieved the consistency of wet sand. He raised his cup to Szonja when he caught her looking and winked.

Inside, the nondescript building was a different world entirely—Szonja felt as though she had stepped through time. All the men and women were dressed exactly like Rina and Aron—the same muted colours, the same cuts and hem lengths. Perhaps the exhaustion of the trip had blinded her to it, but Szonja took in her own sister's appearance, really looked at her for the first time since she had arrived in Los Angeles the previous day. Rina wore a thick black skirt, formfitting but coming down past the knees in a way that necessitated small, delicate steps. Her arms were covered by a long-sleeved shirt over which she wore a dark green knitted vest. Her long brown hair, which Szonja had seen piled on top of her head or swinging from her shoulders a thousand times, was cut into a neat bob and covered with a scarf.

Rina must have noticed her looking; she shifted under Szonja's gaze and adjusted her vest self-consciously. "Come, women are this way," Rina said, leading Szonja, Hannah and her younger sister, Abby, to the far side of the room, which was bisected by a large white partition. Aron had disappeared into the pews on the other side wordlessly.

Szonja sat between the two girls. Rina handed her a prayer book and flipped through it to point out where they would begin. As the prayers started, Szonja felt an overwhelming sense of restlessness come over her—for a while she tried to follow the phonetic script, brushing her finger across the thin paper of her prayer book, but she understood little to nothing of its meaning apart from the occasional *amen* punctuating the monotone like a finger tapping her on the shoulder, reminding her disapprovingly to stay awake. She would have been comforted to hear some of the less than pious thoughts going through the minds of those around her, but when Szonja noticed a neatly dressed nine-year-old sitting at the end of their pew dutifully mouthing the prayers, she thought that even some of the children seemed to fare better than her.

She was relieved when, fifteen minutes into the service, after a vigorous bout of fidgeting, Hannah slipped from the wooden pew and disappeared towards the back of the room. Rina didn't seem to notice, so during a particularly long-winded section of the service, Szonja stood to follow her.

The back of the room led onto wood-panelled hallways—at first Szonja thought they were wallpapered, but the pattern turned out to be the markings of thousands of names etched one after the other into the wood with their dates of birth and death, each life indelibly stamped and yet covering only the length of a forefinger. Hannah had wandered into one of the small rooms that sprang off the oppressive hallway and found a stack of colourful children's books among the dour-looking siddurs. Szonja sat down on the cool tile beside her.

"This one is about a family of bears," Hannah explained, with a sweet solemnity. "A mom bear, a dad bear, and two little bears." She looked up into Szonja's eyes and said, "They don't behave well."

At the house they had a lunch of hearty stew and soft white bread. Her sister had clearly learned how to cook since she'd last seen her, although she'd taken as her template some other mother; there was no trace of Mrs. Imre's anaemic salads here.

"What did you think of the synagogue?" Aron asked as they sat drinking coffee while Rina cleared some plates. He spoke to her in English with the occasional Hungarian phrase thrown in clumsily and used a combination of English and Hebrew with the kids, so it was a wonder anyone understood the other at all.

"It was very nice . . . though I don't have much to compare to."

"Yes, I understand your parents didn't often go when you and Rina were children."

In fact, they had never once been to synagogue with her parents, but Szonja did not want to say much, feeling that whatever version of their youth Rina had presented to Aron was best preserved that way. "These things are different back home."

"Yes, I suppose that explains it." He smiled at her, his eyes friendly but the dip of his head giving it an air of condescension.

"What does it explain?"

"Oh, well." He paused, a little uncertain. "Your behaviour today."

Szonja might have been incensed by this, but she was too confused—for the past twenty-four hours she had felt like an imprint of herself, her body there to give an impression of her presence but her character left behind somewhere in her sleep. She could not imagine any part of her behaviour being objectionable.

"I'm sorry, did I do something . . . ?" She stopped short of saying *wrong*, feeling enough like a child as it was.

Aron took a sip of his coffee thoughtfully and paused for long enough that it seemed their conversation had ended. "You know, Hannah is turning five soon," he said finally, rubbing a napkin slowly between his thumb and forefinger. "She does not read properly yet in any language. But words are our gateway, the letters are the bricks that make up the road that leads us to God. She does not have the tools to walk that road—not yet. But God sees her toiling—every day she adds more bricks—and soon she will walk alongside the rest of us. God knows this and awaits her patiently."

Szonja was at a loss for how to respond to this speech. Should she pretend that God was a reality to her, an entity whose thoughts and hopes she could fathom? She felt ridiculous even thinking in these terms. But Aron was not finished yet.

"I took the liberty of speaking to Rabbi Raskin after service. He's happy to take you on—as a favour to me. You can join the Hebrew class at the learning centre on Tuesdays and Thursdays." He leaned forward and patted her hand on the table. "You will create your bricks too, sister, don't worry."

Los Angeles, 2001

Sonia can see the traffic cop eyeing her like a carnival prize as she walks towards her car, which is double-parked across from the school entrance. But before she can make an escape, Cecily Auerbach, a mother from Mila's class, spots her with a gaze like a heat-seeking missile and homes in on Sonia, so her best efforts to look studiously in the other direction are for naught. She is so close to her car now, but Cecily is proving to be more athletic than her beige chinos and Banana Republic button-down suggest.

"Yoo-hoo!" Cecily calls in the manner of the mother in a laundry-detergent commercial calling the kids in from the garden. She swerves erratically around pedestrians and cars until she reaches Sonia.

"Cecily—you are a vision! You could be in a commercial," she says, and Cecily is immediately, predictably pleased. Sonia has found that turning her less than hospitable thoughts just a degree or two generally makes convenient compliments out of them. Cecily smooths some invisible creases in her shirt, momentarily forgetting the purpose of her *yoo-hoo*.

"Oh, that's right," she says, recalling herself. "Now, Sonia, tell me, is it true what they say?"

Sonia looks skyward, taking her time to adjust her sunglasses, aware of Cecily's excitement and, being possessed of a flair for the dramatic, wishing to prolong it. "Yes," she answers solemnly, although she has no idea what the woman is referring to. It does seem that whatever "they say" generally tends to be true, though, and Sonia has found it's always better to sound in the know. In any case, she reasons to herself, a little mystery can only serve to spice up a conversation with Cecily Auerbach.

"Oh, but that's marvellous," Cecily says, planting a light hand on Sonia's forearm.

"Isn't it just?" Vague enough, certainly.

"Well, I'll be going too, of course, so if you have any questions..." Sonia doesn't say anything—if you wait long enough, she has learned, people usually provide all the information you need. But Cecily, with her eyes round and alert like a child's drawing, looks like she'd hold her own under an interrogation.

"You know, I think I'm all set," Sonia answers finally.

Cecily tilts her head to the side a little, like she doesn't quite believe this. "Well, I don't know how you do it with everything else going on," she says, looking at Sonia's car, a 1985 Buick Century station wagon that's seen better days, as though she might spot *everything else* in Sonia's life through its windows. Of course Sonia is aware of Cecily's meaning—since moving here ten years ago, she has perfected not only her English but also the little-known subdialect spoken exclusively by suburban mothers. What Cecily means by *everything else* is that Sonia is, by all indications, a single mother; what she means by *how you do it* is that Sonia *doesn't* do it—that is, doesn't quite measure up to Cecily's standard of parenting and involvement in school life.

Cecily Auerbach believes herself to be a self-aware person. Then again, how would she know if she wasn't? She doesn't think about it, though, so it's safe to assume that she is not. Self-aware, that is.

She is, however, almost as confused as that train of thought. Cecily believes she has been welcoming towards Sonia: She has invited the awkward daughter over for playdates with Megan, has offered Sonia countless roles on the PTA committee; she has several times bought an extra latte "by accident" and shared it with her on the off chance the ritual might spark conversation. And yet she is still unsure where Sonia is from, what exactly it is that she scurries off to do after school drop-off and which of the men she practically parades around Mount Washington could have spawned that strange child of hers. There is a lot that Cecily doesn't know, including the fact that the more she wants to know, the less likely it is that Sonia will yield to her curiosity.

While Cecily ponders the limits of her knowledge, Sonia slides onto the leather seat of her car and makes her apologies, then glides past the traffic cop with a smile and a nod.

A question is posed in the cereal aisle of Albertsons:

"Milosh, any idea what it is that Cecily Auerbach thinks she and I will be doing together?" Mila darts her eyes from the box of Reese's Puffs in her hand to her mother for the briefest moment. "No?" she says slowly, hopefully.

"She seemed awfully excited, very convinced, in fact, that I was going to be doing something that she is also doing, and I usually make it a point not to do the things that Cecily Auerbach is doing—not because I don't want to be in her company, you understand, although that's definitely a consideration, but because, Milosh, we all like to think of ourselves in a certain way, and the way I like to think of myself can best be summed up as not being like Cecily Auerbach, so you see, if I were to do something that Cecily is doing, it could be damaging to my self-ima—"

"You're chaperoning!" Mila finally blurts out. There is no defence against her mother when she decides to wear you down with words, although usually this trick is reserved for others: the dry cleaner who wants to close shop just as she arrives; the man arguing for the last parking spot she's slipped into right in front of him, that sort of thing.

"Chaperoning, huh?"

"The trip to San Francisco."

"Yes, there is that trip to San Francisco . . ." Sonia says, losing some of her moral high ground. "Remind me again."

"The school orchestra. We're going for an end-of-year concert hosted by the Palo Alto Youth Symphony Orchestra."

What Mila understands instinctively but cannot at this stage of her cognitive development quite put into words is that children are, for the most part, braggarts. Perhaps this is being harsh; it would be more accurate to say that bragging is their only form of communication (and for some this never changes—we've all met that person). In any case, it is conceivable for a couple of children at Mount Washington Elementary School to have the following conversation:

"My mom packed me pizza for lunch."

"Well, my mom is bringing me pizza at lunchtime."

"My mom owns the pizza shop, so I can get pizza whenever I want."

"I like pizza." (There's always that one kid who doesn't get it.)

And although Mila, with her anthropological eye trained on the fifth-graders in her school, can understand this process, might even be able to emulate it with a little effort and a slant view of the truth, she lacks a fundamental understanding of its purpose. And when Mila doesn't see the purpose of something, you would be hard-pressed to get her to do it.

This is all to explain that when Mila signed her mother up to chaperone the Mount Washington Elementary School Orchestra's trip to San Francisco, it wasn't due to some misguided attempt to impress her classmates or a feeble attempt to make her mother impressive to their parents. No, it was a way to get around her mother, who would never have agreed to go unless coerced in such a way. All things considered, a better reason than showing off.

"Yes, that one, the Palo Alto one, of course," Sonia answers. "And yet I don't remember signing up to chaperone."

Mila sighs. "I signed you up, okay?"

"Of course it's okay, sweetheart," she says, picking up a box of Froot Loops and examining the back. "We'll just have to make sure to sign me *off* as soon as possible so they can get someone else in. Don't want to be rude."

"Mom, you have to go, they're expecting you."

Desperate measures had to be taken when Mila discovered that the name Anthony Greene appeared not only in her mother's digital inbox, but also in their actual mail. Sifting through Sonia's email led her to realise that the other kind has always been jealously guarded by her mother. Although Sonia is usually quite happy for Mila to do chores and fetch things for her, she has never once asked her to bring in the mail. And the one time the mailman arrived at their house the same time they did and offered their stack of envelopes to the "young lady," Sonia snatched them right out of his hand, as though he had offered her a rusty razor blade and a syringe. So Mila had the idea to rifle through the box's contents while her mother was out one day and found a variety of bills addressed to unfamiliar names. Some of them had clearly been sent to the wrong place (one to Rina Cronenberg and one to Jadranka Antic), and Mila threw them in the trash. But there was one that was too familiar to ignore. She couldn't risk opening it, so the envelope was placed back inside the mailbox carefully, but it got her thinking nonetheless. If Anthony Greene was getting mail delivered here, perhaps he was that mysterious person she'd heard referred to as "the man of the house"—door-to-door salesmen sometimes asked after him and her mother once snapped at a woman in the supermarket who offered her a free beer sample to share with this elusive figure. Their man of the house was absent, that much was clear. But there was a man named Anthony Greene who happened to be in San Francisco, the exact place where Mila's school happened to be taking a trip.

And so, at some point Mila must tell her mother that in a couple of weeks she will have to accompany herself, thirty other children, a few teachers and a handful of enthusiastic parents to San Francisco; that they will share buses, cars, accommodation and meals with these people, and that it all involves a *lot* of inane chitchat and very little privacy. It will also have to be revealed that a certain man named Anthony whose emails have been languishing unanswered in Sonia's inbox for a while now will be awaiting her in San Francisco, having received a series of poorly spelled emails requesting his presence at Pier 39 on the twenty-ninth of June. Mila may be a clever child, but she has not thought that far ahead. But she has seen enough straight-to-video movies to know that things are sure to resolve themselves by that point. First, though, her mother must cooperate.

"Well, this is one good thing about being a habitual underachiever in the PTA sort of areas of life—no one really expects anything of you. And rightly so, in my case—"

"You have to go," Mila says again, loud enough this time for the lady down the aisle to glance their way.

PORCUPINES

"Mila, I don't have to go, actually," she says, the former lightness of her tone gone. "I've told you before, spend too much time with people, and those people start to—"

"Ask questions about your life."

"Precisely, and that is something we just don't like," she says, giving a little shrug. "We just don't."

Mila looks her mother squarely in the eye then, her mouth set in a hard, angry line, and takes the only gesture of defiance at her disposal in that moment—she throws the box of Reese's Puffs into their shopping cart and stomps off.

"I don't let them have the sugary stuff either," says the lady down the aisle who's been trying to listen in on them—without much success, it seems. "Sugar is slow death," she adds with a meaningful nod.

"Yes," Sonia says, putting the Froot Loops in her cart, her mind wandering to an imaginary San Francisco peopled exclusively by Cecilys. "Yes, a slow death."

After a frosty ride home, they arrive to find a large brown package at their door brought to them by Alonzo, the moustachioed UPS deliveryman. UPS men are the single most frequent visitors at the Imre household. With the concurrent increase of Sonia's reputation as a seamstress and decrease in package delivery costs, it made sense a couple of years ago to move all her dressmaking work home. Materials and designs were dropped off, dresses and accessories were whisked away, money landed in Sonia's account and she never had to venture downtown to the studio she used to work at when she first moved to the city with its stern Serbian seamstresses who talked over her head in a quick-fire Slavic rhythm.

Alonzo is Sonia's favourite deliveryman—he is always up for some chitchat over the packages and gives away details about his personal life at the gentlest encouragement. As much as Sonia avoids talking about herself, she is often struck with a pang of longing for someone else's intimate dramas in a way that not even reality television can satisfy.

"Something exciting, Ms. Imre?" he says, the words muffled slightly by his thick moustache. Sonia sometimes wonders if Alonzo is aware that his facial hair looks uncomfortably pornographic, especially when considered in conjunction with his job. But then again, the man's eyebrows are almost as thick as his moustache and they slope down at the sides, like hapless caterpillars sliding off a slick leaf—all in all, he doesn't strike one as being aware of the tropes of pornography.

"I sure hope so," she answers absently, eyes lingering on his moustache a second too long. She can't remember what it is that she actually ordered, but seeing the package now, she hopes it will be something that might distract Mila from the bitter note they left things on in the grocery store. Perhaps something they can share and delight in together, something that might inspire them and bond them even closer.

It is, however, a vacuum cleaner.

Mila looks at it dispassionately after Sonia divests it of its cardboard clothing. It is a round little robot vacuum, the first of its kind, its packaging announces. The box makes other excited exclamations about its various fixtures and functions: "'Three speeds!' 'Ultrasonic sensors!' 'Self-drive!' 'First-class object detection!'" Sonia reads these out with the enthusiasm befitting their gleaming red font and excitable punctuation, but even to her own ear, she just sounds like a forty-year-old man at a Star Trek convention, and the most she can elicit from Mila is a "Cool" before she goes back to cleaning their goldfish tank.

Still, Sonia is immediately fond of the little contraption. Certainly it is better than her ancient corded vacuum, which she has to drag around the house like a reluctant dog on a leash. It is shiny and new and no one else has it—it makes the perfect distraction, for her, at least.

The robot is not theirs to keep, however; Sonia is just trying it out before placing a larger order for a businessman who sells hard-to-come-by electric goods to nouveau riche clients in Eastern Europe. *Businessman* is perhaps too strong a word for someone she met a couple of years ago outside a Best Buy in Burbank, even if he was wearing a suit and did give her a crisp white business card. Who knows what kind of radar alerted him to Sonia as a good prospect, but Marek had asked her in the parking lot if she wouldn't mind going into the store and purchasing two PalmPilots with cash he'd give her; they'd placed a limit on the amount of goods you could buy in one transaction and he had clients in Romania absolutely desperate to keep their lives organised in a little plastic machine.

Sonia recognised an opportunity when she saw one, and before handing him the PalmPilots, she wore the man down until he agreed to stretch the production line to two and let her deal with procurement in the future. The other week they had hunted down the last available HitDiscs, miniature music players that came with teeny-tiny cartridges that played tinny versions of Sugar Ray's greatest hits. Sonia demanded a good cut of that one, and Marek made his usual threats of severing ties. But he was a sentimental man, he said; the only reason he kept her on was that she was a fellow Eastern European, a fact he guessed and she grudgingly admitted to. These days, she is Hungarian only when business requires it and Jewish only when a Jehovah's Witness knocks on the door. It's simpler this way.

The little robot zigzags its way around the living room, changing course when it bumps up against a wall or the leg of a chair. It does get stuck occasionally, and Sonia watches it apprehensively, not sure whether it is better to help or let it figure things out on its own. Which, when you think about it, is a lot like raising a child.

Los Angeles, 1989

LOS ANGELES HAD MANY THINGS TO ENTICE AN EIGHTEEN-year-old girl from the Eastern Bloc—the never-ceasing sunshine and the promise of the ocean nearby, however false; the significantly increased probability of running into Patrick Duffy from *Dallas* on any given day; and then, of course, the shopping. Attending Hebrew school twice a week, despite its many possible merits, would not be likely to crack the charts. And Szonja, who had never been particularly academically minded and in fact was dreading the start of her university course back home in a mere few months, certainly had not planned on spending her time among schoolchildren. She broached the subject with Rina the following week while Aron was at work.

"Did he really mean it that I should go to Hebrew school *twice* a week?" There was something especially oppressive about the multiple.

Rina was gathering clothes for laundering and kept at her work as they talked. Szonja had noticed this about her sister in the short time she had been here—she fluttered about the house without cessation, always occupied in some task that kept her gaze forward. Szonja could not be sure if she imagined it or if it was intentional, but Rina had not faced her more than once or twice since she'd arrived; consequently Szonja had become overfamiliar with her sister's back, her shoulders, the side of her face, the little birthmark on her left ear, which she had not noticed in all the years she'd had the opportunity to look at her sister.

"You'll like the rabbi, Szonja, he's quite a character," Rina said as she went through her daughters' bedroom.

"Yes, I'm sure he is, but I thought . . . I mean, if anything, shouldn't I be going to English classes while I'm here?"

"Your English is great, Szonja, everyone at the synagogue said so. Several people mentioned it, actually. But you've always been better at languages than me—I've been here for five years and I still seem like a foreigner."

Szonja thought that had less to do with her accent and more to do with her sartorial choices, so at odds with the barely there denim and slip dresses of Los Angeles. They had both picked up English well enough during their father's postings, after all, but she refrained from saying so.

"It's been years since I've used English properly," Szonja said. "I can see the confusion on people's faces when I speak. Even when they understand me, they're straining. I'll never make friends that way."

Rina sighed. "Friends? Sounds like fun," she said as she discovered a stash of dirty clothes hidden under Hannah's bed. Rina pulled out one garment after another, an endless parade of colourful fabric she seemed to have stowed there for unknown reasons. They looked at each other for a moment, then burst out laughing.

"These are my friends, it seems," she said, piling the clothes into a hamper.

"Rina." Szonja stopped her sister from moving out of the room.

Rina turned to face her. With one arm holding her basket wedged to her side, she took the other hand and brushed back

Szonja's hair. "If it's important to you, we can find you a class at the community college. But at this rate you'll be in classes all week—I won't even see you."

"I'll do Hebrew school once a week and English class once too—the rest of the time I'm all yours." She had, after all, come to see her sister as well as Patrick Duffy; she and Rina had become all but strangers during Rina's five-year absence. "You need better friends," she said, picking up a sock from the basket in Rina's arms.

"That much is true."

If Szonja had any qualms about the less than auspicious location of the city college where she would undertake her English classes—being as it was across from a strip mall—she might have been comforted by the fact that most things in Los Angeles were across from a strip mall. In any case, she was too excited to be out of the house to care much where she went. Although she enjoyed being with her sister and getting to know her nieces, as anyone who's ever been a houseguest knows, there is no amount of voluntarily undertaken chores that will make you feel less like a chair placed awkwardly in the middle of a room.

Rina drove her to the college after dropping off the children at preschool. As Szonja said goodbye at the community college's entrance, Rina looked almost wistful, like she might just park her car, get out and join Szonja in class, leaving her chores for another day. But the hesitation lasted only a moment before the click of her indicator signified her departure and Szonja was left, for the first time in her life, alone in a foreign city.

Rina had told her not to expect too much from the college, but Szonja was immediately captivated by the place. As she walked through the hallways, which were lined with noticeboards and placards on one side and opened onto a courtyard on the other, she saw a wide variety of classes and activities enticingly marketed to students. It seemed at once marvellous and completely frivolous for a person to be taking Introduction to Pottery or Esoteric Dance when her own education had been a strict Prussian diet of mathematics, literature, history and languages.

Outside her designated classroom, she saw a crowd of students assembled and waiting for their instructor—the group was so diverse in age, race and nationality that, if placed in any other location, it would be almost impossible to guess what they could all have in common.

She was approached immediately by a girl of a similar age who introduced herself simply as "Tatiana, Yugoslavia."

"Szonja, Hungary," she answered in kind.

"I had a feeling. The rest of the Europeans in the class are from the West, except that girl over there, Nadja." She pointed at a girl standing on her own by a trash can. "She's from Moldova, so east of Hungary, which, according to the people west of everyone, apparently makes it lesser than Hungary."

"'Better than Moldova'—our new national slogan."

"That's funny." Tatiana was the kind of person who would tell you that rather than laugh at your joke.

"Thanks."

"It's not easy being funny in another language. I've tried."

Szonja explained that during her summer breaks back home, she had worked at a sound company that translated movie scripts for voice-over actors. "I spent a lot of time trying to figure out why *Caddyshack* is funny."

"And why is it?"

"Still not sure—I suppose it's the kind of humour that doesn't translate."

In fact, Hungarians loved nothing more than to discuss the generalised sense of humour of other nations. The British, to their ears, had none; the Germans loved puns in an unsophisticated way; and of course, American humour was coarse and reliant on the scatological. Hungarian humour was, naturally, the golden mean.

"So is that why you're in the accent class?"

"What do you mean?"

"This is what we call the accent class—the students here all aced their placement exam, and we know English better than your average American high-school student, but . . ."

"We have accents."

"Some worse than others. Regina over there is probably a genius, but I can't understand a word she says. Myself, I still struggle with the w's." It was true, Tatiana pronounced every word that had a w in it with a v, and vice versa—or, well, wice wersa.

Their instructor was a mild-mannered woman in her forties who seemed somewhat unsuited to the profession of teaching; she led the class with a weary placidity that allowed for the most gregarious students to wrest control from her almost as soon as the lesson started.

Tatiana had clearly taken it upon herself to guide Szonja through the turbulent social entanglements of their class, and she continued her instruction at lunch. "Okay, that's Tito and Vera, they are a couple and disgusting. Every day they eat lunch together and they share their food."

"Horrible."

"Yes . . . Oh, you're joking again? No, it really is horrible, just watch."

It soon became clear why Tatiana had immediately drawn Szonja into a group with herself and another Yugoslavian, a man named Peter who was there for an academic seminar on fluid dynamics. Despite the jovial mixture of nationalities in the class, alliances had been formed on a geopolitical basis. Three Armenian women talked to no one else, and a group of men made up of a Greek, a Spaniard and a Cypriot (or "the Olives," as Tatiana called them) preferred one another's company too, even though the eldest was in his sixties and the youngest was possibly below drinking age. The melting pot seemed more and more like the little containers of food on an airplane, divided into small aluminium compartments that made it all look less appetising.

The Hebrew class on Thursday was walking distance from Rina's house, so Szonja undertook the journey on her own. Rina and Aron's synagogue ran a small Jewish learning centre where the Hebrew classes were taught and the rabbi held deep dives into Talmudic study for the more enthusiastic in his congregation. Meanwhile, his wife gathered the women in the congregation at themed events with cutesy names that attempted to marry terms from the zeitgeist with appropriate synagogue-sanctioned activities via the power of alliteration. She was nothing if not creative in these endeavours. When Szonja entered the little building, she saw advertisements for "Lattes and L'Avoteinu" and "Tots and Talmud," among others.

She was relieved to see that her class was not in fact made up of children around Hannah's age. Somehow Aron's comparisons between them the other day had her imagining a roomful of four- and five-year-olds playing with LEGO bricks. There were a couple of shy-looking teenage boys seated in a far corner, one man with a sombre expression around her own age and a slightly older woman who, although dressed the part of an Orthodox Jewish wife, looked more like she had been deposited there at the whim of some anthropologically minded aliens. The group was like a summer remedial class for Jews who had fallen behind.

"Ah, welcome, Szonja, please take a seat here." The rabbi greeted her at the door and introduced her to their teacher. At synagogue, Szonja hadn't had a chance to get a proper impression of the rabbi, and in any case, bearded men all looked a little bit similar to her. But standing across from the rabbi, Szonja realised he wasn't as old as she had initially thought—his beard was flecked with grey and there were lines around his eyes, but they were also alert in a way she found certain older men's weren't, the ones who felt they'd seen enough of the world to make up their minds about it and no longer needed to focus on the details. But Rabbi Raskin looked straight into her eyes, and even though she couldn't quite make out the emotion in them—kindness? Curiosity? Pity?—she felt it eased some of her apprehension in coming here.

They began the class with exercises aimed at teaching them the alphabet, after which they were tasked with copying out the letters over and over again in their notebooks. There is nothing quite so infantilising as following the dotted lines of a letter with the nib of your pen, needing the assistance of those little guardrails to form the most basic element of language. And yet, once Szonja had done a few pages of her workbook, she found it quite mesmerising to watch the motion of her hand across the paper, so divorced from active thought but somehow, slowly, through repetition, building towards knowledge. It struck her as ironic that the very texts she might use this knowledge to read would most likely instil in her a shame towards the corporeal, and yet here was proof that her body could feed her mind.

After some time spent with these individual efforts, they were paired up to practise some basic phrases. Szonja was joined by the frightened-looking woman, and they used a dictionary to tell each other banal details about their lives, which had about a 50 per cent chance of being correct and were even less likely to be true: "I live nearby," "My favourite colour is blue" and "Wednesday is my favourite year, aside from beetles." Szonja had marvelled at the process of language learning before, but now, a turn of the kaleidoscope showed a more despairing image—if this was how she was to reach God, she was worried He might soon give up on humanity altogether.

After class was over, with her fingers numb from use, Szonja walked down the hall of the learning centre, passing by the rabbi's office. He addressed her like they were continuing a conversation from moments ago, asking how she had found the class.

Szonja stepped into the doorway of the room and looked around as though the office might hold inspiration for her answer.

"A little dull?" he ventured.

"I'm not much of a linguist," she said. The rabbi smiled as though he understood she did not want to be here.

"And how are you finding it in Los Angeles?" he asked.

"Hot, mostly."

"You can imagine how we struggle under the beards. They were more suited to our forefathers back east."

"I'm sorry to tell you, but the beards have gone out of fashion there too."

The rabbi laughed, an easy, comfortable laugh.

"You are right, of course, it does not suit the modern custom, and neither does the clothing." He shook his head a little as if to say *It's all a bit silly, isn't it.* "My father never wore a beard—all my life, I saw him shave every morning. He had one of those old-fashioned brushes; no foaming Gillette for him. He would lather up his whole face and shave it with a fascinating sort of precision—always, always the same strokes, moving from left to right, wiping the blade." The rabbi looked at an indistinct point in front of himself as though his mind were projecting his memory there. "And then I found some old photographs of him before the war, and you know, I did not recognise him, because of course he had a beard! Not quite as fulsome as mine." He smiled up at Szonja a little, stroking the facial hair in question. "But a respectable beard nonetheless. When I asked him about it, he said he shaved it because it felt dirty. Only years later did it occur to me to wonder—what made it feel dirty? And who was the first to shave it for him? And when they did, what grew in its stead?"

Szonja was engrossed by the rabbi's story—she was not immune to a well-crafted narrative, and much like the rabbi's delayed questioning of his father, it occurred to her only some days later that there might have been a reason he chose this particular anecdote to share with her the first time they spoke. And even though she knew, to some extent, she was being manipulated, she couldn't help but admire the finesse with which he did it. And after all, every story is a manipulation in one way or another.

Los Angeles, 2001

You would be hard-pressed to find an individual who hasn't contemplated the life choices that led them to sit in the clear plastic seats of the Mount Washington Elementary School teachers' lounge. Certainly, each teacher who passes through after being bullied by children a fifth of their age or before they are required to tell a parent that their precious child has stuck yet another pencil sharpener up his nose has thought long and hard about the unfathomable ways one's life can go.

On this particular day, as Sonia sighs deeply, she senses keenly the many disappointed souls that have passed through this room—or perhaps what she senses is the smell of Mrs. Dennis's three-bean dip marinating in the corner. Either way, she regrets her involvement in the situation. Mrs. Flores stands in front of them gesturing at a whiteboard on which she has outlined the orchestra's trip to the Bay Area in letters that seem to Sonia almost aggressively rounded—each *o* and *b* its own little balloon, ready to burst. The fifth-grade teacher has a penchant for loose-fitting paisley smocks and always wears a beatific smile that only thinly masks a tenacity that would have served her well in a career as a lobbyist. And then there's the fact that she's a big fan of grammar. It's hard to imagine being a very good person if you're that invested in grammar—there's a reason why they call them grammar nazis.

As Sonia stares at the board, she wonders what a handwriting analyst would make of Mrs. Flores, and her attention slips a little, which is likely why she misses the moment when Mrs. Flores takes volunteers for "activity leaders." Had Sonia been paying attention, she might have raised her hand at an enjoyable activity such as "chocolate-making class at historic Ghirardelli factory" or a harmless one like "picnic in Golden Gate Park." She might even have volunteered for the "trip inside the infamous Alcatraz." Instead, the activity she is left to arrange for forty ten-year-old children is a trip to the Historic Button Museum. Even Mrs. Flores, who has written this particular itinerary item on the board with a little drawing of a button where the *o* in *Historic* stands—well, even she seems uncertain as she bestows the dubious honour on Sonia.

Awoken from her reverie, Sonia learns that they are to spend almost a week in and around San Francisco with the kids in the Mount Washington orchestra, an unusually robust organisation for a small public school and open to all grades, although mostly peopled by fifth-graders like Mila herself. There are a few enthusiastic young orchestra members who play simpler instruments that produce fewer tones (and at least half of those tones are produced by banging the instrument against the wall), but this trip is exclusively for the more accomplished players.

"Won't the other children feel left behind? They don't get a neat trip to San Francisco," asks a concerned father. Concerned for someone else's child, that is. Sonia nods in agreement, though this thought would not have been even the forty-sixth to occur to her in the moment.

"Certainly it's a huge privilege," Mrs. Flores says with a smug lift at the corner of her mouth. "But these kids have worked extremely hard throughout the year to perfect their playing. I've also asked each of them to prepare a little talk on their experiences, which they will present the week after the trip, to show that it's been a learning process, not just jolly good times." Mrs. Flores laughs, the sound springing a lonely echo around the room. Although this doesn't quite add up to fair compensation, the concerned father leans back in his chair, less concerned, and they continue going through the details of the trip.

After the itinerary, very little of which seems to revolve around the concert that gave purpose to the whole trip, has been thoroughly reviewed, Mrs. Flores announces a coffee break. Sonia cups her hands around Styrofoam gratefully—the coffee smells a little nutty, like the warm sesame oil her neighbours cook with, and tastes much better than it should, given where they are.

"I wonder whether it might somehow be arranged for Mrs. Flores to stay locked in Alcatraz on this trip." Linda Park has approached Sonia at the back of the room. She is the mother of a quiet girl in Mila's class who tends to blink more than seems necessary for the regular moistening of her eyeballs. Sonia is relieved to find that Linda has no such problem.

Sonia laughs a little, gauging whether it is safe to proceed in mocking their surroundings. "Harsh. I was just thinking whether it might be time to consider homeschooling."

"I heard the Bennets did that, right after it was suggested that Mr. Bennet come in and build the stage for the sixth-grade talent show."

"Oh yeah, and how's that working out for them?"

"Their son looks right on track to become a cult leader, and the daughter has become a competitive knitter."

"Aspirational."

"Very." Linda laughs lightly. "So, you're Mila's mom, right?"

"I am, unless she's done something embarrassing."

"In our household I'm the one who's a constant source of embarrassment—my daughter is Kathy."

"Of course, sweet girl," Sonia says, although the only thing she can recall in that moment is the blinking. Sonia is not particularly familiar with Mila's class; it hasn't seemed important to get to know other children when her own child is often a mystery to her. But now she wonders if the woman has approached her because their daughters are friends.

A few days ago, looking to deprive the ants in their house of her daughter's leftover lunch, Sonia had gone through Mila's bag and found a library book with a pleasantly squeaky plastic encasement wedged inside a binder. *How to Be Cool in the Sixth Grade: Thirty Cool Rules to Rule the School.* The title alone was alarming; the contents were worse. A supposed fifth-grader called Camy Baker gave her advice to other girls on how to stand out in school. Some of these were obviously aimed at making the adults' lives easier (*Don't smoke! Be kind to teachers!*), but some was just plain bad advice (*Be the nicest person in the class!*—Camy had clearly never met a fifth-grader, despite claiming to be one). Later that evening, as she and Mila watched a reality show about toddler beauty pageants in Sonia's bed, Sonia was distracted from the television, staring at her daughter, who had somehow, in the span of an afternoon, become a stranger to her again.

"No," Mila said when she caught her mother looking.

"No what?"

"Don't even think about it. I'm not entering a pageant."

Sonia laughed and turned back to the television, momentarily relieved—Mila was still Mila. "Just thought it was time for you to earn your keep."

But now, in the Mount Washington teachers' lounge, she is reminded again of her discovery—that inside this school is the social terrain that her daughter, it seems, wants to "rule," with the help of an asinine book clearly written by an adult with a firm handle on the correct use of *whom*.

She looks around the room at the other mothers and fathers and thinks that each of them has their own little imprint in that classroom, a little part of them that split off and grew into a slightly altered version of the original. Is it possible that all these pairs are like her and Mila? The two of them are like the playground game where you spin around holding hands, the centripetal force keeping you from falling down—unless your hands slip out of each other's grasp. But no, of course they don't feel the same; they aren't pairs, after all. There are spouses and other children and dogs and grandparents—a whole host of other beings keeping them all upright. But Sonia tells herself that she prefers it this way—the two of them know how to hold on tight.

Then again, as Cecily Auerbach approaches her with a look of manic enthusiasm, Sonia thinks perhaps it would have been nice to let go of Mila's hand for just one week, while she takes her trip to San Francisco.

Los Angeles, 1989

IF SZONJA HAD BEEN ASKED TO GUESS WHERE HER FIRST INVITAtion to a party in America would arrive from, she would never have considered Dovid, the sombre and diligent man in her Hebrew class. And yet, there in front of her was a Xeroxed copy of a handdrawn flyer for his band's concert. He handed these out to everyone in the class, seemingly unaware of the likelihood that any of them would actually go. Rivka, the scared-looking woman Szonja was often partnered with, looked like she might faint as she took the flyer from Dovid with trembling hands.

Szonja didn't particularly care for Dovid—he seemed competitive in a petty way, only smiling after successfully answering one of the teacher's questions. She had assumed he was extremely observant and committed to learning Hebrew for that reason, but it turned out his only devotion was to music. The purpose of the Hebrew classes had been to impress a woman he was seeing who had recently gotten into Kabbalah, but while he was there, he seemed to feel he might as well be the best in class.

It mattered little, though, whether she enjoyed his company or not, because Szonja recognised Dovid's party as the perfect opportunity to go out for the first time in Los Angeles. Szonja was still at that age where she had a need, common among young people, to be always going somewhere, preferably at night, with low visibility, preferably to a cramped space where there were three people to every square inch of her skin—bumping, scratching, burning with a carelessly held cigarette. She felt it impossible to go on any longer with each night at her sister's home spent in the same way: an elaborate dinner prepared by Rina, enjoyed by Aron, disregarded by the children, for the most part, and afterwards, the cleanup, the kids' bedtime routine and maybe a late-night talk show if they had the energy (though Aron made it known that he would prefer not to have a television in the household at all). Szonja had never been around a young family, with the attendant tedium of raising small children, nor had she ever partaken in Orthodox Jewish practice, with its attendant tedium of prayer and ritual, and so in her mind, the monotony of one became irrevocably tied to the monotony of the other, and the appeal of both were, perhaps unfairly, diminished.

However, she was reliant on Aron and her sister's goodwill, and their car, so it seemed like the perfect moment to ease them into a different kind of nighttime routine—even Aron couldn't object to a party thrown by *Dovid* from *Hebrew school*.

At her next English class, Szonja invited Tatiana, who said yes even before Szonja had a chance to finish what she was saying. Tatiana was spending the year with her great-aunt, who liked to pass their evenings regaling Tatiana with stories of her youth in Yugoslavia. The irony of these evenings preventing Tatiana from enjoying her own youth was lost somewhere in the fog of her nostalgia. In any case, Tatiana needed this evening even more than Szonja did. She reminded Szonja to "borrow" an old ID card from her sister, something Rina wouldn't miss, while Tatiana planned to use her neighbour's driver's licence. Tatiana also took it upon herself to locate a point a ten-minute walk to the venue to which Szonja could direct Aron and Rina and where Tatiana would meet her so that they wouldn't suspect the girls were headed to a seedy-looking nightclub called Coconut Teaszer. Hebrew class notwithstanding, Coconut Teaszer was unlikely to inspire confidence in Aron, who had probably never tasted a coconut, let alone spent the evening getting sweaty in its namesake.

When Rina and Aron dropped her off at the address provided, Tatiana was already there, walking down the driveway of a nondescript one-storey house as though she had just locked its door.

"Do you know these people?" Szonja asked, looking back at the dark windows of the house behind them as they waved goodbye to her sister.

"No, I just got here. We'd better move before they think I'm trying to rob the place."

In the club's bathroom, they changed into clothes Tatiana had brought for them—leather miniskirts and T-shirts with band names Szonja didn't recognise. They left their clothes in a bag on the windowsill to change back into later and Szonja had told Rina that Tatiana's aunt would drop them off after the party—it was not as though anyone had told her that leather miniskirts were strictly forbidden, but having become familiar with her sister's wardrobe, Szonja felt it was safer to arrive home in the appropriate attire.

On the main stage a band was playing melodic rock songs with enough distortion on their guitars to warrant their vaguely punk outfits.

"Is this Dovid's band? They're pretty good!" Tatiana looked impressed for a moment, then spotted a sign beside them, said, "This way" and swivelled Szonja towards a crooked staircase leading to the basement, a much smaller room. There they found Dovid's band playing to ten enthusiastic fans and twenty people who looked like they'd wandered down there in search of the bathrooms.

"This might require tequila," Tatiana said, and they wove through the crowd and went back upstairs to the bar, where, even with their borrowed IDs in hand, they struggled to get the attention of a bartender, both girls being relatively small in stature.

Tatiana scanned the crowd for someone who might take pity on them. She pointed to a man walking their way. "Well, this tall man seems to be offering himself up for the task."

"Dovid, hi!" Szonja said as Dovid approached them at the bar. "Are you done playing?"

"Just taking a break," he said. "I'm glad you came." He still had the sombre expression she was familiar with, but it seemed more solicitous than arrogant outside the classroom.

"Tatiana, this is Dovid, from my Hebrew school."

Dovid laughed. "It's Anthony, actually. Dovid is just a Hebrew name I chose for the class. You know, like how we choose a Spanish name in Spanish class? That one was easier—I was always just Antonio."

"Well, Dovid, Antonio, Anthony—it's a pleasure to meet you, I'm Tatiana, and we were just after a drink."

"Allow me," he said, and towering over a group of people at the bar, he ordered them a round of tequilas.

"So how's it going with the Kabbalist?" Szonja shouted over the noise of the band as they moved closer to the dance floor.

Anthony looked confused for a moment. "Oh," he said. "She's unimpressed by my Hebrew vocabulary."

Szonja felt the alcohol and the thrum of the bass guitar work their way through her, and she smiled as her limbs loosened up, joining in with the dancing crowd. At some point Anthony went back to play the rest of his set, and Szonja and Tatiana moved between the two concerts. As they dragged each other across the club,

Szonja briefly imagined that the person holding her hand was Rina. An alternate universe in which they spent their time together dancing rather than cajoling two small children into behaving well. This seemed so impossible now, even ridiculous, to think of her sister in her prim Orthodox dress and patent leather shoes scuffing the sawdust strewn across the floor, her neat bob swaying to the music.

Around one a.m. Szonja lost track of Tatiana, who had said she was going to the bar a couple minutes or possibly half an hour ago. Their clothes were no longer on the windowsill of the bathroom when Szonja went to check, and as she emerged, she bumped into Anthony.

"I think your friend left with our bass player," he said, then added, noting the look of concern on her face, "Don't worry, he's a nice guy, I've known him since high school."

"Oh, Tatiana can take care of herself, but I have been left to my own devices, it seems." It occurred to Szonja then that it was unlikely that Tatiana had ever actually intended for her great-aunt to take them home. She felt suddenly panicked, like a child lost in a supermarket aisle. Was she going to have to find a pay phone, call her brother-in-law in the middle of the night to pick her up? Or find a taxi in this unfamiliar place?

"We've got a van for our equipment. If you don't mind waiting until we pack up, we'll take you."

Szonja sat on the curb outside the club as Anthony and his remaining bandmates loaded their things into the van. She was still a little tipsy, and the street in front of her had turned into a fun-house mirror—all the beautiful outfits suddenly garish; the makeup on the women clown-like and disturbing.

She rode in the back of the van, wedged between an amplifier and a guitar case, and when they arrived at the house on Glenville, Anthony helped her out.

"Thanks, Dovid—I really owe you one."

"Actually, it's Anthony," he reminded her, then, offering his hand, he added, "Greene."

"Anthony Greene," Szonja repeated, smiling and savouring the syllables. "Thanks for the lift."

She crept up to the house and went in as quietly as she could. As she closed the door behind her, she could see Anthony waiting beside the van. He waved goodbye tentatively.

Inside, the house was hushed, and she breathed a sigh of relief that Rina and Aron hadn't waited up for her—the clothes would have been difficult to explain, never mind the sawdust in her shoes and the cigarette smoke in her hair. But as she started to climb the stairs, she heard a small voice behind her.

"Szonja?" It was Hannah, bleary-eyed in her long pyjamas that she had inherited from another girl in their congregation but hadn't quite grown into yet.

"Hi, sweetie, why aren't you in bed?"

"I wanted a snack, where have you been?" she asked, all in one breath. Hannah took in her outfit with a curious look, and Szonja reached for her niece's hand and led her to the living room, where they were less likely to be heard.

"Don't tell anyone," she said, leaning down to whisper to Hannah, "but I went dancing."

Hannah looked at her sceptically, as though she couldn't fathom how this was a good way to spend time. "Come, chicken, I'll show you." She took Hannah's hand and twirled her around, approximating a slow swing dance. Hannah giggled a little and tried to follow along; Szonja's steps were still a little unsteady, and she realised she was still feeling the effects of the tequila.

"Szonja? What are you doing?" They hadn't noticed Rina in the doorway of the living room, watching them. "Hannah, please go to bed. And if you've had food, please brush your teeth again. Now."

When Hannah was out of the room, Rina turned to her sister, and as she looked at her—her leather miniskirt, her hair sticky from dance-floor sweat—Rina's face took on an expression somewhere between hurt and confusion.

"Okay, it's not all that bad, Tatiana and I just went dancing a little," Szonja said preemptively.

"You said you were going to a Jewish boy's party."

"Well, that's true, it was probably just a different kind of party than you imagined."

Rina sighed. "Why didn't you just tell us where you were going?"

Szonja gestured at her clothes and hair. "Would you have let me go to a nightclub?"

"You're eighteen years old and I don't tell you what to do," she said. "It's just—we were expecting my grown-up sister rather than a teenager who sneaks around and comes back to my house in the middle of the night smelling like an ashtray."

A feeling of regret passed over Szonja but was quickly shoved aside by petulance. "Yes, well, you wouldn't know who to expect."

"What do you mean?"

"You chose to be absent for all of my teenage years, so I'm sure it'd be easier for you to just pretend I went from being a child to an adult while you've been living it up in America. *Sorry* for trying to have some fun." She wasn't sure what she was arguing for, but her words seemed to have found their mark. Rina sat down on the arm of one of the couches looking like a teenager herself, her small, delicate frame sagging in a too-big nightgown.

"Yes, we've missed a lot in each other's life," she said, looking down at her hands. "And I'm sure you've noticed, because you constantly look at the four of us like aliens, that we have a different lifestyle than what you're used to."

Szonja laughed a little, but then, seeing her sister's expression, said, "Well, yeah, you could say that."

"And it seems I was right . . . I can tell you've just been itching to say something, so come out with it, then."

"Well, of course I have, Rina—I mean, what the fuck? I've tried to be polite about it, but where has all this come from? We've never been religious; we've never even been to synagogue."

Rina stood up. "*You've* never been—this would have been a completely normal part of our lives had our father not decided to inculcate us with shame towards our religion."

"Oh, okay, I get it. Is this why you've got the rabbi telling me stories about this great shame of the Jews? It's all a bit heavy-handed, don't you think, bringing up the Holocaust?"

"Well, you also seem to have inherited our father's penchant for paranoia. I don't control the rabbi, Szonja, I don't even know what you're talking about."

"Okay, so, you're going to tell me that this would have been your *lifestyle* back home if it weren't for our father? Is this why you had to leave? Some great religious oppression you suffered at the hands of our tyrannical father? You're living out some sort of fantasy—"

"I'm not the one who came here expecting a great American adventure."

"Well, I wasn't expecting to be bored to death—that much is true."

"I'm sorry that my life isn't suitably entertaining for you. I didn't ask you to come here so you could judge the way I live."

"No, you didn't ask me to come, you couldn't care less what the rest of us are doing back home."

"Oh, sure, it's me who doesn't care. If you didn't just bury your head in the sand, you'd have noticed that our father hasn't spoken to me for years. And you act like it's none of your business."

"What are you talking about? Mom and Dad call you every month—they talk to you practically more than they talk to me, and I live with them."

"Yes, Mom talks to me, she calls me. Dad has found some excuse or other to be conveniently busy every single time. He's fixing the kitchen sink, he's running an errand, he's doing work in the garden. We don't even *have* a garden! As though I'd forget that!"

Szonja looked down at her feet—she could feel that they were both on the verge of dissolving into laughter at the idea of their father inventing a fake garden just to avoid talking to Rina. If she just looked at Rina, this argument would be over. She felt how easy it would be to let go, to let it all simmer down, but resentment came up in her chest like bile. It was Rina who'd decided to leave their family, to leave her as the sole witness to five years of their parents' heartache and resentment.

"Look, it just seems to me like this is all Aron—I'm sure the Jewish Stepford Wife thing seemed fun at first, but come on—"

"It's called having a family, Szonja. And having a faith. And I'm not sure what's so wrong with either." Rina sighed and sat down again. "Do you think so little of me that you can't fathom how I would make a choice for myself?"

Szonja thought for a second. Part of her mind urged her to bite her tongue, but it had always been the weaker part. "No, to be honest—I can't imagine you'd choose this. Choose him." She thought of all the things she had imagined her sister choosing over their family—a glamourous life in America, a life that was worth the sacrifice of even Szonja herself.

Rina shook her head. "Well, I love him—I love his steadfastness, his confidence, his belief in something greater. I love him."

"Repeat it enough times and it'll be true?" Szonja asked, but, feeling the cruelty of her own words, she changed tack. "Rina, this isn't who you are."

"Well, as you've pointed out, I don't know who *you* are." Rina looked down at her hands like they might provide the answer. "And you don't know who I am."

Their voices had gotten louder and louder as they spoke and must have woken Aron; he came into the room then, looking groggy with sleep. Szonja sighed, expecting even more censure from him, but he simply looked at Rina, took her hand and, without another glance at Szonja, they went back to their room.

PART II

Washington, DC, 1984

People never actually grow out of being read to at bedtime—they just stop. Or perhaps they call it something else: It's the TV's flicker that lulls them to sleep instead, or the rustle of the radio, or perhaps, as the day ends, their partner recounts in a lovable monotone the minutiae of the hours that led to its close.

At the age of thirteen Szonja would certainly have said she was too old to be read to if asked, but thankfully no one asked, and so her sister had the privilege of reading to her every night in the small room they shared on Upton Street at the diplomatic residences in Washington. They'd gotten through a fair bit of the German and French canon since their father had been stationed in the United States and were just now in the middle of *Candide*—none of it was suitable material for a thirteen-year-old, certainly, but Rina had to get through her reading somehow. They were now both homeschooled by their mother, and their father expected them to keep up with the Hungarian curriculum, having a deep-rooted mistrust of the American education system (and the Swedish system, and the French, and any other education system they were obliged to take part in). Even so, Rina, at nineteen, was a little late in taking her matura exams, due to the frequency of their moves and shifts in her education.

So Rina tried to keep up with her reading, and Szonja kept up with Rina's reading too, inadvertently. She struggled and grew restless through Balzac and Stendhal, and she could make no sense at all of Hoffmann, but Voltaire, finally, was fun. Candide bounced from one misadventure straight to the next in short little chapters, his eternal optimism battering against one obstacle after another.

"One more," she said. Candide had just suffered through a terrible earthquake, and Szonja wanted to know what was next for him.

"Fine, but it's getting gruesome. If you're too scared to fall asleep later, don't come bothering me."

Szonja reminded her sister that Rina wouldn't even be home this evening to bear witness to her struggles, so Rina read on about the Lisboans rounding up people, including the unfortunate Candide, for a ritual sacrifice to stave off further calamities.

"You know why they took the two Portuguese men?" Rina interrupted her own reading. Szonja was impatient to find out how Candide would get out of being burnt alive, but she indulged her sister, who, after all, was doing the hard work of the actual reading. "They're Jewish—see, it says they rejected the bacon-larded chicken, and that's why they were chosen to burn."

"So? They picked Candide for no reason at all," Szonja answered.

"But Candide survives the story—the whole book is about him, so you know he will." This seemed to bother her sister enough that Szonja felt it might be callous to ask her to continue reading. Rina had been particularly sensitive to injustices against the Jews lately, having recently coaxed out of their reluctant parents their family's Holocaust statistics (two survivors of Buchenwald, a one-way trip to Auschwitz and one to Treblinka). Rina was at that age when picking at these scabs felt somehow important.

Szonja could hear the front door open and their mother moving down the hall towards them, the end of her evening with Rina hastening along with her. "One more," she said, though she felt even as she said it that it was a little desperate and entirely futile. Rina would be on her way soon.

Their mother knocked gently on the door as she nudged it open.

Rina straightened and tried to suppress a smile. She shut the book and set it on her desk as she got up to go. "Is it Mrs. Kardos?" she asked. Rina adjusted the hem of her skirt in the mirror while Mrs. Imre took her seat and began to stroke Szonja's hair as they both watched her. Mrs. Kardos, a wife of one of the diplomats working at the embassy, was taking her to Friday-night dinner at a relative's house. Mrs. Kardos was something of a celebrity among the ambassadorial staff, as she had been a minor theatre star back in Hungary, the apotheosis of her work being a turn as Hedda Gabler. Mr. Imre had once commented that she must be an asset to her husband in her ability to perform at social events, but in reality she was ill at ease among the straitlaced statesmen in Washington. Her aloofness, however, made her all the more intriguing to them. When Mrs. Kardos asked Mr. Imre if his daughter might be interested in helping her fundraising efforts for the dilapidated Dohany Street Synagogue back in Budapest, no one had thought much of it—perhaps they were even a little proud to have Rina singled out in this way, proud to have a daughter interested in charitable work rather than malls and movies. But things had soured in the weeks since then. Now Rina slipped away Friday evenings to attend synagogue service with Mrs. Kardos, as though having spent all this time talking about the importance of a place of worship, she now felt compelled to make use of one.

"You look beautiful," Mrs. Imre said, and Rina quickly tore her eyes from the mirror. She looked at her mother curiously, which recalled Mrs. Imre to her question. "No, it's your father's guests—the ambassador needed a third for Ulti. One of the attachés has a stomach bug, I think."

Rina folded her arms. "And now you're hosting?" She went over to her mother and began plaiting her hair so that the three of them were now a little totem pole of care.

"Oh, hardly . . . two men, two wives, some pálinka, some pogácsa." Mrs. Imre waved a hand in front of her, dismissing her own effort, but her daughters knew the kind of strain a spontaneous hosting of the ambassador put on their mother. A game of Ulti went on for hours and was always an opportunity for social and political advancement if you got into the right one.

"I can't be expected to just go to sleep, can I, if you and Dad have guests coming and Rina's going out?" Szonja said this with a studied nonchalance. She had gotten used to her sister's social life by now (specifically the fact that it rarely included herself) and with an instinct for emotional self-preservation had stopped asking Rina to spend time with her. Her forced indifference had paid off so that now it was almost real.

Rina and Mrs. Imre shared an amused smile as Szonja got up from her bed and changed out of her pyjamas before either of them could protest. "Well, since you're both dressed, let's make an appearance, shall we?" Mrs. Imre said, but no one made a move to leave the comfort of their bedroom and exchange it for the cool civilities outside it until they heard Mr. Imre down the hall telling his guests stiffly that the girls were around here somewhere.

By the time they emerged, the guests had assembled around the small dining table, and Mr. Kenéz was shuffling a deck of Hungarian cards, the familiar hearts, acorns, bells and leaves fluttering under his thumbs. The ambassador looked worn, the thin skin under his eyes revealing the purple of late nights they had all been obliged to work since Reagan's blustery rhetoric had reignited old tensions across the Eastern Bloc, rousing even Hungary from its complacent middle ground, its comfortable "refrigerator Communism." This week they had all been in flux as the leaders back home deliberated for one whole excruciating week over whether the Hungarian athletes would join the boycott of the Olympics in Los Angeles along with their Soviet allies.

The men at the card table made their rounds of cautious obligatory statements on the topic. It was common knowledge that the CIA watched everyone in the Hungarian embassy. It was also common knowledge that half the ambassadorial staff were state police from back home, watching the other half of the embassy staff. And it was also true that all of the embassy staff kept an eye on their neighbours—out of habit, just in case. All that was left, really, was for everyone to stare at themselves in the mirror suspiciously.

"None of our boys needed to prove themselves," the ambassador said. *Intelligence suggests that 90 per cent of our athletes would defect as soon as the games were over.*

"They're still sore they didn't get to host in '80," Mr. Kenéz said. *Moscow got there first; now here's our punishment.*

"What even is rhythmic gymnastics?" asked Mrs. Kenéz from the sidelines. *Why must I sit and watch them play cards?*

"Twenty, one hundred," Mr. Imre said, putting two cards down, placing his bet, even his inner monologue suppressed by the depth of his reticence. Whether his restraint was habit or disposition was hard to know at this point, though some events in life had certainly pushed him in the direction of discretion. Like many of his colleagues, he had been educated at Karl Marx University, where fierce competition for foreign ministry work led students to report each other to the police for even the smallest infraction to gain even the smallest advantage. So he had become fastidious to a fault. But then, he had also had his education a safe distance from the disillusioning Soviet Union; he was a true believer in the principles that had by now receded to mere rhetoric. He believed in hard work, modesty, equality. This was what he was known for—he had made his career on the back of this reputation, but he was not exactly well liked and therefore seldom asked to play Ulti.

"Well, what do you make of it, Géza?" Mr. Kenéz pressed him.

Mr. Imre paused as his younger daughter came up to the table with a plate of pogácsa at her mother's behest. He held his cards in one hand, a cigarette in the other, its ashen tip in suspense over a glass ashtray. "Crime rates in Los Angeles are exceptionally high, so they are better off staying away," he said simply, at the same time indicating to Mrs. Imre with a small jut of his chin the ashtray beside him, replete with shells from the sunflower seeds Mrs. Imre ate to calm her nerves.

"I heard that there are people sleeping on every street corner," Mrs. Kenéz added.

"Well, the weather in California sure sounds great," Mrs. Imre said as she cleared the offending mound of shells from the ashtray in front of her husband.

Rina, sitting to the side and nursing the lukewarm glass of vermouth she'd been allowed, quietly added that she knew some people with family out there and they had said it was quite a pleasant place to live, really. It was hard to say if anyone heard her, but the next comment came from her father, who asked her to fetch another bottle of wine from the kitchen. As Rina stood up, her tights caught on the leg of her chair and a ladder revealed itself down her shin—she made flustered excuses and left to find another pair in her bedroom just as the doorbell rang and Mrs. Imre, with Szonja in her wake, went to let in Mrs. Kardos.

"Julikam," Mrs. Kardos exclaimed in the doorway, using the possessive and diminutive at once, pressing her cold cheeks against Mrs. Imre's. Szonja went to hang her coat, playing the part of the docile and helpful child while taking the opportunity to run her hands along the luxurious silk.

"Rina is just getting ready . . ." Mrs. Imre looked towards the living room, where the noise of cards shuffling and flapping against the table could be heard. She hesitated only a moment, thinking her husband would not want the woman to linger in their home, but then the protocol hardwired into her took over and she asked Mrs. Kardos if she would like to step in for some coffee while she waited.

Mrs. Imre made both of them strong coffee on the stovetop, thick as tar, the way they liked it back home. Mrs. Kardos sat on her chair by the kitchen table, back straight like she was waiting primly outside an audition room, but when her hostess turned towards the stove, her face slackened and became pensive; when she caught Szonja looking, it morphed quickly into an expression of benevolence, a wise confidante, and it changed again when Mrs. Imre turned to serve the coffee, shifting imperceptibly into brow-arched hauteur. Szonja felt repelled by the woman but yearned to get up close to her, to run her hands along the metamorphic rubber of her face.

"Julikam, is this where you hide out from the tedium?"

"Hmm?"

"The apparatchik Ulti party."

"Oh, they're a lovely bunch, really . . . ," she said softly.

"It's okay, sweetheart. We are all bound by duty to be here for one reason or another. We are not bound by anything to find it interesting."

Szonja giggled but Mrs. Imre only smiled a little, caught between politesse and deference towards her husband and guests. It seemed unfair to Szonja to have her mother, whom she loved dearly, in such proximity to glamour when it could only diminish her in comparison. Mrs. Imre was quiet and careful in her movements and expressions; whatever her personality had been originally, it had been nudged in a specific direction, pressed through the mould of her husband's contours, so now, to all but those who knew her best, she was the consummate diplomat's wife.

But Szonja often wished that others could see her version of her mother. She had been the one to teach her a love of the theatre. Back home, Mr. Imre and Rina went to plays out of duty, the former to show his colleagues that he attended the right kind, the latter for the purpose of rounding out her education and pleasing her father. But Mrs. Imre and Szonja went for pure pleasure, for the feeling when the lights came low over the life of the audience and all that remained was the brightly lit stage, its curated objects and painted faces. They went to plays that were tried and true and ones that were new and experimental; they went to the big theatres but also to theatres that were out of government favour, the ones where actors and directors in political exile washed up to do penance. Mrs. Imre was a near contemporary of Mrs. Kardos, so she had spent her youth in imitative admiration of the woman, even going as far as cropping her hair close when she saw Mrs. Kardos play a spirited, pixie-cut Masha in a modernised *Three Sisters*.

And now they were both "protocol wives," moored in Washington for as long as their husbands served there, attending functions in muted skirt suits, smiling and shaking hands.

"How is your beautiful daughter?" Mrs. Kardos asked mildly as she stirred her coffee. Even though she had meant no slight on Szonja, the younger girl bridled at the implication and offered boldly, "She's right here, miss."

"Szonja!" Mrs. Imre said, waving her hand towards her as if it could subdue her. But Mrs. Kardos just laughed and said, "But of course, here is one beautiful daughter. I was just wondering how the elder is. I was sad that she couldn't make it to our little Friday get-together last week—I assume a young girl like her was out with friends?"

"She was at a ballet with her father," Mrs. Imre answered, and then, as though this required further explanation, "I would have gone, but *La Sylphide* is a particular favourite of Rina's, so I gave her my place." Mrs. Imre felt bad for passing the burden of her official duties to her daughter, even though Rina never complained. This was her fifth posting with Mr. Imre and she'd found herself weary and more often tired at the prospect of such events, more often tired in general. Her daughter's English was better than hers as well, and Mr. Imre seemed these days to prefer Rina's company anyway, so Mrs. Imre had slowly slipped into the neglect of her duties like a warm, enveloping bath. It also allowed her to spend time with her younger daughter in a way she hadn't had a chance to with her elder. Of course she knew both girls with the depth of any mother: their habits, their likes and dislikes, the personal histories of their lives. But Szonja she'd gotten to know almost as a friend, one she shared interests and jokes with, in a way she never had with Rina.

Something in the swirling complexity of guilt in Mrs. Imre's answer had given Mrs. Kardos the in she needed—she did not know precisely what was going on in the Imre household, but she felt intuitively the right button to push.

"Oh, but surely a young girl like her ought to be with other young people her age, not at fusty piano concertos and ballets!"

Mrs. Imre stared down and stirred more sugar into her coffee. Szonja looked between the two women, and despite her interest in their glamourous guest, she couldn't help but feel protective towards her mother, who was so easily suppressed by the stronger voices around her. "Rina spends time with me and I'm young," she told Mrs. Kardos.

Mrs. Kardos laughed again. "Aren't we the spirited one? But you see, there are some things you are *too* young for—just you wait a couple years," she said with a wink.

"I do everything Rina does—we listen to the same music, we read the same books. I'm her best friend." Szonja was at once wary of everyone's sudden interest in Rina's social life and offended at the lack of interest in her own.

Mrs. Kardos had lost patience with the younger daughter and turned back to Mrs. Imre without answering her. "Rina's met some wonderful young people these past months—we must encourage her in making friends with some of them, perhaps even more than that," she told her conspiratorially. When Mrs. Imre only nodded in a polite, noncommittal way, Mrs. Kardos grasped her hand across the table and looked her directly in the eye. "Oh, Julikam, you must help her along, Rina looks up to you so," she said, although she had no way of knowing this. When Rina returned, with fresh tights and colour in her cheeks, Mrs. Imre and Szonja watched wordlessly as Mrs. Kardos ushered her out into a foreign world.

Why Mrs. Kardos took such an interest in Rina was a mystery to the whole Imre family. Perhaps it was her penchant for romanticising the lives of young women in her social circle, a way of regaining some of the lost romance of her own youth. Or perhaps it was just a habit of framing life as a drama, which sometimes required a little moulding and cajoling to fit Aristotle's principles. It might also have been a genuine interest in seeing her young friend find a life of faith and love. Or, as Mr. Imre would later say, perhaps she was working for the CIA.

And then, of course, there was also good old-fashioned boredom. Often the simplest explanation is the right one.

Mrs. Kardos had invited Rina to participate in the fundraiser for the synagogue without any specific intent; she'd simply cast her as one of her repertory players, banked for later use. But when she saw the way Aron looked at the young girl at the first meeting of the fundraising committee, she resolved to help Rina see herself reflected in his admiration.

And even the steadiest young person will waver in the face of first love. When Mrs. Kardos had introduced her to Aron, whose mother was distantly related to Mrs. Kardos herself, Rina didn't think much of him. This was no slight to Aron's looks, which were perfectly adequate to interest a young woman predisposed to be interested. But Rina was a late bloomer and hadn't yet acquired the habit of some of her contemporaries of sizing up each man she met in terms of his suitability as a companion. What she saw was a man several years her senior apparently devoted to charitable work; what he saw were dark brown eyes that stilled the world around them like an anchor and a girl who seemed serious-minded enough to possibly build a life around their religion. His thinking, clearly, had been borne along on a faster, headier train than hers.

By the time Aron walked Rina back to their house that night and she invited him in to say hello to her parents, the card game had dimmed to a drawn-out end. Szonja had dozed off with her head in her mother's lap but was roused when the door opened to reveal her sister and the solicitous young man whom she had met only in passing at the embassy's outreach events for émigrés.

Aron bent his knees until he was squatting in front of Szonja. Except she was thirteen years old and not only resented the patronising gesture but was in fact too tall for it, so she had to look down at his awkward frog body as the man smiled broadly and offered his hand to her.

"Hello, young lady," he said in the tone of a much older man and in the accent of a foreigner.

"Hello, old man," she offered. Aron blinked twice and then laughed, looking up at Rina, the sudden movement pushing him off-balance so that he had to perform a bit of a Cossack dance before he straightened up to his full height.

"Your sister says you are enjoying *Candide*," he said after he had righted himself, but he forgot to put it in question form and had to continue on his own. "It's a great one. 'Man was born to live either in convulsions of misery or in the lethargy of boredom.'"

Szonja didn't immediately grasp its meaning, but she thought, looking at her sister's new beau, that *lethargy of boredom* had the right ring to it. However, a glance at Rina confirmed that his recall of the classics had done the trick—she gave him that private smile of pleasure Szonja recognised from watching her sister read. That smile that meant that whatever enjoyment her sister was having was miles away from herself and not to be shared—and now there was this man on the far shore with her.

"Géza, your daughter has a suitor—you haven't said anything about this," the ambassador said, the conversation in the hall having made its way in snippets to the card table. "Come, let's see this young man."

PORCUPINES

Rina and Aron stepped shyly into the room, and the men stood to give strong two-handed shakes.

Aron introduced himself haltingly in Hungarian.

"Aron's grandparents are from Transylvania originally," Rina told them and received a polite round of *Oh, is that so*s. Rina herself seemed surprised to have chosen this particular fact to share about Aron when so many more were at her fingertips. Over watery coffees, he had revealed to her the little details of his life that only someone poised at the precipice of loving him would have found interesting.

"We met at your fundraiser for the Dohany Street Synagogue," Aron offered.

Mr. Imre tensed up reflexively at the mention of the synagogue, directing his eyes briefly to the ambassador. Even among just the lower rungs of the embassy, there was a Herzl, a Kohn and a Klein who had been transformed by the magic of deed poll to a Fodor and a Varga and a Horvath sometime in this century, but Mr. Imre resented the association he had worked hard to shed.

Although at first he hadn't minded letting Rina participate in the fundraiser, one intolerable event had piled onto another in the past weeks since Mrs. Kardos had taken a shine to his Rina. He had watched her spend interminable hours speaking to Hungarian-Americans, Jews who had emigrated decades ago (centuries ago even, judging by the speed of their speech) and had such fond (and tedious) anecdotes about the times they had gone to just that synagogue in Budapest. They all shuffled in with their long coats and a whiff of the shtetl still about them; these people who had come to the most advanced country in the world seemed not to have advanced beyond their voodoo and ritual. Mr. Imre, a Hungarian, a

Jew, in America, had nothing to say to these people. But Rina was enraptured by their insipid stories and seemed content to sit for hours with the mustiest of them. And then, the boy—the son or grandson of one of these old sacks of bones—came to these events much more often than a young man ought to, a normal young man who worked and had a life. And now Rina was going to synagogue and peppering her talk with foreign words.

"So what's the harm?" Mrs. Imre had asked him. She was glad to see Rina getting out of the house a little more and thought, a little selfishly, that perhaps she could direct her morbid questions about the suffering of the Jews towards someone else for a change.

"The *harm*?" he asked incredulously. But then, unable to vocalise what actual harm it might do, he was forced to leave a suggestive blank as an answer and allow his daughter to go to synagogue. For a while Mr. Imre would make excuses for his daughter's increasing absence from embassy events. He told people she was unwell, that she was studying, that she had studied so much she'd become unwell. He would have felt ridiculous saying that his clever young daughter was praying.

Mr. Imre might have sneered at Aron's devoutness, but perhaps he would have felt differently had he known that somewhere in Brooklyn, Aron's extended family belonged to an even more stringent orthodoxy, that his parents had taught him English and Hungarian in addition to the Yiddish commonly used in their community. That they had allowed him to be educated in ways they themselves hadn't been. But the Imres did not know any of this. One family's black sheep is another one's straight and narrow, and so it has always been.

"Would you like to join us, Aron? We were just finishing up but we can start another round if you're interested," Mr. Kenéz said, his wife sagging back onto her chair defeatedly.

"Oh, no, thank you, I am not a betting man," Aron said.

Mr. Imre, worried that Aron might launch into some prim religious censure of the card game he had just hosted, decided to politely hasten the departure of all his guests and thanked them for their visit. He shook Aron's hand again and pointedly thanked him too, so they all shuffled awkwardly out into the foyer to put on their shoes and coats.

"Dad, can we talk?" Rina asked when all the guests had finally left and Mrs. Imre was wiping the crumbs and wine stains from their dining table.

"It's been a long day, Rina, we can talk tomorrow," he said without looking up at her.

"I'd rather . . . we talk now," she said, a small quiver in her voice.

Mr. Imre gave his wife a quiet look, and she shuffled their younger daughter to her bedroom, several hours past her normal bedtime, then rejoined them in the living room.

Lying on her bed, Szonja could hear her father's voice, the volume of his words going up and down in rhythm with his paces across the living room so Szonja heard about three out of every ten words.

". . . that's what you said . . ."

". . . I just think it's . . ."

". . . up your socks . . ." And so on, in maddening, nonsensical abridgement. They were arguing about Aron, that much was clear. She crept closer to her door and opened it to hear better.

". . . we cannot be together otherwise."

"And what does marriage look like to you, Rina? Does it involve shaving your head and vowing subservience to this boy you hardly know?"

She mumbled something Szonja couldn't hear, to which Mr. Imre responded, "Do not disrespect your mother, Rina."

There was a long silence, and it seemed like the discussion was over, but then Rina spoke again. Szonja strained to hear her muted voice.

"I have always, *always*, done as I am told. I have never disrespected you. I wish . . . I just wish you would trust that I know my own mind."

And after that—silence, and Szonja knew that she had not missed any words; Mr. Imre simply declined to answer his daughter.

When Rina finally came to bed, Szonja could see her in the dim light of their room preparing for sleep in her slow and methodical way, as though nothing out of the ordinary had happened that evening. After a while, Szonja crept up to her bed. "I don't want to dream of ritual sacrifices," she said, and Rina opened up her covers and shifted a little to the side to let her in. Szonja could feel her sister's shaky breaths, felt her tense body beside her, until sleep, blissfully free of earthquakes and fires, finally overcame her.

That night, as the house settled into uneasy slumber, the members of the Imre family each told a story to soothe themselves—the same time, the same setting, the same players. But these stories, told and retold over the years, would come to rest on each other unevenly, like a sloppy deck of cards.

Rina told a story of her self-assertion: She had only ever wanted to live up to the regard her father had for her, but now, for the first time, she wanted something for herself. Not just Aron but all that he represented—a life of stability and community and faith in a way she hadn't known before. She told herself that she had never put a toe out of line, so wasn't she allowed one act of rebellion? And wasn't it her *own* life she was altering? She told herself her father would understand eventually, would come to love and respect Aron the way she did. Her mother could return to the faith of her forebears with her, and her sister could be brought up in the solidity of it.

Mr. Imre said to himself that his elder daughter knew him well enough that she understood him. He would not have admitted this to anyone, but he had always thought his younger daughter, even accounting for her age, was somewhat frivolous, not at all predisposed to serious thoughts and a little too easily enamoured of the bright, cellophane-wrapped culture they had found themselves in. He hadn't had much need to verify his assumptions when he and Mrs. Imre had so easily, so seamlessly aligned themselves one to each daughter, so Mrs. Imre could have her giggles with Szonja, and he had Rina—dutiful, serious-minded Rina. That is, until she'd started that nonsense with the Jewish boy. But he had been clear with her, and he didn't need to explain himself further. He didn't need to tell her that marrying an American man would make his job untenable. That having an American daughter left him open to blackmail, to being turned. That the defection of a beloved child would lead people to wonder whether he would follow—and wouldn't he?

He had three more years of work to do here for his country, so she could wait out those three years, and then, if she still thought that mumbling incantations over candles was important, she could go and marry this young man, though he doubted any of it would last longer than a few months. He didn't need to explain this—Rina knew his word was final.

Mrs. Imre repeated uneasy assertions to herself too. She had supported her husband in his decision to tell their daughter that she could not marry. But she had also conveyed to Rina her sympathy, had she not? She had allowed her to spend time with the boy; she had been a vessel for Rina's many thoughts on faith and family. Her conduct could not be faulted; she had expressed kindness and understanding to everyone, had put each of her family members so far ahead of herself that she wasn't sure of her own mind on the matter anymore. But surely that was enough to keep the peace. These thoughts would prove flimsy comfort in the years before the wall fell, when people believed the intransigence of the conflicts that kept them apart.

Szonja, for her part, was a swirl of impulses: She could see her sister straining against the confines of their family and felt a nascent interest in running her hand along those boundaries too; she could see her mother falter as her habit of pleasing everyone came up against immutable opposition between those she loved most; she saw her father, strong, inflexible and out of her reach. And eventually, as Szonja reluctantly folded away the bright, promising life she had enjoyed in Washington, DC, she could not help but admire her sister, who had been braver than all of them in going after just what she wanted.

Lost Hills, 2001

NEITHER THE CHILDREN'S ATTENTION SPAN NOR THEIR BLADDER capacity are deemed sufficient for them to make the trip to San Francisco—approximately six hours by bus—in one go, therefore it has been decided that an overnight stop will be made in the unfortunate location of Lost Hills, California. This town has little to recommend it apart from the fact that it sits a couple of hours north of Los Angeles and is accessible by a major highway. There it stands, awaiting travellers who have decided to take the fast route instead of the scenic one along the coastline; there it waits, knowing that even these men and women of an optimising bent, these individuals immune to the poetry of a dramatic cliff drop, will grow tired of the highway, will need a rest or, at the very least, gas. Despite the potentially damaging effects of this slight to the morale of the good people of Lost Hills, they welcome the school bus of children with enthusiasm.

"We've cleaned the pool special," says the man at the front desk of the Lost Hills Inn, leading some to wonder what state it could have been in before their arrival. "I hope the kids packed their swimsuits," he continues, leading some to hope fervently that they have not.

But there is no keeping children from a pool, and as the alternative is a visit to Lost Hills Wonderful Park—a misnomer of some proportion—there really is no choice. Sonia watches from a faded sun lounger as Mila performs her fifteen-minute stretching routine while the other children cannonball into the pool, sees her daughter put talcum powder in a swim cap before plastering it over her head as the other kids load water balloons—and she wonders whether this trip will be the moment she finds out her daughter is destined for a lifetime of loneliness.

But Mila seems not to mind; she swims her laps, politely winding around the rest of the children playing, and when she is satisfied with her exercise, she props herself up on the pool's edge and sits with her feet dangling in the water.

Mila has, until recently, had no qualms about her social standing—after all, her mother doesn't bother keeping up friendships, and she looks happy enough. Mila has viewed her class from a position of emotional remove, observing the undulations of their little society but making sure not to involve herself too much. Each year, school begins, and a certain pack of girls and boys might seem to a less discerning onlooker to be the "popular" ones—but Mila has found these to be false gods, propped up by surprising growth spurts or interesting summer holidays they can relate anecdotes from. But as the year goes on, the shifting of alliances topples them, until finally, sometime around March, they calcify into whatever formation they are currently at.

This year has left her in a loose coalition with Kathy Park, a shy girl with dry eyes, and Sergio Mendoza, a boy who is too polite to be widely liked but who will go on to be a wonderful boyfriend to many vulnerable women later in life. The three of them are not so much friends as spare parts—the bolts and screws left over after assembling furniture, thrown into a Ziploc and forgotten about. Mila has accepted this with the habitual equanimity of an outsider, but something has shifted lately; she has always known her place, but she's never been aware of her power to change it. Like someone roused from an overlong afternoon nap, she has woken up a little disoriented and wondering what else could be made of the day.

And so she is at a loss for what to say when Megan H swims up to her seat at the edge of the pool and says, "I like your swimsuit."

Mila looks down at her suit—a standard-issue black Speedo—and decides not to let this compliment unduly go to her head. Megan H is decidedly among the upper echelons of their class, far above the other Megans, of which there are five in total, at least two of whom are on this trip. There's Megan C, who is kindhearted but dumb, and Megan A, who is smart but mean-spirited. Then there's Megan L, who is restless and sporty, and Megan B, who has no discernible qualities whatsoever—a sort of blank-slate prototype Megan, if you will. Mila imagines that the Megans are God's little experiment—He keeps trying different combinations until one day maybe there will be a perfect Megan. But until then, it is down to the likes of Mila to remember which is which, a heavy burden to bear, since offering Megan C Hot Cheetos, which are clearly Megan H's favoured snack, could render Mila a social pariah for the week. Mila might be aloof, but she is not entirely immune to the social pressures of the fifth grade.

"Thanks," she says simply, and before she can make any further error, she shifts herself back into the water and swims a few more laps.

Each child is assigned to a room with a chaperone, three to one. Mila shares a double bed with her mother while Megan H sleeps on a single and her most dedicated friend, Riley, is relegated to a trundle bed in the corner.

"Take a good look around, girls—if you ever find yourselves in an establishment of similar quality as adults, it's time to rethink your life choices," Sonia says and Megan and Riley giggle from the bed where they are playing travel chequers. The two of them are prone to giggling as well as generous amounts of elbow nudging and eyerolls.

Mila does not attempt to insinuate herself into the girls' game—she has been on the receiving end of too many "This is an A and B conversation, so C you later" type remarks in her school career not to know better. In any case she has brought with her a library book on the composer Dmitry Shostakovich, whose music they are to play in San Francisco, to keep herself entertained in the inevitable lulls of such a trip. The book's cover has a rough pencil sketch of Shostakovich's profile, a benign rendering that has softened the oppressed intensity of his eyes from early portraits. Mila has been carrying it around with her everywhere, and the image has become stamped onto her imagination to the extent that any mention of an adult man now evokes this figure. It is just as well that there are no actual images of Shostakovich for her to compare it to—the man consistently sat for portraits with the bearing of someone in a hostage video. (Russian portraiture does seem to leave something to be desired—one look at Rasputin will leave anyone questioning Boney M. for life.)

Upon seeing Mila reading, Riley remarks derisively, "What's that, a book about your grandpa?" It is unclear how this constitutes an insult, and yet it is understood that it *is* an insult, and Sonia, overhearing it, tenses up immediately. Looking at her daughter cling to her library book, Sonia suddenly remembers her daughter's rulebook back home, which advises girls to set their own trends in order to be cool. She wonders if Camy Baker was quite specific enough about the kinds of things that were likely to catch on.

"What have you learned today, Milosh?" she asks, sitting down on their shared motel bed.

"It's about Shostakovich," Mila says, partly in response to Riley, who has long since lost interest in receiving an answer to her question. "He wrote his first opera when he was only thirteen."

"Oh." Sonia glances at the cover with the severe-looking man. Something about his face and her daughter's factoid sounds familiar. "That *is* impressive."

Upon hearing Sonia call it impressive, Megan ventures over cautiously, takes the book from Mila, flips through it like a magazine, then returns to her game with Riley. Mila observes this series of actions, opens her mouth to say something, but there is no obvious way to parlay it into anything further, so she returns to her book.

Although it was Mila herself who volunteered her mother to chaperone this trip, and she had her reasons for doing so, she has found it strangely unsettling to see her worlds—school and home—collide in such a way. Seeing her mother in her leather jacket and her Ray-Ban sunglasses, her hair a shade of brown that is indistinguishable from black, sitting on the school bus taking a paper bag of juice and crackers from Mrs. Flores or helping a classmate unstick a jammed zipper is like seeing a dog trot into your classroom and start teaching your class.

Of course Mila has seen her mother interact with her peers—it is nearly unavoidable. Sonia will drop Mila off at a birthday party and politely decline to stay for cake; she will take her to swim practice but stay in the car reading a magazine while the other parents sit on the bleachers gossiping; she often warns Mila, "If you ask people about their lives, they're bound to ask about yours. And if you tell people something interesting about yourself, there are bound to be follow-up questions." And yet, seeing her among the other parents, the schoolchildren, the muted pastels of the Lost Hills Inn, Mila realises her mother is like a tropical bird in a highway underpass—she is by far the most interesting thing around.

Sonia is unaware of the critical gaze cast by her own daughter, but she is very conscious of the scrutiny of the other parents and teachers. Thus far she has managed to stick to the company of the children, but she has been informed that the chaperones will be gathering in the "lounge" of the Lost Hills Inn for a mixer after the kids have had their lights-out. There is nothing about this event that doesn't fill her with dread, but Cecily Auerbach has already been around all the rooms to chivvy along the children in their nighttime routines and to remind the parents of their social obligations. Sonia briefly considered pretending to be asleep, but as she was standing by the closet fully dressed when Cecily entered, this seemed unlikely to work.

"All right, kiddos, make sure to keep the giggling to an acceptable decibel level so we can all pretend you're sleeping," Sonia says as she touches up her mascara in a mirror that seems to shrink in on itself like it's embarrassed to be placed on the wall of this room. Sonia goes to kiss Mila good night, then thinks better of it and throws all the girls air kisses as she heads out.

The lounge of the Lost Hills Inn is possibly sadder than its rooms, which makes sense when you think about the amount of socialising that is bound to go on at a two-star motel adjacent to the highway. But the man from the front desk (Dalton, his name tag announces) is there again, doubling as tender to a makeshift bar, looking as enthused about the prospect of serving them drinks as he was about their swimsuits—that is, to an uncomfortable degree. Dalton has never seen the movie *Psycho*, but if he had, he would surely resent the connection everyone is certainly making in that moment.

The teachers and parents have all gathered there, sitting on well-worn sofas and a few uncomfortable-looking chairs. There are eight chaperones in total, three teachers and five parents. Sonia is familiar with Cecily and with Kathy Park's mother, Linda, as well as Mrs. Flores, Miss Anderson and Mr. Rodriguez. There is also Dave, the only father to accompany them on the trip, who wears a surprised expression, as though he can't quite comprehend how he's found himself here, and another mother, whose name Sonia will not be able to remember even by the end of the week but who she will continue to refer to as Lisa.

"Nice cold beer, missus?" Dalton asks as Sonia sidles into the room.

"I'd better not."

"Oh, go on, Sonia—we have designated chaperones, so we're allowed." Linda Park has come up to the bar. She pays Dalton for two beers and hands one to Sonia.

"Let me guess—Cecily?"

"No, actually. Cecily has the secret sauce . . . I mean, Cecily secretly likes the sauce . . . God, that's hard to say. Perhaps I'm the one with the secret sauce. Can you tell I don't get out much?"

"Depends on how many of these got you into this state."

"Too few, Sonia, too few."

Sonia takes a hesitant sip of her beer—she is in no way a teetotaller, but being the sole caretaker of a child for the past ten years has rather reduced the opportunities for the casual enjoyment of alcohol. She and Linda settle into lounge chairs, and with the beer loosening her muscles at a surprising pace, Sonia dares to go against one of her very own edicts: She asks Linda about her life. And

Linda is happy to provide details, telling Sonia about her mother-in-law moving in with them, about her job as a social worker, and about her daughter's struggles with math. All of it completely normal, uncomplicated, banal even, and yet Sonia can't help but ask for follow-ups and elaborations. And when Linda reciprocates her interest, it's easier than she imagined to swerve the question—she offers to get them each another beer, proposes a trip to the restrooms. She tenses up only momentarily when Linda makes a casual remark about Sonia's assumed family, but after a little fumble, she sidesteps this by pointing out the awkward way Mrs. Flores strokes her own bottle of beer.

For a moment—really, only a very brief one, and even that she will deny later on—Sonia is glad to be able to sit back and drink a beer while someone else stands guard. But there is a price to pay for this comfort, and it is their company. And apart from Linda, who is rapidly growing on her, it's very dull company indeed. But then again, it's been a while since she's had better.

Los Angeles, 1989

SZONJA WAS USED TO TIPTOEING AROUND PEOPLE'S EMOTIONS, HAVing lived with a sullen father and a fragile mother for most of her life, so she was quite comfortable navigating the displeasure of her hosts—she had never thought, though, in all her excitement to come to Los Angeles, that she would be reverting to her old roles from the suburbs of Budapest. Nothing about Los Angeles had said to her *small lives, quiet pleasures*. But as she was not desirous of another blowout with her sister, her pleasures did indeed remain small and quiet, mostly confined, ironically, to the Hebrew classes she had so chafed against.

In the breaks, Szonja and Anthony walked down to the convenience store a block from the learning centre where there was a whole world of lurid plastic-wrapped confectionaries she was unfamiliar with. Anthony accompanied her around the store with a bemused expression as Szonja gradually made her way through all the offerings.

The intimacy generated by a night out together had forced Szonja and Anthony to bypass the usual preliminaries—they were now somehow indisputably friends, and yet she didn't know all that much about him.

"Are you even Jewish?" she asked one day as they tried to discern nuances of flavour among the different colour Skittles on their way back to the learning centre.

Anthony widened his eyes in mock horror. "Have I not proven myself enough?" He waved around his satchel stuffed with loose sheafs of paper—handouts and exercises from class.

"Well, you did say you were here to impress a girl. And then there's the fact that you're not even called Dovid. I'm not quite over the deception."

"Yeah, I guess Anthony Greene doesn't scream *yeshiva*," he said, dipping his head apologetically. "I'm Jewish on my mother's side and, I believe, Catholic on my father's—though neither is particularly serious about it, as you can probably tell by their decision to get together and procreate."

"And also that their son is awful at Hebrew."

"Only when compared to people who actually speak it."

"Which is much too harsh a measure."

Anthony smiled—a rarity, it seemed, even in his best moods. It was as though his face were arranged in such a way that made it uncomfortable. Szonja wondered about the Kabbalist girlfriend briefly, but to ask him would upset the tenor of their fledgling friendship, and he was only her second friend here—it did not seem worth the satisfaction of her curiosity.

"Is your mother pleased that you've taken an interest?" she asked instead.

Anthony hummed a little and finally said, "I think she finds it amusing. She likes to say that she's just a 'deli' Jew—you know, not particularly interested in the liturgical element, but she makes her brisket and kugel and all the rest. How about yours?"

Szonja wondered which angle to approach the question from to make him understand the strangeness of her faith, or lack of it, Rina's faith, faith in general—but their languorous walk finally deposited them at the door of the classroom, and they divided shyly before she could formulate the thought properly.

In class that day they were practising words related to Shabbat—*bracha*, *erev*, *kiddush*—and putting them to use by inviting each other over for a Friday-night meal.

"Why don't we, actually?" Anthony said after they'd stumbled through a stilted conversation about who's making challah.

"I'm not much of a baker—" Szonja said.

"No, I mean do Shabbat," he said. Szonja looked to Anthony in question—she had gotten the impression that Shabbat dinners were unlikely to be held at the Greene residence—but he just smiled expectantly, clearly enjoying her confusion. "Come to my house, I think my mother would love it." Szonja looked a little alarmed at this. "No, my mother loves to host, there'd be loads of other people, there always are."

They made plans to have dinner at Anthony's house the next week, and as they left the learning centre, they passed Rabbi Raskin, who smiled widely at them—Szonja had no doubt he would feel it was a job well done if he brought two young Jews together, much as if they were to finally string together a coherent sentence in Hebrew.

Szonja had feared that her fight with Rina would result in the end of her English classes—as was often the case for those on the precipice of adulthood, she had not quite realised yet that others could no longer dole out punishment for her misbehaviour; the censure was confined to the stiff backs and averted glances, the overly solicitous remarks at the dinner table. Rina still drove her to the community college, still packed her brown-paper-bag lunch and asked her how her day had been, as they slowly adjusted to a different vision of each other than what they'd begun with when Szonja first landed at LAX.

During their next class, the theme of which was "common American idioms," their teacher patiently tried to explain the illogic of phrases like "That's just fantastic" and "Don't be a stranger" and why believing something in America meant you had to purchase it. Despite their perfect grammar, the students still occasionally stumbled into the misuse of figurative language, so they partnered up and practised some common expressions.

"You help someone . . . ," Szonja prompted.

"I give them a hand," Tatiana answered.

"Your signature is your . . ."

"John Hancock."

"Something suits you, you like it . . ."

"It's up my alley!" Tatiana answered defiantly, like a game-show contestant in the last round. "Are these sounding a bit sexual to you?"

"Get your mind out of the gutter," Szonja replied. "That was going to be our next one, actually."

"Really?"

"No," said Szonja. Tatiana huffed—her form of laughter. "Okay, how about, if you watch out for something . . ."

"I keep an eye . . ." Tatiana answered more soberly, the missing word making it sound a little sinister.

During the break, they finally had a chance to debrief their night out. Szonja was ready to forgive Tatiana for leaving her to fend for herself at Coconut Teaszer, but she need not have prepared for such a show of magnanimity, as Tatiana turned out not to be remorseful in the least.

"How was the rest of your evening?" she asked simply, and Szonja realised that of course Tatiana would not understand the implications of their evening of revelries, that Szonja's night out brought up old resentments the way the Pacific regurgitates plastic at high tide. *Hello, did you think you could forget about me?*

She didn't bother to explain, and Tatiana in any case was consumed with a sudden fervour for the bass player she had spent the night with and continued the conversation herself, talking about another club he was planning on taking her to and when they should all go together. Szonja wanted to join her, but something of her sister's censure must have wormed its way in, because she found herself weary and reluctant to make more plans behind Rina's back. And making plans with her consent would require Szonja to brave the topic she and Rina had been skirting around for days, so she made noises of approval without any words of commitment.

Tatiana was not so easily fooled, however, and on their way back to class she fell into step with Szonja and said, "We don't have to go if you don't want," with an air of earnestness at odds with the less than dramatic nature of their undertaking—it made Szonja think Tatiana had understood more of what she was experiencing than she had thought. "We can do something else—and perhaps your Antonio would like to join us?"

"Not *my* Antonio," she said. "There's supposedly a girlfriend. Although she is suspiciously absent . . . and then he asked me to come have dinner at his parents' place."

"Interesting." Tatiana wiggled her eyebrows.

"I don't want it to be like *that*." Szonja wiggled her eyebrows back.

"Why don't you want it to be like *that* with the nice American boy—don't you think it would be fun for it to be like *that* with the nice American boy?"

Szonja considered this for a moment—would it be fun? "He's just a little too self-serious."

"Well, that is what these American boys are like—they are loud and self-important. I blame the excessive consumption of beef."

"I'll make sure to ask Anthony how much red meat he consumes," Szonja said, rolling her eyes. "Or maybe you can ask him yourself at dinner next week?" she asked hopefully.

Tatiana sighed. "All right, yes, I will come to meet beefcake's family with you."

Szonja gave her friend a delighted squeeze. "I don't think that means what you think it means," she said as they took their seats.

Mrs. Greene ran the kind of household where guests were welcome. Parties were held, dinners were hosted, houseguests were given the softest towels—and yet it was unclear whether this tendency was born of enjoyment or habit. She was not the shimmering hostess, the locus of conversation, but she eased the way for everyone else with a brisk, unfussy kindness. Only at the end of an evening, when she collapsed in a seat at the dining table and proclaimed, "That's it, I'm done," did everyone become all at once aware of the depth of her endeavour. Then they would all rally around her—Anthony's sister collecting dishes, Mr. Greene loading them, Anthony serving coffee in little porcelain cups and saucers piled onto a gilded silver tray. It took three people to fill the void of activity she left behind once she'd decided she was done for the day.

It reminded Szonja of her own mother, who had quickly learned to be hostess to any number of influential figures and dignitaries when her husband had joined the foreign ministry. But although she performed her duties with perfect decorum, she never seemed at ease in the role—when she collapsed at the end of the day, it was in the privacy of her own room. Mrs. Greene would stay there at the centre, near the evening's dying embers, holding herself close to the warm glow of her own achievement. And in turn, Szonja would come to love holding herself close to the warm glow of Mrs. Greene's personality.

When Szonja had first mentioned her plans to her sister, Rina looked at her blankly.

"You want to voluntarily go to a Shabbat dinner?" she asked, eyes narrowing.

"Well, it won't be like *that*," she said, and whatever "that" was, Rina correctly understood it to be different and better than the experience she herself had provided. Shabbat was the focal point of Rina's week, an opportunity to invite over friends and acquaintances from the synagogue and the girls' school, but it was somewhat lacking in ease and liveliness. Most weeks Shabbat manifested in doing various things with a chicken—indeed, Rina seemed always to be in the process of doing something with a chicken. And although all this work only bemused Szonja, she could tell that there was some unknown significance to her sister's efforts and tried to make up for her callousness by asking Rina's advice on how to approach the dinner at the Greenes'. Her sister gave her an old copy of *How to Be a Jew* that had been on her bedside table and showed her some passages on the Sabbath that she had underlined in pencil. The thought of her sister thumbing through a little guide on how to live her life before she went to bed every night made Szonja at once want to hug her and shake her, but she took the book anyway.

She had an opportunity to introduce Anthony to her sister outside of the Jewish learning centre later that week, where they made polite conversation about how nicely the new landscaping had turned out. "Anthony seems nice—why haven't you mentioned him before?" Rina asked.

"I have—" she began, but then Szonja realised she had only ever mentioned "Dovid"—whose name was irrevocably linked with debauched nights in Los Angeles's seedy clubs. "Well, I didn't really get to know him until recently." Which was true enough.

Szonja was surprised to find that the friendly chaos of the Greenes' household didn't overwhelm her as much as she'd thought it might. That was not to say that she got many words in on her first visit there, but she was folded into the household without much ceremony, which was a relief after the friction of the past month in her sister's house.

She and Tatiana were introduced to Mrs. Greene standing in their wide kitchen before dinner. Anthony's mother was an age difficult to determine in the eyes of someone in her late teens, but Szonja thought she was tiptoeing around her fifties in all likelihood. She had on a formfitting brown T-shirt that looked like it came in a pack with four others in the greige colour family and pleated trousers in a plaid that made no effort to match. Her appearance could best be characterised as having an absence of thought.

Mrs. Greene gave Anthony a stack of plates, their rims adorned with little birds chasing each other into infinity, and said, "Make yourself useful." Tatiana, without any offer of assistance, followed him out in order to pepper him with questions about his bandmate, who had clearly lost her number. When they were alone,

Mrs. Greene turned to Szonja and asked softly, "What would you usually have for dinner back home?"

No one in Los Angeles had expressed any particular interest in Budapest or her life there, and Szonja had quickly adapted to this absence of curiosity by focusing conversations on the ephemeral—who she was in any given moment became not an accumulation of her past experiences, most of which had taken place in locations too obscurely foreign for people to contemplate, but the minutiae on that particular instant: the Los Angeles sun, the traffic on the freeway, the music of the moment making its boomerang rounds on radio stations. If this made her less substantial or interesting, it also made her light and easy in a way she enjoyed.

At Mrs. Greene's question, Szonja pulled her mind back, a little reluctantly, to the kitchen of that suburban Budapest apartment: green linoleum on the floor, a pitcher of lukewarm, sickly sweet tea on the counter, her mother's workmanlike cooking, her own quiet assistance—chopping vegetables with a small paring knife. A broad-shouldered Romany man would come knocking on their door every month to ask if they had any knives that needed sharpening. Her mother would roll all the knives up in a kitchen towel and bring them to him. Later she would say something awkward, although meaning well, about how it was good to encourage honest work.

In that moment Szonja could not think of a single dish that had actually been made in that kitchen. She realised Mrs. Greene was peering at her, that she was taking too long to respond.

"Are you missing home, sweetie?" she asked, and something in her frank, unpitying expression compelled Szonja to answer candidly.

"Not at all," she said, the truth of it slotting into understanding in that very moment. "'There's no place like on the way'—my mom used to say that about me. I was always happy to be moving, which we did a lot, because of my father's job."

"Gosh, well, you have come to the right place . . . we're all constantly sitting in traffic, so we do spend most of our day 'on the way.'"

"On the way to such exotic locations as the dry cleaners," Anthony said, entering the kitchen again.

"As though you've ever graced a dry cleaner with your presence, my son." Mrs. Greene held Anthony's head in her two hands and kissed his forehead; Anthony was a good two feet taller than his mother, so this necessitated a little stooping on his part. Mrs. Greene's playfully sharp words seemed reserved for Anthony—she was much gentler with her two daughters—and Szonja wondered if this meant that she favoured him less or more.

Anthony's younger sister, Julie, who lived at home as well, was joining them with her friend Emily, who seemed put out by the presence of the two older girls and made ostentatious displays of familiarity with the rest of the family. There was also Anthony's father, Rick, who was an almost exact replica of Anthony—tall, gangly, bird's-nest-brown hair—but on his weathered face was an exuberant smile that Szonja had never seen on Anthony's, and it made him look, strangely, almost younger than his son. He seemed just as excited about the new napkins as he was about the arrival of his elder daughter, Marnie, and his grandchildren. And finally, their neighbour and Anthony's childhood friend Nico rounded out the table. A slightly stocky boy with soft sandy hair, a year older than Anthony but still living at home—he sat down with the ease of someone who was often cooked for.

In the half hour it took to sit down to dinner, it seemed like they would never settle: Mrs. Greene ran back to the kitchen for some forgotten essential on three separate occasions, springing up from her chair as soon as she touched it; Julie and Emily disappeared into Julie's bedroom for twenty minutes at one point; and Marnie had to wrangle her children to the table a good few times, as they continually crept back to the TV in the living room, like sleepwalkers.

When they were finally seated, Marnie looked at Szonja and, as though she had just noticed her, asked over the hubbub, "Are you Anthony's new girlfriend?"

"Oh, no, I'm just a friend." Szonja was conscious that even this truthful answer awkwardly raised the possibility of another, and she felt for a moment exposed and unsure why she was there. But it seemed Marnie didn't much care either way.

"Oh, okay. So, Mom, why are we doing this Shabbat thing? I thought it was Anthony's girlfriend who was religious." Marnie gestured towards Szonja with her fork, on top of which perched a plump, ash-grey piece of gefilte fish. She kept waving the fork in her direction, as though Szonja were an old sock and she wanted to know who'd left it on the couch.

"She's not religious, she's spiritual . . . she practises Kabbalah," Anthony said, a little defensively and also a little uncertainly.

"We're not doing it for anyone's benefit, dear. This is your own heritage and it's good to ground ourselves with rituals sometimes," Mr. Greene answered. No mention was made of the fact that Mr. Greene himself was not Jewish, although he did pass on the duties of the Shabbat ceremony to his wife, something Szonja had never witnessed in her sister's home, where the lights and the blessings were divided strictly by gender: Rina said the blessing over the candles and Aron the blessing over the wine.

Mrs. Greene had brought two mismatched candlesticks to the table and said the prayer over their soft light, after which Mr. Greene clapped enthusiastically, as though she had given a performance. The wine for the blessing was served in generous portions and they toasted to Mrs. Greene and all that she'd provided.

After dinner, when all the other guests had left, Szonja, Anthony and Tatiana went out onto the back porch, and Anthony brought out a joint, its astringency mellowed by the smell of camphor trees all around them. Szonja tried to seem unaffected by the grandeur of Anthony's childhood home, which was a classic Craftsman two streets from the one that had been in *Back to the Future*.

"People go by there to take pictures of it all the time," he said, rolling his eyes. And then, catching Szonja's expression, he sighed. "Yes, we can go take pictures later if you want."

"The one where Marty lives?" Szonja asked.

"No, the one where his parents live—in the past. I think the other one is somewhere in the Valley," he said, then added, "Where I will definitely not be going."

Tatiana admitted that she hadn't seen the movie yet, Yugoslavia being several years behind in their cinema screenings.

"You're not missing much. All the fifties nostalgia is embarrassing, isn't it?" Anthony said.

"I don't know—we were having a revolution in the fifties, and I don't think anyone's nostalgic about it," Szonja said. Anthony looked alarmed at his faux pas and offered an apology.

"No, we do have nostalgia for the fifties," Tatiana said. "At least, my auntie Jadranka does. I'm pretty sure she has a picture of Tito in her wallet."

Anthony wrinkled his forehead a little and said, "Well, in any case, I'm not sure what the appeal is of taking pictures of some random house on the street."

PORCUPINES

"Some might find this beautiful, Antonio," Tatiana said, indicating the area around her. The backyard, though small, had a little pond and a brick fireplace that looked like it had never been used. "Some of my family back home live on the fiftieth floor of a council house that's one in a block of twenty—concrete all the way down. You can see how something like this might be attractive."

"Okay, sure, I can see how the scale of those blocks could be dehumanising."

"I wouldn't turn my nose up at it either," Szonja said. "They're apartments for the masses, but it was the first home with electricity and water for many."

"Of course—it must have been a huge deal," he said quickly. "Essentially building the middle class. It's amazing what was accomplished in just a few decades."

"All right, Stakhanov, calm down."

"Don't fetishise the system, Anthony," Tatiana said. "People *died* for it," she added with an ominous widening of her eyes.

"No, of course I'm aware there have been atrocities in the name of Communism."

Szonja shook her head. "But there can't be revolution without bloodshed."

Tatiana nodded along meaningfully.

"Okay, what is happening here?" Anthony asked, looking between them. "I'm just trying to say I understand that you're coming from a different perspective."

"Well, for starters, Anthony, Tatiana is from Yugoslavia and I am from Hungary," Szonja said slowly, as though she were teaching a foreign language to a small child. Anthony looked a little embarrassed. "So you see, Anthony, these are two different countries."

"They are in Europe," Tatiana said, taking over. "That's another continent."

"A continent is like North America," Szonja said. "Which is different than the United States of America."

"All right, all right, I get it—big dumb American here," Anthony said, laughing finally.

"Beefcake," Tatiana said, smiling at him indulgently and then giving him a big kiss on the cheek.

In the next few weeks, Szonja spent more and more time at the Greenes' house, sometimes without Tatiana and occasionally even without Anthony. Mrs. Greene offered to take her shopping and teach her how to play bridge; she invited her to the Rose Bowl for a game, and any number of other activities that Szonja had never had a desire to participate in before. It felt at once like Mrs. Greene was taking an interest in her and also like she would offer her time up to anyone at all, and the uncertainty of this made Szonja want to prove herself to be worth the attention.

Rina was happy to have her over at the Greenes'; Szonja's interest in spending time with a fifty-year-old Jewish mother seemed wholesome, if a little odd, and infinitely preferable to going out behind her back, widening the gap between them even more. She could not have guessed at the unfavourable comparisons that were being drawn in Szonja's mind as she shuttled between the two households, which, despite both being Jewish, could not have felt more different.

The Greenes' dining table was a revolving door of strangers. There were recurring guests—Mr. Greene's mother, a woman who had clearly once been as tall as her son, and although age had diminished her height, she still carried herself with the stature of someone bigger, straight-backed and purposefully gentle in her movements. Marnie always arrived with her husband and three kids in tow, and Julie brought a rotating cast of friends.

Whenever outsiders grace the presence of a tight-knit but open-hearted family such as the Greenes, they have the option of sticking together on the periphery or creating a quick hierarchy based on proximity to the centre. Some guests, such as Julie's friend Emily, make clear their choice is the latter, and yet despite Emily's outsized efforts, she received no more or less attention.

But there were other outsiders who were friendlier, like their neighbour Nico, who had grown up riding his bike around the Pasadena suburbs with Anthony and was often around the Greene household. He would show up for dinner in his flip-flops with wet hair, like he had just come down from his room into his own dining room. He was quiet and unobtrusive—he would lean back in his chair and occasionally ask for more of some dish and smile. There was a calmness to him that meant he either did not have problems or did not have the depth of thought to consider them.

"Doesn't your mother cook?" Marnie often asked him.

"No one cooks as well as yours," he always answered smoothly, and Mrs. Greene would squeeze his shoulder like he was one of her own.

This scene played out more than once, and it was clear from his rehearsed part that he was a repertory player they all loved having around.

Although her interactions with Nico were not frequent or lengthy, Szonja appreciated that he took the time to smile at her and say hello even when everyone else outside of the Greene household was more interested in the Greenes themselves. And his smile was warm and easy and uncomplicated; when he passed by someone, squeezing behind their chair or manoeuvring beside them in the kitchen, he touched their arm gently first—he was frictionless.

So one day when they walked out of the Greene house together and Szonja was about to say "See you later" in that hopeful American way she had learned to do, he smiled and touched her arm gently, then kissed her, and she found she didn't mind.

And on another evening, when Aron was stuck at work and couldn't pick her up and Nico offered to drive her home, she didn't mind that. When they stopped at his house first and he smiled and touched her arm gently and led her up to his bedroom, she didn't mind that either.

Coloma, 2001

ONE MIGHT WONDER WHAT KIND OF MOTHER WOULD MAKE OUT with her ten-year-old daughter's elementary-school vice principal next to a vending machine full of Funyuns. Sonia certainly does as she tiptoes back into the motel room where her daughter and two other innocent girls are sleeping, blissfully unaware of an act they would certainly have called "gross"—not on moral grounds, but rather from pure distaste, in the way only children can express it.

Why is this a reprehensible thing to do? Is it the fact that he is her child's educator? Is it that Cecily Auerbach would suffer a stroke if she found out? (To get what she so longed for—Sonia's involvement in the Parent-Teacher Association—but to have it perverted in such a way!) Is it that she barely knows him?

Or—was it their location, next to the Funyuns?

Sonia can't quite put her finger on what makes her uneasy about this brief, inebriated tryst with Mr. Alvarez. It isn't that she worries a complicated relationship with him might deprive Mila of a father figure; it isn't that Mila might get too attached to the man as a result of their closeness. No. What really bothers her is her own questionable motivation—was she momentarily attracted to him because Mila's silly stunt called her attention to his fatherly potential? The idea of some primal, Freudian impulse overriding her good sense and taste is disturbing indeed.

Then again, it might simply have been his mournful brown eyes, his proximity and that third bottle of beer within the space of an hour.

She had been talking to Dave outside the rec room of the Lost Hills Inn after the stifling heat of the room and the even more stifling boredom of the conversation it held had propelled her outside. As meek as Dave had seemed at first, a mere five minutes after he joined her outside, he was expounding on the amount of protein contained in various foodstuffs with reckless abandon.

"Now, peanut butter has a high protein content relative to other nuts and nut butters, but some people think the fat content negates some of those beneficial qualities."

"Oh, reall—?"

"Yes, but as I told Davie Jr. after his soccer practice, his muscles are fatigued, his body's telling him to replenish his macronutrients, including fat, so in that case, peanut butter is a great choice."

Dave spoke with continual reference to his own digestive system and its various thoughts and feelings. It was clear that he was the kind of father whose entire life revolves around his child's various sporting achievements, to which he contributes little but takes much credit for. Unfortunately for Dave, though, his son was not interested in sports. Unfortunately for everyone else, this didn't seem to give Dave pause.

Thankfully, Sonia was saved from finding out what Dave's stomach was telling him at that very moment: Mr. Alvarez joined their huddle outside, smiled at Sonia and bashfully asked for one of her cigarettes. Dave, possibly offended by their reckless treatment of their own bodies, retreated to the room to regale someone else with the ins and outs of macronutrients.

"I wouldn't have pegged you for a smoker," she said.

"More of a pipe man?"

"Ah, self-awareness—such an endearing quality in a man."

"You said it, not me."

Sonia has always thought that that first drag tells you so much about a person. Mr. Alvarez held the cigarette confidently, not waving it around or rushing the stub angrily towards his mouth. When he wasn't smoking, he held the cigarette towards the floor. Enjoyment mixed with a little shame, but no posturing. He smiled at her and said, "Thanks for this."

And then one thing led to another—a truly unsatisfying way to relate any process, but in this case it does accurately describe Sonia's hazy recall of the night's events. There was indeed one thing (the sharing of cigarettes), and she presumes it led to the other (her face in impolite proximity to that of Mr. Alvarez); whatever the connecting logic was, it escapes her in that moment as she slides under the thin, tightly tucked sheets of the motel bed.

When they get back on the bus the next day, Megan H sits down next to Sonia. Sonia shoots Mila a despairing look, but Mila just shrugs her shoulders and sits down in the seat behind her. Sonia smiles thinly at the young girl and looks out the window, where Dalton is waving them off—it worries her a little, how attached this man has gotten to their little party. Some people's lives are just too lonely to contemplate.

"How old are you?" Megan asks her, and Sonia understands immediately that she will not be left in peace for the next couple of hours. She sees Mr. Alvarez shuffle onto the bus as well—she can't stop calling him Mr. Alvarez in her mind, even though she is pretty sure he revealed his first name was Daniel the previous night. It seems for a moment as though he might say something to her, but he thinks better of it and sits down next to one of the children, whose face reveals such despair that Mr. Alvarez immediately stands up and moves to a free two-seater.

They stop for one bathroom break, during which the chaperones hand out apple juice and tapioca pudding to the children. Linda unloads the juice boxes while Sonia stacks the puddings, one over the other, in an effort to look productive as she allows her alcohol-fried cells to recover in peace.

"I can't get Spandau Ballet out of my head," Sonia says, "ever since Cecily sang 'Gold' last night at karaoke."

"There was no karaoke last night," Linda says.

"That was just . . . Cecily singing?"

"Yep," she answers with a resigned nod, then turns to the brown-haired girl approaching the table. "Megan, honey, would you get the other cooler from the bus, please?" The girl rolls her eyes a little but turns back to the bus.

"How do you manage to tell all the kids apart?" Sonia asks.

"Half of them are called Megan; I took a shot."

Sonia laughs, then winces at the sudden pang of a headache it brings. "I'm not sure those beers were such a good idea after all, Linda."

Linda assesses her: "This looks like more than the one beer I recommended," she says, raising her eyebrows faintly.

"True . . . I am regretting my decisions last night," she says in the exact moment Mr. Alvarez reaches over and picks up one of the juice boxes. He blinks rapidly, looking from Sonia to Linda and back, pausing for a beat too long.

"Please, Mr. Alvarez," Linda says slowly in that lean-down, hands-on-thighs tone, as though he were a child in need of coaxing. "Feel free to take one."

He looks down at the juice box in his hands and mumbles a thanks.

"This is what being around children all day, every day does to you," Linda says, and Sonia follows her gaze from Mr. Alvarez to Mrs. Flores, a woman well into her fifties, dressed in a flower-print pinafore dress, enjoying her own tapioca pudding with eyes-closed ecstasy.

Sonia tries to stifle another laugh as Cecily joins them at the table and says, "Looks like we're having as much fun as we did last night." Sonia wonders for a moment whether Cecily knows exactly the kind of fun she had last night or if this is just her way of trying to join in, at which point Megan approaches them with the cooler.

"You poor thing, why are you carrying that, it's much too heavy for you," Cecily says, relieving the girl of her load. The girl eyes Sonia and Linda for a moment with the shrewd look of someone about to tattle.

"You know, in some countries, ten-year-olds already work and support their parents and they don't complain," Sonia says mildly. Cecily's mouth forms a little surprised O—clearly this is the wrong thing to say, and Sonia beats a quick retreat. "I don't mean that we should have our children work . . . I'm just saying, there's a certain amount of preciousness about childhood in our age that is historically unprecedented." Sonia is beginning to sound like she sends Mila down to the mines to earn her keep, so she resolves to stay quiet for the rest of the day.

Despite herself, Sonia is excited to reach San Francisco. Although the landscape has changed outside the bus window at the rate of a time-lapse video, she has become bored of looking at trees and fields, whatever colour they come in. There's no amount of bucolic scenery that can trick a city heart, which thumps at the sight of a cluster of buildings in friendly proximity. And she has never been to San Francisco—she allows her sense of wonderment to leapfrog over her cynicism for a brief, brief moment. She is, however, to be disappointed, as, unbeknownst to her, before they reach that other gleaming metropolis of the Golden State, they are first detouring to a place two hours outside of San Francisco, the Marshall Gold Discovery State Historic Park. Yes, all those words truly are in its name—concision was clearly not its founders' strong suit.

You can imagine Sonia's surprise when she alights from the bus—after a brief nap against the cool windowpane—to be greeted by an Amish couple. At least, a couple that seems to be Amish, judging by their clothes, the woman in full skirts and bonnet; the man in vest and britches with a jaunty hat.

"Good day to you, sir, ma'am," they say enthusiastically to each child coming off the bus. Most of the children avert their eyes; the more loquacious of them mumble a hello back, but Mrs. Flores does an excited little curtsey that looks uncannily like one of her own fifth-graders requesting a bathroom break.

Sonia is aware that a simple "Where are we?" would draw too much attention to her confused, post-inebriated state, so when she passes the couple, she says, "Hello," and looks meaningfully into the woman's eyes, hoping perhaps to nonverbally communicate the question.

But the bonneted woman just becomes flustered. "Good morrow, good lady, and welcome . . . on this fine morrow!" she says with a strained smile. And now Sonia has scared the poor Amish woman.

PORCUPINES

Sonia falls into step with Mila. "Milosh, what in the world is going on here?" she asks from the side of her mouth.

Mila blinks up at her mother, coolly assessing her, and finding that there is no cause for concern (her mother isn't having a meltdown or reprimanding her), she informs her, "We're here to pan for gold."

"Ah . . . yes, naturally." Sonia has at times felt blessed by the quietude of an introverted child, but for once she wishes she had raised a girl with true American verbosity, the kind who provides much more information than necessary in any given situation.

But the clues pile up—more people dressed in nineteenth-century attire; a table where three women are cross-stitching and speaking about the harvest in loud, theatrical voices; and a couple of troughs and sieves set up in front of them. The children all gather around the troughs, and the man who greeted them at the bus launches into a speech about the history of the Gold Rush—except he speaks resolutely in the present tense and sprinkles his lecture with old-timey phrases at odd intervals.

"Now, it isn't just Americans down here—people been coming in from all over: France, Germany, Portugal, the—"

"Netherlands?" Cecily interjects excitedly. Sonia has deduced that Cecily's family, although proudly American, has some vague ancestral ties to Europe; she can't quite remember the exact configuration of it. It's always unclear with Americans whether this is a good thing or not—so proud to be Italian American one minute, then derisively labelling women in heels as *Eurotrash* the next.

"I don't rightly know, ma'am," the man says with an exaggerated twang, reminding his audience that he is desperately trying to stay in character. He also seems to think that old-timey speech is anything spoken with a Southern accent.

It appears they are actually going to be panning for gold. ("*Gold!*" Sonia thinks now, every time the word is mentioned, which is about every five seconds.) They are all given wading boots and pans and led to a quiet stream on the American River. The water is surprisingly clear, and it laps against Sonia's shins pleasantly. The mountains beyond the stream look verdant and full of possibility, and Sonia smiles to herself, thinking that this gold-prospecting business couldn't have been all that bad after all—spending your days splashing around with dreams of gold ever hovering in your mind. (Clearly, Sonia has not been listening to the Amish fellow's mentions of disease, overcrowding and food shortages. Then again, no one in 1849 listened to the warnings either.) Cecily gives her a sharp look, and Sonia realises she's been smiling at all the children diligently sifting through silt as though pleased with the sight of child labour. She quickly gets back to the business of panning before Cecily decides to call child services.

The children are unusually engrossed in the task before them. That is, until they are not. Once they've put in about half an hour of prospecting work, the signs of restlessness begin to show: After Riley finds a speck of gold that turns out to be a bedraggled sequin with a Las Vegas past, a boy named Austin is the first to realise they've been duped into believing one of them might *actually* find gold. The conclusion indicates a surprisingly mature mind; however, his response—using his pan to pour muddy water down the shirt of the poor Amish man—is less promising. The children are directed back to the changing rooms, and once they are dry, they all settle in on the park benches scattered around the banks for a picnic lunch, the faint whiff of river aerating around them as they eat.

Sonia watches as her daughter tentatively shares some more fun facts about her Russian composer with her friend Kathy. (And here's a fun fact: Fun facts are never, in fact, fun. But calling them *a spontaneous overflow of information without context* doesn't quite roll off the tongue.) Kathy smiles politely, and Sonia feels a surge of grateful affection for this child who does not dismiss her own oddball daughter out of hand. *Rule number fourteen: Be the smartest person in the classroom—* but then Sonia remembers that, somewhat confusingly, rule number twelve was something about not pretending to know more than you do, and she curses Camy Baker and her rules to rule the school.

"And his most famous opera was *Lady of Minsk*," she hears Mila tell her lunch companion.

"*Lady Macbeth of Mtsensk*," Sonia corrects her. Mila looks up at her mother, eyebrows raised, and Sonia is no less shocked at having had this random bit of information at her fingertips. She returns to her juice box, contemplating just what else the recesses of her mind might have stowed away.

Across from her sits Sergio, whose round face and even rounder, guileless eyes make him seem a good year or two younger than his classmates.

To compound his image of youthful naïveté, Sergio has clearly, this very day, developed an understanding of the concept of history and has gone wide-eyed at the magnitude of its implications. Now that she has revealed herself to be a person of knowledge, she is in his crosshairs.

Just as Sonia begins to relax into the quietude of forty children eating ham sandwiches, he addresses her. "Mrs. Imre . . . back in the Gold Rush . . . did they have toilets?"

"There are toilets at the main house, dear," she says absently, massaging her temples.

"I don't have to go," Sergio says thoughtfully. No doubt he has been asked whether he has to go so many times throughout his childhood that he has lost all natural sense of his own bladder. "I was just wondering . . . back in Gold Rush times . . . did *they* have toilets?"

"They would have had some form of toilets, yes," Sonia answers with a pretence of conviction she doesn't have. How do children always manage to ask questions that reveal the paucity of knowledge they'll be growing into?

"But did they . . . in the Gold Rush . . . would they have had toilet paper?"

At least the boy is making good use of his past-perfect conditional, even though he stumbles over the *have*s and the *had*s like a clumsy contestant at a dressage show. His wide eyes bore into Sonia's.

"Yes, I imagine. Not like what we use today, but they would have . . . wiped with something or other."

The contemplation of what these alternatives might be lays sufficient claim to Sergio's mental faculties to keep him quiet for another few minutes, but Sonia is unable to relax. Between Megan's newfound admiration of her, Sergio's continued historical Q and A ("But would they have had ham sandwiches? What kind of sandwiches would they have had?"), Cecily's watchful gaze and the guilty glances Mr. Alvarez has been throwing her way, there are altogether too many people for Sonia to be avoiding at once.

Los Angeles, 1989

Mr. Chajit pointed to the board and said, "These are the minor mistakes, errors, faults." He was portly and avuncular and, like a walking thesaurus, had the habit of using three equivalent words when one would suffice. "Faults like 'It's your fault,' not the San Andreas Fault." He paused, presumably for laughter, although no part of his steady inflection had implied that it was a joke. "Unlike the major ones, you get to make up to fifteen minor errors before you fail, flop, flounder."

"Deep," said the boy next to Szonja. He could only have been a couple of years younger than her, but his long limbs rag-dolled on the chair like a child's. By the sounds of it, he'd have more trouble staying sober for the driving test than actually passing it. Szonja had thought the class would be full of people like him, teenagers who were compelled to be here in order to get their licences, but it seemed some older learners had thought it prudent to go through the course as well. Szonja herself couldn't believe that you could get a driver's licence here without sitting in a classroom to learn the rules first, and not having had a licence back home, she thought it best to get the full extent of the training provided. Beyond that, she'd found the idea of being among real Americans in this most banal of circumstances to be extremely exciting. Sure, she'd gone to Hebrew classes, but they were a subset of

Americans, their allegiance more to one another and their own version of the God under which all Americans believed themselves to be indivisible. They marked themselves out as different. The English-language classes were filled with foreign students playing at Americanness as much as she was. But here, finally, in the first-floor classroom of Wheeler's Wheely Good Driving School, was the wonderful reality of the America she had come to see: The teenage potheads! The divorcées striking out on their own! The middle-aged men who'd lost their licences to DUIs! *Such stuff as dreams are made on.*

Rina was late picking her up from driving school, and in her harried state she wedged her car into the lot with a jagged imprecision that Mr. Chajit would certainly not have approved of.

"Sorry, I was stuck talking to Mrs. Ernst at pickup," she said as Szonja slid into the passenger seat she was excited to be trading in for the driver's seat soon. "How was it?" Rina asked.

"Really great—there were such characters in the class, Rina, truly, you couldn't make them up."

"Trust you to find entertainment in the dullest of places," she said, but the words held no edge; they were only fond and amused. Rina hesitated before speaking again, a moment easily masked by her brisk manoeuvre out of the parking lot. Finally, she said, "You know Mrs. Ernst, the woman I was just talking to, she's an interesting character too. She runs a Jewish philosophy study group for women and she was asking if I wanted to join. You know I love to read—not that I have much time now, but it could be interesting, you know?"

Szonja was engrossed by the view outside—she liked to read the signs on all the shops as they slid past, offering everything in the world that no one needed—so she answered with a vague noise.

"Do you think you would want to come with me sometime?" Rina asked, trying not to sound as though she needed company. If she ever missed the attention she had once commanded from her little sister, Rina made sure to keep it folded away somewhere within her.

"Sure, maybe," Szonja answered, and she didn't mean for her noncommitment to sting.

After the driving-theory course, Szonja took the compulsory six hours of lessons at Wheeler's. She was assigned to drive with Mr. Chajit himself in his red Mazda, as she was the only one in the class who'd opted to learn on a stick. "Now, in these intersections you want to stay alert, you want to stay vigilant, you want to stay . . ."

"Switched on?" Szonja provided—she'd started to think in triplicates now herself. It was annoying, somewhat irritating and a little aggravating.

"That's right," Mr. Chajit said. He spoke in a soft, low voice with an unnervingly even cadence, as though his pupils were easily spooked horses. Szonja proved to be a quick study, driving with enthusiasm and speed if not finesse. She had a feel for switching gears but never managed to look in every mirror before turning. Certainly she proved to be better at it than her sister, who now rode shotgun with her as Szonja took her learner's permit out on the road.

In an effort to keep every single soul gridlocked in freeway traffic, even temporary residents were allowed to get a licence in the state of California. The city was torn between keeping its inhabitants tied to their cars and keeping its immigrants from finding life too convenient. But the cars, the freeways and the almighty oil won out—for a while, at least. And so, even though she wouldn't be in America long enough to get her permanent licence, Szonja got her training wheels. She wanted to get as much practice as she could while she was here, in this city made for cars. During the day she begged her sister for the opportunity to drive for the most mundane of purposes and so began to accompany Rina on rounds of errands—to the pharmacy, to the dry cleaner, to the jumble sale, where they purchased the girls' future wardrobe (things were not looking up for them sartorially). All of these activities gained an unprecedented sheen of thrill with Szonja in the driver's seat (a thrill for both of them, albeit for different reasons). But she did her best driving at night; there was something at once illicit and soothing about taking the car out late. Although not *very* illicit—it was her sister's Subaru she was driving, after all, the back seats still sticky with whatever Hannah and Abby had spilled the day before. The sun still pushed night into the late hours where Rina and Aron were usually too tired to tread, but Rina nevertheless roused herself after the kids had been put to bed and the dishes cleared away and sat beside her sister, giving advice that she had been given herself but never bothered to take.

At night, with no errands to run, their drives lacked purpose. It had not occurred to Rina to take her sister sightseeing in Los Angeles because she had lived there long enough to forget that there were sights to be seen. In any case, Szonja had wanted to be the opposite of a tourist. But now, as they glided through the dusky streets, Rina pointed out the places that had inspired wonderment in her when she had moved to this odd, sprawling city with her new husband five years ago. She pointed out those places that Aron had taken her—the Museum of Tolerance, Canter's Deli—but also, because Szonja loved the movies, they drove past the Chinese and Egyptian Theatres and Hollywood Boulevard. For the first time since arriving in Los Angeles, Szonja imagined her sister arriving in the same place, how she must have been compelled to make the most of it, having left her family and country behind on the gamble of one man's promise of love. But the image did not warm her to her brother-in-law—having never experienced love herself, Szonja could only think that some coercion had to have taken place to bring her sister here, where she stood in her life like a chiaroscuro in reverse, all the brightness of her surroundings rendering her once-spirited intellect drab and dark.

But it was somehow easier to speak freely when they didn't have to speak freely to each other's faces, and the car slowly became the conduit they needed in order to get to know each other again. In the benign anecdotes and professions of odd preferences, they began to take a more distinct shape in each other's minds once more.

If Rina was disappointed when Szonja told her that Anthony could occasionally relieve her of her shotgun duties, she didn't show it to her sister—the demands of her young children enveloped her so immediately that she might not have had time for resentment, which wasn't in her nature anyway.

Anthony came to pick her up in Pico-Robertson with his grey Ford Escort, which looked like it should be driven only by men in equally grey suits, and suggested they go somewhere new. "To keep things interesting," he said, even though discovering the same couple of streets and their shadow counterparts had seemed interesting enough for Szonja. She felt there was something slippery about Los Angeles—no matter how many times she traversed its roads or how well she came to know its freeway system, it wouldn't plant a firm flag in her imagination. In this way it became addictive, the Sisyphean task of figuring it out, little by little.

"So where are we driving, then?" Szonja asked as they settled into their seats. Anthony told her to just follow his directions, which led them on the 405 heading north for what seemed like forever until their exit suddenly deposited them into a grid of unremarkable suburban streets.

"All right, here we are," Anthony said after she parked the car on one of them. He got out and Szonja followed suit. Looking pleased with himself, Anthony spread his arms out towards the house they had stopped next to.

"I feel like you're about to say 'Ta-da,'" Szonja said.

"Ta-da," he said. "Come on, you don't recognise it?" They looked at each other, then back at the house. "It's the McFly house."

Szonja looked at it—plasterboard, short driveway, garage. "Oh, that's not the house," she said.

"Yes it is."

"But it really isn't."

Anthony looked at a piece of paper he had drawn a rudimentary map on. "Well, it can't be far."

So, they continued to drive through a sprawling network of squat one-storey houses. The hum of transmission lines could be faintly heard, as Szonja had turned the radio down to afford the moment its reverence, now that she knew that reverence was due.

When they finally found the right house on Roslyndale Avenue, she got out of the car and stood right in the middle of the street to take it in.

"Hmm," she said after a minute.

"Okay, now, this is definitely the right one," Anthony said. "Don't tell me it isn't."

"No, it's just . . ." Szonja looked at the house again, trying to rouse that feeling of excitement the movie had given her. It was definitely the right one, but of course, without the sheen of a camera lens, the McFly house looked just like any other house—all promise of adventure sapped from it. Which made sense, really—the McFly family had to be in a state of perpetual lassitude until adventure came knocking on their door. But the wideness of the road, which had allowed for the DeLorean to make its thrilling exit, now just felt like too much unfriendly concrete separating people. "Not what I expected," she said finally. And they stood there, tilting their heads this way and that, as though the house might reveal itself at a different angle.

"You're a bit of a brat, aren't you?" Anthony said. Szonja raised her eyebrows and looked at him—for a moment they were suspended in the possibility of an argument, but then she burst out laughing.

"I am," she said without remorse. "And the only balm for my disappointment, Anthony, is a corn dog by the beach." They got back into the car, and as she drove down the road, Szonja tried to superimpose the house from the movie onto the one that she had just seen, dialling up its brightness and colour, its contours becoming more crisp and satisfying, until they were one. The image of the real house and its disappointment faded quickly as they got back onto the freeway that rolled towards the ocean (actually, it rolled right into another freeway by a Costco somewhere in Irvine, but that was an adventure for another day).

As they slid onto the driveway of the house on Glenville Street, the hazy blue of the sky had finally relinquished itself to darkness, but Szonja could see the light from a lamp in the living room still on. Almost as soon as she'd spotted it, the light flickered off, and Szonja, giddy with the remembered smell of salt air and the freedom of an empty highway, did not think of Rina sitting in her house, waiting for her sister's return.

"Szonja drives like a maniac," Hannah declared from the back seat on their way to a new farmers' market.

Szonja turned her head to Rina and raised her eyebrows as she changed lanes.

"Eyes on the road, please," Rina said, hand gripping the side of the door.

"Have you been complaining to my niece about my driving?" she asked. "'Drives like a maniac.'"

"Must be something from the TV," Rina answered innocently.

"One day, Hannah," Szonja said, locking eyes with her through the rearview mirror, "your aunt is going to teach you how to drive."

"No, thank you," Hannah answered.

"You're killing me, buddy," she said, at which point Abby burst into tears, and Rina assured her that no one was killing anyone.

Szonja continued her efforts to convince a four-year-old of her driving skills as they parked, trundled out of the car and made their way through the maze of stalls. Szonja was in the middle of a long-winded explanation of how slow driving could be just as dangerous as fast ("It's okay to be wrong sometimes," Hannah answered in the tone of a *Sesame Street* aphorism) when she noticed a familiar figure.

"Mrs. Greene?"

For a moment Mrs. Greene contracted her eyebrows as though she couldn't place Szonja without the context of her son beside her, but she quickly recovered and enveloped Szonja in a hug and the smell of plain soap. Szonja pointed her sister out in the crowd, and Mrs. Greene led the way to the barrel of avocados Rina was inspecting.

"Hello there," she said in a broad California voice. "You must be Rina."

After introductions were made, Mrs. Greene engaged Rina in conversation while Szonja shifted her weight from one foot to the other like she was a small child waiting for the adults to finish talking. The feeling was exacerbated by the fact that Hannah and Abby were doing just the same beside her. Looking at Mrs. Greene and Rina together, Szonja thought her sister seemed absurdly young, too young, certainly, to be classed with Mrs. Greene and other matronly women with households and children and opinions on the firmness of Pinkerton avocados.

But Mrs. Greene was athletic and had none of the brittle fragility of Szonja's own mother, which was who she saw, suddenly, in Rina, with her wide blinking eyes and nervous hand-wringing.

"What brings you all the way down here?" Rina asked. "I understand you live in Pasadena."

"We do!" answered Mrs. Greene. "But I like to come to Fairfax for the kosher butcher and the market." She said this in a hushed tone, leaning into the gap between their group, as though they were all enthusiastic devotees of kosher butchers, which, to be fair, at least one among them was. Rina visibly relaxed, being on firmer footing now with Mrs. Greene.

"We just love your Szonja, I have to say."

"Oh, that's nice," Rina answered. Even after five years in America, she had no way of countering this kind of unwarranted effusiveness. "I know she enjoys spending time with you all."

"Well, you must join us for dinner too sometime!" Mrs. Greene said, patting Rina's delicate forearm a little too heartily, so she dropped an avocado she had been idly squeezing.

"Yes, of course, I'm sure it would be nice."

Szonja winced at the stately and studied tone of her sister's English; it was somehow less noticeable at home and at the synagogue, but in the face of Mrs. Greene's elongated American vowels and her ease of communication, Rina sounded like some foreign dignitary. Szonja's attention bore inward then as she considered whether she sounded like Rina to Mrs. Greene's ears, stilted and decorous, and she suddenly regretted making the introduction, which must have turned the dial of her image just a little bit more towards foreign.

"Let me show you where the best artichokes are, honey," she heard Mrs. Greene say. She was the kind of woman who assumed that everyone was as invested in artichokes as she was, but when she called you "honey," "sweetie," "darling" in that warm conspiratorial way, it was easy to forget that you didn't even like artichokes. Mrs. Greene led them to a small tucked-away table between a pickle stall and a spice vendor only to see a woman in deep consideration of the last few artichokes.

"Oh, honey, no, no, no," Mrs. Greene said to the woman, gently touching her elbow. "You don't want to be getting these right now."

The woman looked slightly affronted. "Yes I do."

"Well, how were you going to prepare them?" she asked as though she were speaking to her children, demanding reports of their homework. The woman explained about a *Good Housekeeping* recipe uncertainly.

"No, no, no, what you want right now is some nice snap beans. Make a nice little rice pilaf with some whitefish, a little pesto—gorgeous." She went on to describe in detail where the best snap beans were to be found in the market until the woman inched her shoulders lower from their defensive height and eventually got out a piece of paper to jot down a quick recipe for radicchio salad.

When the woman was gone, Mrs. Greene turned back to the stall and purchased three large artichokes with a wink, then offered them to Rina.

"No, really, you keep them," Rina said with an edge to her voice that sounded a little censorious to Szonja's ears. But Mrs. Greene could not be dissuaded.

"Now, when you've made these, you tell me they're not the best artichokes on the whole goddamn planet," she said as they parted ways in the parking lot.

"I will."

"You won't," Szonja corrected her.

"Yes, that's what I meant," Rina said, fumbling for her keys.

When they were back in the car—its seats warmed up, the seatbelt buckles almost impossible to touch—Szonja told her sister that she needn't worry about Mrs. Greene's invitation to dinner, that she invited almost anyone and quickly forgot about it.

"Don't worry, Szonja, I wouldn't impose."

Szonja narrowed her eyes. Then she opened them up wide. She repeated the process in the hopes that it would keep her awake. When she caught her sister looking at her, she tried to revert to a neutral expression of interest; Rodin's *Thinker*.

They were at the learning centre, where Rina's Jewish philosophy study group was hosting a rabbi whose book they had all been reading about Jewish joy. The man's thesis seemed to be that they should all enjoy food, and his grinning insistence on the sanctity of wine implied that he may have already partaken of some.

"I thought you said this was a Jewish philosophy thing," Szonja whispered to Rina, who was respectfully following the man's words.

"The guests are a little hit or miss," she said from the side of her mouth.

Szonja had offered to take her sister, thinking she could wait in the car with a nice stack of *People* magazines and her secret stash of cigarettes, but her sister had looked a little queasy when she got out of the car.

Rina and Aron's house was only just within walking distance of their synagogue, most of whose members lived a few streets' worth of affluence closer. Aron was still a little stiff from his ultra-Orthodox upbringing, and Rina often felt lumped in with Soviet refugees whose complete lack of religious practice was a bridge too far for some. ("I heard the Soviets traded them in for agricultural machines," one of the old ladies at the synagogue had said when a Russian couple and their two young children quietly shuffled in for service, and it was impossible to know now whether in place of Rina's head, they all saw a tractor or a combine.) All of this resulted in a back-footed scrabble for social purchase that was a little hard to watch, and Szonja felt bad for how nervous it made her sister, the low stakes of socialising among these people. So she'd offered to join her and very soon regretted her magnanimous gesture.

Finding it impossible to sit still after twenty minutes, she mouthed to her sister that she was going to the bathroom. Instead, she wandered out into the small courtyard of the learning centre, where some landscaping had been attempted with mixed results, so that it looked a little like the tufts of greenery added to a small-scale model of a building and its surroundings, meant to indicate the intent rather than the outcome. There, she found Rabbi Raskin pacing up and down, his hands by his sides but his fingers flexing and unflexing nervously.

She was too close to pretend not to have seen him, so Szonja walked up to him slowly and asked if everything was okay.

"Oh, yes," he said, smiling. "It's just habit—I used to smoke, in a different life, and now, if I'm given a five-minute gap between one thing and another, my body thinks it's time to go outside and light up. My fingers are the last to get the message." He put his hands in his pockets resolutely.

"Is it . . . not allowed for you?"

"It is and it isn't," he said. "Like almost anything in Jewish law, it is open to interpretation. But I suppose I should set a good example at the least."

"So if I have a cigarette now, you probably have to leave," she said. "And then you wouldn't have a chance to provide me with words of wisdom. Which is worse?"

"What ever makes you think I would burden you with my 'words of wisdom'?"

"Just a hunch."

"I feel so mischaracterised," the rabbi said. "And after admitting to a former life of smoking . . ."

Szonja smiled. All this talk of smoking really made her want to light up now, and she turned a little to begin extricating herself, but the rabbi just turned with her and they began to walk back towards the event.

"But you know, your question reminds me of something," he said after a while. "Have you ever heard the parable of the porcupine?" Szonja shrugged apologetically. "No? Well, the great German philosopher Arthur Schopenhauer had this theory that mankind was like a group of porcupines in the winter." He paused a little too long, and Szonja thought perhaps Schopenhauer wasn't such a great philosopher after all, but then the rabbi continued. "They felt the cold, so they all huddled together for warmth. Then they felt the prickle of one another's needles and sprang apart. Together, apart, together, apart—and so on into infinity. This was mankind's lot, he said."

"That's depressing," Szonja said.

"Ha, indeed," he said. "Not quite as cheering as today's guest here. But smart man, that Schopenhauer. Though, unfortunately not a fan of the Jews. Perhaps he did not know us well enough," he said, gesturing towards the building; the event had recessed and people were chatting animatedly. "It seems, to me, at least, that these are not his porcupines." He winked at Szonja and joined the hubbub.

When Rina found Szonja, she suggested they take their seats again; on a whim Szonja said, "But what if we don't?"

"Well, you can stand if you want, but I'm tired," Rina said.

"No, I mean what if we skipped the second half," she said, to which Rina's response was a sad little "Oh." "We could do something else instead—just you and me?"

Rina took surprisingly little convincing, and after a phone call from the reception desk had been made to inform Aron that she'd be late coming home, they were on their way. In the car, Rina asked Szonja what she and the rabbi had discussed.

"We were talking about woodland creatures."

"Oh, sure," Rina said. "As you do."

"*Tango and Cash*!" Rina pointed to the sign outside the movie theatre. "Let's watch that. That's the one where Tom Hanks is paired with a sweet slobbery dog to solve crimes."

PORCUPINES

It was not the one where Tom Hanks was paired with a sweet slobbery dog to solve crimes. That was *Turner and Hooch*. *Tango and Cash*, it turned out, consisted of Kurt Russell and Sylvester Stallone getting their shirts wet, blowing things up and being subjected to an astounding amount of violence. This led Rina to whisper-shout, "When is the dog introduced?" to Szonja every five minutes until it became clear that neither Tom Hanks nor a slobbery dog existed in the universe of this movie. However, once their expectations were adjusted, they did find something to enjoy in the film.

"Oh, he's kind of cute in glasses," Rina declared when Stallone appeared in a neat suit and spectacles, wielding a delicate little gun.

"Well, it's important that everyone know that."

"What?" Rina asked, a little bit of popcorn still in her mouth.

"You're being really loud," Szonja said, laughing.

"No I'm not," she said, eating some more of her popcorn, then added, "This movie is loud. And anyway, there's not a soul in this city who speaks Hungarian."

After an hour, Rina excused herself to go to the bathroom. The denouement had become pretty apparent at this point, so Szonja followed her out to the restrooms, where she heard her sister retching in one of the stalls.

"You okay in there?"

"Too much junk food," she said when she came out. "I'm not used to it." She rinsed her mouth and asked if Szonja wanted to go back in for the end of the movie.

"Are you still hoping Hooch will show up?"

"I don't think either of those men should own a dog."

"That is the most scathing criticism I've ever heard from you."

Emerging from the theatre, Rina and Szonja felt that quiet thrill of arriving on the same street but a different world—it was now dark and balmy, the last rush of cars had petered out and the streetlights had come on. Szonja convinced Rina to take a little walk so she could finish her box of Hot Tamales before they got back in the car.

"These are disgusting," she said, contemplating a little red candy between her thumb and forefinger. "Want some?"

Rina looked a little queasy again. "Well, you've really sold it, but I don't dare."

"Right, sorry," she said, and she tipped the remains of the box straight into her mouth. "How do you think Aron's handling the girls' bedtime?" she asked as they rounded the corner back towards the movie theatre. Szonja had witnessed the utter lawlessness of Hannah and Abigail in the hour before bed, and didn't envy her brother-in-law the task.

"Oh, Aron could put anyone to sleep," Rina said, which made Szonja snort. "No, I didn't mean it like *that*." A nervous little patch of red appeared on her forehead. "I just meant he's a competent father."

"Of course, he's very competent," Szonja said soberly. "And he can certainly put anyone to sleep."

Rina swatted her sister's arm but smiled a little despite herself. For a moment, even as they walked back towards the car, back towards Rina's life, her children, her duties, Rina was able to share her sister's worldview, where respect could tip at any moment into ridicule. But this was not a place for Rina to dwell—she could not abide absurdity hovering on the periphery. Some need to live their lives conserving the sanctity of their beliefs or risk tipping into the abyss.

When they arrived home—a full three hours later than intended—the girls were already asleep, but Aron was waiting in the dining room.

"Where were you?" he asked, and Szonja was about to defend her sister, but something in his expression—regretful and drawn—stopped her. "Your father called." And then he told them their mother had died.

When Rina finished talking with her father, she looked at Szonja and nodded towards the receiver, but Szonja just shook her head. "He's hung up anyway," Rina said. It had taken a while to get a hold of him, and when they did he had been groggy and curt, but he told Rina the gist of what had happened: that she had been ill for some time but refused treatment, that she had been rushed to the hospital only at the end.

Szonja, Rina and Aron sat down around the dinner table with the weight of people whose legs will barely hold after a long journey.

"Is she to be buried today?" Aron asked. This seemed like such a nonsensical question to Szonja, her mother being so recently dead as to be almost alive, but her sister responded, "They're burying her tomorrow morning."

"Wait, but how are we supposed to be there?" Szonja asked.

"We're not," Rina said without looking at her.

"The burial should be as soon as possible," Aron said simply. "It's the custom."

Szonja didn't know what he meant at first. "It's not her custom," she said when she understood.

"It's Jewish custom," he said, folding his hands over his knees, like he was used to having the final word.

"Our mother wasn't religious, as you know."

Rina was roused from her blank reverie to say, "Please, I haven't told the children yet."

"They never met her," Szonja said, a note of petulance creeping into her voice.

"Hannah and Abby respect and love their bubbe," Aron said, and Szonja rolled her eyes at his sanctimony—what did he know of how anyone felt about anyone? He followed the mandates of Judaism as though he were a robot leafing through a manual on humanity.

"Our family will be the ones to decide how she's buried," she answered, picking up the thread from earlier, even though it cost her to say it—even the oblique acknowledgement faded her mother's image just that bit more. "Our father wouldn't want a religious ceremony."

Looking resolutely at the table, Rina said, "It was her choice."

"Oh, come on, how would she even know to choose that."

"She asked me about it a couple times on the phone lately. She was just curious, that's what she said. Wanted to know what the customs were. So I told her. Well, I didn't know she wanted to put it into practice, how could I have known?" She looked helplessly at Aron. "I told her the basics, and also, you know, about . . ." She faltered, embarrassed. "Well, I told her about the lack of proper burials in the camps—all those souls. She was affected by it, I think."

"You used the Holocaust to convince our mother to have a Jewish burial," Szonja said.

"Could you please assume, occasionally, that I am acting from a place of goodwill?" Rina said. "I was not manipulating her, I didn't know this information would be . . . used. I was just glad she was taking an interest." Rina could have added that the lack of interest from Szonja and their father about this part of her life, the part that now included her husband and two daughters as well, made her feel they rejected not only her, but Aron, Hannah and Abby too, which sometimes tipped rejection into anger.

"Right, okay."

"Szonja," Rina said, "I might wonder why it is, in fact, that I didn't know and why you didn't know that she was ill in the first place."

"What do you mean?"

"She had cancer, Szonja, our mother had cancer—she more than likely had it a few months ago, when you were sitting at home with her. How in the world did you not know about it?"

"She didn't tell me," Szonja said, her forehead wrinkling faintly.

"Maybe if you had paid a little more attention to people other than yourself, you would have noticed something was wrong."

"Well, it's not like I could have done anything about it even if I had."

"You could have stayed home with her, taken care of her in her last days."

"Yes, like you've been taking care of her for the past five years. I think we'd be better off if you didn't lecture me on what we owe our parents."

Aron cleared his throat and the two of them looked over at him. "Oh," he said—he really had only needed to clear his throat, but now he had unwittingly inserted himself into the argument. "Well, there's nothing to do about it now," he said, at once the truest and most ineffectual words.

Coloma, 2001

"Well, aren't we the lucky ones?" the Amish man says, looking at the boys and girls gathered around him.

The indignities of the day did not end at panning for gold and watching adult men and women play dress-up. For the afternoon, the class is divided into three groups, each going on to the activity they volunteered for back in the safety of a Los Angeles classroom. Well, that some of them volunteered for—Mila took the initiative to sign both her mother and herself up for horseback riding, so at least one of them exercised her free will. Sergio goes off to the blacksmithing workshop and Kathy trots off to make homestyle corn cakes at the activity centre's kitchen. The other children have had the foresight to pick activities with their friends—Mila did not understand that you were not meant to choose the activity you thought would provide the most enjoyment but the one that would give you the opportunity to solidify your social circle.

So it is that Mila and Sonia find themselves beside a self-contained group of children who make no effort to include them. Mother and daughter stand there like the first flowers of spring rising over clusters of grass, shivering in the wintry wind.

Watching Mila as she diligently takes in the Amish man's instructions, Sonia whispers to her daughter, "Didn't you want to go to the baking workshop with Kathy?"

Mila wrinkles her forehead, considering this. "I wanted to try horseback riding," she says (*rule number twenty-five: Be adventurous*), but her enthusiasm has clearly been punctured as she looks around, registering Kathy's and Sergio's absence and the fact that it's too late to remedy the situation.

After they are kitted out, a kind-looking man leads them to the stables and begins the process of pairing each child with the right horse. Even the most pragmatic ten-year-old would be excited by the prospect of choice here—children are forever finding ways to understand themselves by externalising their personalities. Favourite colours, favourite numbers, which girl band member they most resemble—a sandcastle of personality built up, bit by bit, from innocuous details and random preferences. It is understandable, therefore, that Mila winces when she is paired with a bay mare called Munch who makes an admirable effort at staying true to her name and never passes a moment without hay in her mouth, working it over with a languorous sideways motion of her jaw and eyes that seem to say she gets no pleasure from this, it just has to be done.

When Munch sees fit to relieve herself of some of that hay she's been working through, the kids point at the pile of steaming horseshit and laugh, because, really, what else is there to do when confronted with an actual pile of horseshit?

"What's his name?" Mila asks, looking at the black horse nudging his nose out of the stable beside Munch's.

"That's Grasshopper," the man says, "he's a wily one." This enigmatic description, the horse's name and the fact that, unlike Munch, his entire head isn't buried in a hay bale, immediately endear him to Mila.

"Can I have him instead?"

PORCUPINES

The man sizes her up. Literally, he sizes her up—the children would be disappointed to know this, but his pairing method is purely based on the height of each child and horse.

"Well, why the heck not," he says after some deliberation, and he saddles up Grasshopper for Mila, leaving Munch to her . . . well, munching.

After a brief demonstration of the correct form and a few turns about the paddock for each rider, they are all led out onto the trail, walking at a stately pace, single file. Her mother rides behind Mila on a tall, dapple-grey horse, looking surprisingly dignified and a little bit like a mounted police officer, with her leather jacket and sunglasses. She sits up straight, as though trying to put as much distance between herself and the horse as possible while still being seated on its back.

Grasshopper, it transpires, has also been named accurately; he moves in a skittish, staccato tempo that occasionally jolts Mila forward in the saddle. On one such occasion, she lets out a laugh, more out of surprise than anything else, but the sound seems to egg Grasshopper on; he moves into a trot and passes by the surprised boy in front of them. Exhilaration turns quickly to fear as the horse, perhaps sensing the conflicting emotions of his rider, continues to gather speed, now passing the group's leader, who tries, unsuccessfully, to grab Grasshopper's reins. The rest of the horses begin to pick up the pace as well, at once confused and excited by this show of insubordination.

And suddenly, the trail becomes a blur—trees, a black mane, the reddish-brown dirt of the ground and then the sky, friendly and blue, like a taunt.

* * *

One broken wrist, two bruised arms, a couple pairs of torn jeans—and one sprained ankle, which is the only damage Sonia cares about, as that ankle belongs to her daughter. The injured kids are driven to the nearest ER by the apologetic stable hand ("I did say Grasshopper was wily, ma'am, I did say") while the rest of the class continues on to San Francisco, discussing the incident in reverent tones on the bus and wishing they had been the ones dramatically whisked off to the hospital, wishing for pain the way only those completely safe from it can.

A short, square-shaped doctor is explaining something to her clipboard as Mila examines the bandage on her ankle, turning to look at it from all angles, as though it were a new toy. Sonia's ears begin to ring, tuning out the words; her vision starts to blur, softening the edges of the scene in front of her.

"Mrs. Imre, are you all right?" the doctor asks, looking up from her clipboard reluctantly.

"*Ms.* Imre," Sonia says. She is apparently not feeling poorly enough to forgo the correction.

"Did you get checked out when you came in, Ms. Imre?"

"No, I'm fine."

"You fell off a horse as well; you need to get checked out. There might be some internal trauma."

"Why would you say that?" In her confused mind, Sonia thinks the doctor is referring to her psychological state.

The doctor looks briefly at Mila as if to ask whether her mother is normally this truculent, but Mila just shrugs. Sonia realises she has sat down beside Mila's examination chair, although she can't remember getting there—after a few breaths, she begins to feel better; the room comes back into focus, the ringing recedes enough that she can hear her own thoughts.

"I'm sorry, Doctor, what I mean is that I feel fine," she says.

"I can examine you now, and you can just fill out the patient registration form—"

"No. No need. I feel fine, as I said. We're just here for Mila." In her mildly concussed state, Sonia forgets that she is allowed here—for years, doctors and hospitals were for her daughter only, while she tried to maintain good health through sheer force of will.

The doctor looks her in the eye—she recognises the expression of someone reluctant to fill out paperwork—and says slowly, "Okay. Well, if you have a headache, nausea, perhaps some confusion"—she raises an eyebrow slightly—"you can come right back in. Just a quick examination."

Sonia hesitates but then nods, and with a brisk "Thank you," she shepherds Mila out of the examination room.

Being knocked off her horse has knocked her off-balance, and outside the hospital, she fumbles to light a cigarette, her hands trembling in their quickness. If only she can take a drag in time, she thinks, everything will right itself again.

The nicotine begins to make its relaxing round of her bloodstream, but just as she closes her eyes for a second, the voice of Cecily Auerbach brings a portent of itself: "What a nightmare, isn't it?"

Sonia opens her eyes, one at a time. Cecily, Megan and Mila are staring up at her, awaiting confirmation.

Sonia sighs and stamps out her barely smoked cigarette, looking longingly at it before it lands in the fathoms of the trash can beside her. "Did Megan hurt herself too?" she asks finally, but the child smiles placidly and doesn't seem much shaken up by the events of the day.

Cecily looks confused for a moment. "Oh, my Megan? No, she's fine, she wasn't with the riding group." Sonia waits for her to explain her presence at the hospital when the rest of the group is likely on their fifth round of "Ninety-Nine Bottles of Beer" in the bus heading to San Francisco.

"And you are . . . ?" she prompts.

"I'm just gathering everyone's version of events—absolutely unacceptable conduct on the park's part, endangering children this way. They need to be held to account."

"To account, yes," Sonia says, because repeating back the end of someone's sentence is the most efficient way to have a conversation in the absence of one's mind.

"Don't know why the school arranged it in the first place—taking such young children horseback riding amounts to criminal negligence."

"Ugh, negligence." Sonia shakes her head ruefully.

"It was Mila's horse that got the rest all riled up, wasn't it?" Cecily asks, cocking her head, her voice rising just slightly.

Mila looks nervously at the adults, and Sonia's instinct to put some distance between themselves and the day's events rouses her out of her stupor. "I think it was a general all-inclusive kind of stampede."

Cecily looks unconvinced but nonetheless abandons this line of questioning. "Well, it's just, first that awful motel, and now this mess? The children deserve a little better, don't you think?"

It seems to Sonia the children generally have a pretty sweet deal. But the answer to *Do children deserve better?* can never be *Not really* or anything remotely noncommittal, as Sonia found out once when UNICEF canvassers knocked on her door in the middle of her nap. Thankfully Cecily assumes the best in her and moves on. "Have you thought about pursuing legal action?"

PORCUPINES

Sonia sifts through the catalogue of her own thoughts. Twice today she has thought about the way Luther Vandross dances in the video for "Never Too Much" (a very specific kind of shimmying motion), but no, she has not once thought of finding someone else to blame for the way her life is going. At the end of the day, it's not the horse's fault if it doesn't want you on its back.

Los Angeles, 1989

WHEN SHE ARRIVED AT NICO'S HOUSE, SZONJA THOUGHT HE wasn't home, but eventually he opened the door, his hair in a friendly rumple, his mouth in a smile that seemed to be for life rather than Szonja specifically. He didn't lead her up to his room as usual, and Szonja wondered if he sensed something different in her. As it turned out, he had just wanted to get his sweater from the living room, but men have been the presumptive owners of many a sympathetic thought where none exist. Once he had pulled on the sweater, he did in fact suggest they go upstairs and take it off.

She hadn't actually intended to come to Nico's house, but when Tatiana dropped her off in front of the Greenes' after their English lesson, she'd found she couldn't press the bell.

Szonja was walking around not telling people about her mother's death. Here was another person whose mental image of Szonja still included two parents; and here was another one. And if that was the reality in so many people's minds, then perhaps her mother, thousands of miles away anyway, was not dead after all, so who was to say that the version she had been told—that her mother was dead and buried—was more real? Because nobody in her life had ever died, she'd felt safe from it, statistically immune. That kind of sadness was for others, not her.

But sidestepping the truth can become exhausting—as Szonja would continue to learn in the coming years—and it was a relief to be with someone whose enquiries need not be evaded. Nico was still warm from his recently discarded sweater; his hands were languorous and his stubble pleasantly coarse. As Szonja loosened under his touch, her mind became pleasantly blank, as if the link between sensation and thought had momentarily been severed and she could finally relax into something elemental.

It would be preferable to say that Nico's views on the matter were considered, but the ethics of his somewhat involuntary involvement in her life would not come to bother Szonja for many, many more years. She was making the same mistake her parents had made—all her ancestors, in fact. Or perhaps it was not a mistake at all. She was making herself a family.

When Nico asked if she had a condom, she said, "Don't worry about it," and he didn't.

As they got dressed, Nico asked if Szonja wanted "a drink or something" and she followed him downstairs, where he got her a can of Dr Pepper and led her to their sunporch. It was companionable, after all, sitting there and listening to Nico tap his fingers on the top of a can, her legs splayed out on the steps below her, warmed by the sun. Her mind wandered into all the places she had avoided in the past weeks. Her mother, yes, but also her father, always inaccessible but even more closed off in his grief; her sister, burrowing into her own family and their various observances. Who knew it had been her mother all along who had kept the idea of a family from becoming hollow?

"Nico," she said, and he startled a little, like he'd forgotten she was there. "Is your family religious?"

"Very much so," he said.

"How much is very much?"

"I go to church with my mother and my cousins every Sunday. We do our best."

"Do you believe in heaven?"

When she asked him this question, it must be stated, Szonja intended to draw comfort from his faith, despite her indifference to her own. She had expected bland moralising at worst and the comfort of ancient texts at best.

"Yes, I do," he said, still smiling. And then he added, "For those who have taken Jesus into their hearts, definitely."

Szonja almost laughed, the words sounded so strange, like he'd read them from a pamphlet. Eventually she said, "You do know the Greenes are Jewish, though, right?"

"I have no problem with that," he said, as though it were as simple as that.

"But . . . you don't think they'll go to heaven."

He raised his shoulders a little as if to say it wasn't up to him.

"My mother is Jewish too, you don't think she'll go to heaven?" She didn't have the heart to use the past tense yet. Perhaps he could sense the rising tension in her voice because he sat up a little straighter and looked at her for the first time since they'd sat down on the sunporch.

"Listen, this is just what I believe," he said finally, and then, leaning back in his chair, he added, "She could always get baptised."

Szonja let out a laugh that surprised herself, and then she laughed a little more until her shoulders shook and tears sprang from the corners of her eyes. Nico smiled at her uncertainly, pleased with the result but unsure of the cause.

Szonja wiped at her eyes, caught her breath and said, "True, she could always just get baptised."

The thing about revelations and disappointments, the flight of high hopes and their descent into pathos, is you still need a ride home after you've had them. Such were the indignities of life without a car in Los Angeles.

Szonja asked Nico to drop her on West Pico Boulevard so she could make the rest of her way to her sister's house on foot. For weeks she had wanted nothing else but to sit in the driver's seat of a car and feel the power of the machine beneath her, gliding across the vast expanse of the city. But suddenly it just felt like something to impede her perspective—the traffic speeding up or slowing down the world around her in a way that was beyond her control. Now, walking along this road, with its delis and synagogues, she felt like she'd suddenly stepped onto dry land, her legs wobbly and yet she was safe. When she reached the house, she sat down on the curb across from it, a river of concrete between them. It was dusk and Rina had started turning on the lights in the house; she could see snatches of movement here and there, as though the family were in a reluctant puppet show.

"You're welcome to contribute something too, Szonja," someone said—it was a man, probably, but she couldn't be sure if it had been the rabbi or Aron. She was lost in the task in front of her. Hannah's favourite stuffed animal—a severe-looking penguin—had ripped its stitches and spewed forth its stuffing in a traumatic fashion, so Szonja had offered to mend it for her. Hannah had been sternly approving of the results and went on a hunt in the house for other injured toys and now stood by her side, carefully overseeing her efforts like a little Henry Ford inspecting his assembly line.

"If you're going to hold me up, I'm going to put you to work," Szonja told her. After threading a bright green plastic needle for her, she showed Hannah how to do a basic running stitch.

Hannah looked at her dubiously. "My friend Miriam poked her finger and she had to get a tentus shot," she explained. "That's, like, another needle they poke into you, and it hurts a lot." Abby came over and examined her sister's hands as though expecting to find these gory details on her, her eyes brimming with fear.

"You'll be fine, just make sure you go slow and your hands aren't under the needle."

Hannah set to work sewing up a pocket, and despite her confidence that Hannah would manage, Szonja was surprised, and a little worried, that she held such authority. She looked up occasionally from her own sewing to find Hannah deep in concentration, her lips pushed out as though about to kiss someone, her chin puckered like old fruit.

Abby was too restless and clumsy to help, but she came up to Szonja's chair and burrowed her face into the animals waiting for Szonja's aid, scrunching them up to her face with a dreamy expression like she'd never felt anything so soft and luxurious.

Szonja reluctantly emerged from her world of stuffed toys and girlhood to find that her sister, Aron and the rabbi were waiting for a response.

"Contribute what?"

"An anecdote, any details you'd like us to mention," the rabbi said. They were preparing some sort of memorial service for her mother to mark the thirtieth day of mourning. After they heard about the funeral from Mr. Imre, Rina and Aron were consumed by their efforts to honour Mrs. Imre in various ways—consulting with the rabbi on what to do now that they had missed the funeral, who said the mourner's prayer and various other details that Szonja had no patience for. Her sister hadn't even tried to persuade her when she'd declined to sit shiva, when hordes of people came to offer their condolences for the loss of a woman they knew nothing about.

"I'm sure you've got plenty," she said to Rina, and it occurred to her that her sister might have little more to say about her mother than the strangers who had sat around their home. Despite the phone calls and letters between Rina and her mother over the years, it was Szonja who knew which soap opera was her mother's most recent favourite (one about neighbours, called *Neighbours*) and what her favourite drink was (a soda brand called Brand) and what paper she liked to buy at the tobacco shop (a magazine titled *Women's Magazine*). (It would be crude to ridicule a dead woman's tastes, so let us blame a lack of free trade for the less than imaginative naming conventions.)

"This could wait," Rina said, indicating her daughter's toys.

"We can't leave them on the operating table, can we, Hannah," Szonja said without looking at her sister. She thought Rina was going to press her, but she turned back to the rabbi and said something about a band her mother had liked a decade ago.

Even if Szonja had wanted to commiserate with her sister, she had, remarkably, more on her mind than her mother's death.

A few days ago she had spent some time in the community-college bathroom squatting uncertainly over a piece of plastic. It had seemed like the right place to do it—Rina's house was obviously ruled out, the Jewish learning centre did not feel quite right for this endeavour and the Greenes' house was a chaotic revolving door of inquisitive and friendly people. It turned out to be less than ideal, however, because people kept coming into the bathroom, and the distraction landed several of the pregnancy tests in the trash. At one point she heard Tatiana come in with another person in their class and she held her breath, as though her friend might recognise the sound of her breathing and wonder what she was doing in the bathroom.

She waited to hear the taps turning on and off and footsteps receding before she came out of her cubicle with the surviving pregnancy test. Clearly she had misjudged the noises, because Tatiana was still there, fixing her makeup. She looked at Szonja in the mirror, then down at what was in her hand—her face remained mercifully impassive. It never did display much emotion, but Szonja took it as a sign of compassion anyway.

"What's the verdict?" Tatiana had asked.

Szonja had placed the test on the side of the sink and said, "About fifty more seconds to go, but I'm pretty sure I'm fucked."

But looking at her sister now, her head nodding along to something the rabbi was saying, Szonja felt calm for the first time in days. She was too young to know how life unspools, one decision at a time cutting out entire alternate worlds, an endless series of bifurcations nudging each person into a life they have no way of knowing if they will like or not. So she was glad of the potential future inside of her. Here was Rina with her husband and her daughters and her rabbi and all the strangers that made up her congregation—but here too was she with a person who could be hers only.

Szonja heard a car pull up outside, the sound recalling her to the plans she had made with Anthony to go driving. She finished up the last stitch of a haggard-looking bear's behind and went to grab her purse.

"Is this really the time to be meeting friends?" Rina asked, her tone uncharacteristically strident. Szonja heard only the censure, not the plea for her company.

"I'm only under your feet anyway," she said without looking at her sister.

Anthony and Szonja went out on the road in his car, this time winding from the flat bustle of the Fairfax roads she'd driven on with Rina to the quiet cul-de-sacs of Pasadena. Lately their drives had become less adventurous. Szonja had stopped going to Hebrew classes in the past weeks, and after Anthony mocked her lack of perseverance, she finally told him about her mother—now he felt it was callous to go "gallivanting around Los Angeles" and chose his locations more soberly, finally landing on a favourite route that deposited them on a hillock overlooking a golf club. They got cheeseburgers on the way and ate them on the hood of Anthony's car, looking down at the players.

"Why is this the best part?" she asked, picking at the burnt-on cheese in the paper wrapper. "And why can't the whole dish be made up of this?"

"Delayed gratification—you wouldn't appreciate the burnt cheese if you hadn't worked through the rest of it first."

"Anthony Greene, you are so smart," she said, taking a piece of cheese from his hand.

She was attempting to lighten the mood—Anthony had just told her about his breakup with Natalie. Szonja had met Natalie only a handful of times, and she had liked her well enough—

whatever they lacked in natural affinity, they had tried to compensate for by giving each other more attention than they gave Anthony, which had greased the wheels of their time together. But she had been gone for most of the fall, so it had been easy to forget her existence. Clearly Natalie had sensed this too and decided to end things before the end became inevitable.

Szonja had her own news to share, though, and she was distracted on the drive back, making Anthony wince as she hit the curb turning into the gas station on their way home. This was the auspicious location—the glare of the Supreme 93 pump outside, the gas station attendant dutifully wiping the shield—where she chose to tell him she was pregnant.

To his credit, it took him only a little time to regain his composure, after which he offered all the right words of reassurance.

"Come over to ours," he said after it seemed he had run out of things to say. "Mom will make you rice pudding."

"Oh, I don't know, I should probably get back—"

"She makes it whenever people are . . . She made it for Marnie each time, and my cousin Marissa." He became more excited as he spoke, as though rice pudding would solve everything. "Come, let's head to mine."

"I don't know—"

"Okay, Szonja, not to sound like a mama's boy," he said, running his hand through his hair, "but my mother always knows what to do."

"I don't know if there *is* anything to do," she said, which he understood to mean that Szonja felt defeated by the enormity of the problem.

"I just want to help," he said, and whether she needed help or not, Szonja wanted the closeness of being helped. And after all, it was easy to imagine sinking into the comfort of the Greene family home. From the image of eating the rice pudding in Mrs. Greene's kitchen, her imagination swiftly leapt to moving in, trailing after Mrs. Greene during the day, sitting at their dinner table in the evenings, driving out with Anthony at night. She was too young and too recently pregnant to really imagine herself having a child in the Greene household; what she imagined instead was a bit like being a child there.

With this vision still in her mind and feeling calmer than she had in weeks, Szonja squeezed Anthony's hand and got out to fill the tank.

Anthony held Mrs. Greene by the shoulders, looked her in the eye and said, "Mother, will you make some rice pudding for Szonja?" Mrs. Greene's eyes widened a little; she looked at Szonja, who nodded and smiled, then back at her son and shook her head. "Well, I will make rice pudding."

Anthony smiled at Szonja reassuringly as his mother began to look through her kitchen cupboards and then draped himself across the living-room couch and turned on the TV.

"Have you ever made rice pudding, Szonja?" Mrs. Greene asked.

"No, I'm not much of a cook."

"It's an important skill," she said. "Not cooking, really, or not just cooking. It's the making something for yourself, something comforting. Something to have in a crisis, something made from scratch. Grab me the cinnamon, would you?" Szonja handed Mrs. Greene the jar. "This is easy as can be—just gotta stir regularly." She worked quietly for a while and all that could be heard was the occasional burst of noise from the living room as commercials came on. The smell of warm milk and spices was making Szonja a little sleepy and she startled when Mrs. Greene addressed her, quieter than before.

"Honey, you know we love you, right?" she said. "And I don't know the details but between you and me, Anthony . . . he's not ready for something like this."

Szonja was racking her brain for what Anthony could be unready for. "Oh."

"Yes, I know he seems very serious for his age," she said. "He puts it on a bit, bless him. But . . ." She arched her eyebrows.

Szonja didn't know how to explain—now that she understood what Mrs. Greene had misunderstood, the woman's initial reaction seemed tame, and yet something about it stung.

"I don't know what the situation is back home, but here in America, there are clinics, there are places you can go . . ." She gently patted Szonja's arm, then turned back to the stove and said, "Let's give it another stir."

Szonja glanced over at Anthony sitting in the living room. He looked suddenly very young, which, really, he was, only a couple of years older than her and still living with his parents, chasing a pipe dream of becoming a musician. But that was his right as a young American man and as it should be. And after all, she was just some foreign girl who had washed up in Los Angeles. She was no one to them when it came down to it, not even to Anthony—they had been friends for just a couple of months. Maybe she could have explained to Mrs. Greene and they both would have laughed. Perhaps she would have helped her anyway, even though the problem was not hers to solve. It could have been fine to lean on them, to lean on him, but sometimes you just don't want to wait and find out if people will disappoint you.

San Francisco, 2001

YOU CAN'T SAY THAT SONIA IS *PLEASED* THAT HER DAUGHTER HAS sprained her ankle, but it is undeniable that there are certain benefits to be gained from it. By the time they catch up with the rest of the group in San Francisco, the students have had to plough on forbearingly with Mrs. Flores's strict itinerary. They have visited the Historic Button Museum and are now at Golden Gate Park for a picnic; they have had one meltdown (Mrs. Flores, mistakenly thinking the Historic Button Museum was closed and cursing Szonja, who was supposed to have organised this outing) and two near-miss bathroom incidents (Sergio, caught up in the history lecture at said museum, and Austin, in protest for not being allowed to take a display button home with him).

Sonia and Mila await the group at the hotel, which is a pleasant surprise after the dubious quality of the Lost Hills Inn. It's a standard-issue greige number more suited to corporate types, who were indeed in the majority until the Mount Washington orchestra lowered the average age and median income considerably. In their room Sonia and Mila lie down on top of the straitjacket-tight bedding and sigh out a synchronous breath.

At some point, Mila, with her sprained ankle perched on top of a pillow, dozes off, and Sonia unpacks her bag. In her nightstand she finds the requisite faux-leather-bound Bible. She is about to move it to the side to make room but instead takes it out and thumbs through the thin pages of the book. The feathery paper and the small type make it appear small and innocuous, and it reminds Sonia of pages she once tried to understand what seems like a very long time ago. And here are the familiar long fingers pointing to where she should be reading, her sister's frame leaning over her in a synagogue pew.

Sonia is thankful for the knock on the door that dispels the image. She assumes it will be a hotel cleaner, but it's Mr. Alvarez standing outside.

"Ah, I'm sorry to disturb you . . ." He waits a beat, presumably for Sonia to contradict him. "I just wanted to check in and see how Mila's doing."

"She's sleeping," Sonia says. "I thought everyone was at Golden Gate Park?"

"We've just come back."

"I see. And how are the other kids doing?" A brief look of confusion on Mr. Alvarez's face. "The other kids who were in the hospital?" she says.

Mr. Alvarez hesitates, his mouth slightly open, on the precipice of speech. It does not seem possible, and yet he looks even more uncomfortable than before.

And suddenly, Sonia feels an inexplicable amount of anger towards the man standing in front of her. "I'm sure they would all love to have a visit from the vice principal," she says coldly. Even though, given the beer, the cigarettes, the Funyuns, she has little moral high ground to stand on, it irks her that the man has come here under the pretext of caring for her daughter.

"Yes, no, of course, I just wanted to check—"

"Mila's fine," she says, and she goes to close the door, but he looks at her with wounded eyes, so she relents a little. "Thank you for checking in."

Back in the room Mila is awake, studiously staring at her belongings spread out on the bed as though she is solving a puzzle. She looks up at Sonia with an expression that is altogether too knowing for a ten-year-old.

Then, without another word, she extends her telescopic music stand with a quick, practised flourish, like a magician pulling an object out of a top hat. She opens her violin case and sets the instrument on her shoulder, poised for music. She is not alone in this endeavour—children from the other rooms can be heard practising different pieces of music, a discordant unity of activity that could have been moving in its collective determination but is mostly just hard on the ears. Mila has learned to tune out the things she does not care about—or perhaps it is a talent she was born with—and so she plays through the noise. Her mother has often asked her what it is that she enjoys so much about playing music (Sonia herself being tone-deaf and averse to hobbies that require daily habit), but Mila doesn't have the words to attach to the feeling, not yet. If she could have expressed herself in language, she might have said that music is a system that makes sense to her. It follows patterns; discord can be avoided with the right combination of notes and the dexterity of her fingers, which she can work towards incrementally. If you practise every day, you get better—the simplicity of this causal relationship appeals to her amidst the chaos of their home life and the complexities of the schoolyard, neither of which has yielded anything discernibly good in direct relation to her efforts. She has control—in her domain of twenty inches, it is just her, the bow, the violin, nothing between them but ricocheting air.

* * *

The same configuration of children and chaperones is maintained from the previous night and with it comes the continued attentions of Megan H, who expresses her newfound appreciation of Sonia by exclaiming "Cool!" to everything—Sonia's suitcase, her clothes, her reckless raid of the minibar; it seems she can do no wrong.

When Sonia retreats to the bathroom to wash off the persistent smell of horses and the American River, Megan's benevolent attention turns to Mila, who is beginning to understand the girl's interest in her swimming attire the previous day.

"Mila, your mom is, like, *really cool*," she says, breathless, shaking her head.

"Thanks?"

"Must be cool to have a cool mom like that." At this rate, Megan will not be winning any vocabulary competitions, but she certainly is clear in what she wishes to express.

"Yeah, well, I'm sure your mom is nice too."

"My mom is a pencil pusher with no imagination," Megan replies without emotion. "That's what my dad said when he left to join an ashram last year."

Riley follows this conversation like a suspicious tennis enthusiast—squinting in turn at her best friend and the strange girl they've never really talked to before.

"Come on, let's go check out Jenny's room," Riley says, dragging Megan with her. Megan allows herself to be pulled out of the room but smiles weakly at Mila as she leaves.

Mila wonders what it would be like to have a friend like Megan, one you can drag around and whisper with, one who sits with you not because there's nowhere else left but because you are her first choice, but the moment is fleeting, and she reminds herself that whatever it is the girls might find in Jenny's room won't be as interesting as what she's going to find the next day on a windy San Francisco pier.

By the time Sonia emerges from the steam of their shared bathroom, the other girls are gone, and Mila is once again sitting on the bed, resting her foot, reading her biography, only the tiniest ripple of disappointment disturbing her face.

"Where have your pals gone?" Sonia asks, applying cream to her face in practised circular motions, looking at her daughter in the mirror.

"They're not my pals," Mila says, lifting her book higher over her face so that only the slight furrow of her forehead can be seen. "And they went to Jenny's room."

Sonia considers urging her daughter to go after these girls, find Jenny—whoever she is—but before she can find the right offhand tone that is best used for the persuasion of a preadolescent child, there's another knock on the door.

"Well, aren't we popular today?" Sonia says, and immediately regrets her wording. "Not that that's—anyway."

"Hair of the dog?" Linda says when Sonia opens the door. "I hear there's a real bar downstairs."

"A *real* bar? Dalton would be hurt," Sonia says, laughing. She pauses and briefly looks back at her daughter. "You go on ahead," she tells Linda. "I might come later."

When Sonia closes the door Mila says, "I'll be fine," bringing the book even closer to her eyes so that in place of Mila's face there is now a disgruntled Russian's.

Sonia wants to say something bolstering to her daughter, something about the mercurial nature of adolescent friendships and how things get easier; she wants to tell her that she won't find what she's looking for in a guidebook on popularity, however tempting it is to outsource the more perplexing aspects of life. But what she lands on is: "Milosh, I think you need to get back on the horse."

Mila finally lowers the book to her lap and looks at her mother with alarm.

"Not an actual horse. I mean, you know, metaphorically speaking, with your friends..." But here she falters because she's not sure there is a metaphorical friendship horse to get back on and perhaps its suggestion will only serve to make Mila even more aware of it.

But Mila has already gone back to her book, satisfied with the absence of actual horses in her future. Sonia should probably get back on the horse too, the metaphorical pep-talk horse, but unlike Camy Baker, she's fresh out of words of wisdom, and she also really wants a beer.

In the hotel's lobby there is in fact a real bar, and the adults, apart from Dave and Lisa, who have been tasked with enforcing curfew for the kids, have gathered across two tables and are discussing the plans for the next couple of days.

"Rehearsals begin the day after tomorrow," Mrs. Flores says, reading from her list.

It has not even occurred to Sonia to wonder, but she is thankful when Linda asks, "What are they playing?"

"They'll be playing Shostakovich's Fifth Symphony," Cecily says proudly, and Sonia is a little relieved to know that there is a reason her daughter is ensconced with the grumpy Russian upstairs.

"Well, not exactly," Mr. Alvarez says. "The Palo Alto Youth Symphony Orchestra will play some movements from the Fifth Symphony. The younger kids will be playing an arrangement inspired by the symphony. Much simpler; a little less intense."

"Don't be modest, Daniel," Mrs. Flores says, patting his hands and then speaking to the others. "He made the arrangement for the kids himself. It's simple and beautiful."

Mr. Alvarez shrugs his shoulders in acknowledgement of the compliment.

"Surely that's not part of the job description?" Sonia asks him, despite having planned to ignore Mr. Alvarez altogether tonight. Mr. Alvarez, it seems, has also planned to be ignored, because his face opens up in delight when he answers. "Well, I offered," he says. "I played and composed a little in another lifetime."

"And here I thought you'd always wanted to be a vice principal."

"You joke," he says, as though he is aware that his face and demeanour belie an understanding of sarcasm. "But no, I did always want to be an educator. I've always wanted to help others realise themselves." Sonia shifts in her seat—she expects him to be embarrassed by his own earnestness, but Mr. Alvarez seems completely at ease explaining his life's journey to casual acquaintances. "But you're meant to want to self-actualise," he continues. "You're meant to want things for *yourself*. So for a while I did. I wasn't very good at it."

"At playing?" Sonia asks.

"At wanting it. Classical music can get very competitive. You have to want it badly." He looks at Sonia for a moment like it's only the two of them having this conversation even though Mrs. Flores is fanning her armpit with an itinerary beside him and Cecily is mumbling something about being indestructible as she annotates her copy. "No, the playing I was pretty good at."

For a while Sonia is left to her own thoughts as Mr. Alvarez tells Linda about his time playing in a pit orchestra on Broadway and Cecily and Mrs. Flores go through the rest of the plans for the trip. There is that specific feeling of being thrown together with a group of people who will disperse after a designated time—the enjoyment of company without the need to evaluate any future purpose. These people do not need to fit into her life or know its details; they need not agree with her politics or have similar hobbies. They are fellow travellers. They only need to sit at a hotel bar and drink beers together.

At some point Dave calls down to the front desk to say one of the kids is vomiting.

"Probably nerves," Linda says when the receptionist comes over to tell them.

"Who is it?" Mrs. Flores asks. The receptionist cocks her head at the note in her hand, trying to decipher her own writing. "Reagan?"

"Oh, thank God," Sonia says. She doesn't bother to explain that she is thankful for the fact of it not being Mila, rather than the fact of the vomiting itself, so her comment just hangs there awkwardly.

"I think you mean Megan," Mrs. Flores says finally, and gets up to go help whichever Megan has deposited her anxiety into the toilet.

"I should probably check on Mila anyway," Sonia says, but Linda goes to get them another beer and she doesn't make a move. With every minute that passes, her concern for her daughter sounds hollower. She startles when Mr. Alvarez clears his throat.

PORCUPINES

"You're doing your best," he says, and perhaps it sounds too intimate, presuming the worries secreted behind her words, because he adds, "We're all doing our best."

Sonia considers him—the weight of a platitude can be foam-light or anchor-heavy, but he doesn't strike her as thoughtless. "Whether or not we do our best is beside the point," she says. "They didn't ask to be stuck with whatever our 'best' is."

Los Angeles, 1989

It happened at a 7-Eleven as Szonja was about to pay for a medium-size cherry-flavoured slushie, which was unfortunate, because she liked cherry-flavoured slushies, and she would never be able to look at them the same way again. Much as people never again eat the thing they consumed immediately before vomiting, this was a post hoc fallacy with no rational basis and yet very human and ultimately understandable.

It was three weeks after she found out she was pregnant and three days before her flight home to Budapest, and the fact of her situation was beginning to filter through, so she no longer worried too much about what she ate, its cost and its relative nutritional value—hence the slushie.

She had walked inland from Venice Beach after a day spent watching the Rollerbladers and skateboarders—a steady and endless stream of people smoothly making their way along the coast. She didn't know where their little highway started or ended, but she liked to imagine putting on Rollerblades of her own and making her way up the coast of California. Of course, she did not realise just how soon she would find her cutoffs and tank top insufficient, as Los Angeles warmth gave way to the Bay Area's winds, but life had not yet ground her down so much that her daydreams contained only what was rational and plausible—she still had one toe in childhood, after all.

When she got up from the bench where she had spun these idle dreams, she felt the light-headedness of too much time spent in the sun. Tatiana was waiting for her at a clinic somewhere in Mar Vista. That her friend had echoed Mrs. Greene's calm practicality when Szonja brought up the topic made it feel all the more like the right decision. A mistake had been made and it could easily be rectified. And so she would have to get a taxi to the clinic eventually, but for now she just began walking vaguely in its direction, stopping at the 7-Eleven to feel the cool air-conditioning on her overheated limbs and to get a slushie, which had won her over with its lurid colours and the satisfying way it churned in its clear vat next to the cash register.

Sometime between when she set the filled cup on the counter and when she reached into her bag for change, Szonja stopped breathing. Her breaths had become laboured even as she walked along Lincoln Avenue, but she had chalked it up to the dry heat of the air she inhaled. But now, standing in front of the bored-looking checkout boy (*Tim*, his name tag announced), she felt like her lungs had suddenly decided to close up shop. She gasped once before leaving the slushie on the counter and exiting the store. She heard Tim say, "Well, what am I supposed to do with this now?" but it came from a distance, the words of a neighbour overheard through the walls.

Outside the 7-Eleven, Szonja kept gasping for breath as she sat down on the curb, her eyes streaming involuntary tears, their salt making its way to her open mouth. She was vaguely aware of being a ridiculous sight, but as life seemed in that very moment to be ending around her, she couldn't muster the presence of mind to care. After a few minutes, or hours, her breath slowed down and she wiped her face with the back of her hand, and noting her brain's ability to command her muscles once again, she deduced that she had not, in fact, died. Tim the salesclerk stood a few feet away—she didn't know how long he'd been watching, but he approached now and held out the cherry-flavoured slushie.

"It's nothing to cry about," he said, not unkindly.

She took the slushie from him and carried it all the way, not to Mar Vista, but back to her sister's, the pleasing texture of the crushed ice melting into pink liquid along the way. In the little bathroom next to the room she shared with her nieces, she poured it into the sink and watched it cut a path on the white enamel until it was all gone.

Aron drummed his fingers on the wheel as they sat in traffic.

"Don't worry, you won't miss it," he said.

"The traffic?" Szonja asked. She had gotten used to the traffic by now, all the idle minutes, a whole life contained inside a car—there was something soothing about being forced to sit still and listen to the radio.

"No, I mean you won't miss your flight," he said. "We left in good time."

Szonja looked at her brother-in-law, his anxious eyebrows and his resolute chin still covered by his mourning beard. To Szonja, suspended in this moment before her time in Los Angeles permanently became nostalgia, everything already felt soft and benevolent. But then she recalled her brittle parting at home with Rina, who had apologised for not taking her to the airport herself but had not seemed remorseful in the least. Rina had been impossible to read in the past weeks, as she'd launched into any activity her mourning strictures allowed with single-mindedness.

"She did want to take you herself," he said. "But your sister . . . has not been feeling great."

"Well, she's been very busy," Szonja said.

"I know all these . . . processes seem strange to you, but there's a reason we do it this way. And your sister, she's found it particularly difficult, not being able to go home at this time."

These words did not rouse her to empathy; they were as empty to Szonja as the prayers mumbled for their mother. But she could have thought of her sister, who had made such a drastic choice for their family back in Washington, DC, only for that choice to become immaterial a mere five years later when the wall fell. Rina had lost the love and companionship of her beloved parents on the conviction that it was a sacrifice that had to be made. How many people made similar choices, believing the ideologies of their countries to be just as intractable as their leaders wanted them to? Szonja could have thought of her sister, who would live with that guilt all her life, now that their mother's death had made her decisions truly immutable; she could have thought to save herself from feeling the same.

"Well, I'd have been happy to give her my ticket, if she's so desperate." These were hollow words. Szonja knew she had to get on that flight; her visa was expiring within days.

"Rina has the children to take care of," he said. "And, yes, she's been unwell, so it was not in the cards for her."

"I think Rina does exactly what she wants," Szonja said, and Aron had no answer to this years-old wound, so he just patted her arm awkwardly.

When they finally reached the airport, Szonja found she preferred the silent companionship of her brother-in-law to getting out and joining the long lines of people dispersing into the world.

PORCUPINES

They sat in the car for what felt like a long time, their eyes trained forward where there was not much to see except the NO PARKING sign they clearly hadn't.

Finally, Aron shifted in his seat a little, the smallest indication that it was time to go, so they got out of the car and he hoisted Szonja's suitcase out of the trunk.

"Take care of yourself," he said, and gave her a hug. *Take care of yourself, take care of yourself, take care of yourself.* These words snagged in her brain and wouldn't shake free.

She waited for the car to drive away, sitting on top of her suitcase, toes skimming the concrete. For the first time in weeks, she allowed herself to think about the future that awaited her at home. Szonja thought of sitting in that suburban apartment—her father, her child, the quiet between them—and how much she didn't want it, not like this. There was no reason not to go home, but that didn't mean there was any reason to go home. So she hailed a cab; it was as simple as that.

After all, America spent decades convincing the world that it was better than the Eastern Bloc. They should not have been surprised when we believed them.

San Francisco, 2001

"Isn't it wonderful?" the woman says. "We have the widest collection of historic buttons in the world right here in San Francisco."

Sonia massages her temples and nods at the guide showing them around the Historic Button Museum, where Mrs. Flores insisted she take the poor children involved in the horseback-riding accident while the rest of the group had their scheduled free time in the park. "No one should have to miss out on the cultural programs." Mrs. Flores, it was becoming clear, was a paisley-covered sadist.

They make for a sad little group: In addition to Mila and Sonia, there is a boy named Jeffrey, who broke his wrist and therefore is no longer playing in the orchestra at all; Riley, who only bruised her arm but is wringing every bit of sympathy she can out of the accident; and a kid named Miles, who hasn't spoken a word. Sonia assumes it has something to do with the accident as well, but she is so thankful for his silence that she doesn't want to risk coaxing him out of his shell. All she wants is to be back in the hotel bed with the curtains drawn.

This time you couldn't blame the Funyuns. There was no seedy motel to act as a backdrop for seedy activities. This hotel couldn't have inspired anything other than a corporate merger. This time,

Sonia knew exactly what it was that compelled her to get close to Mr. Alvarez again. Assuaging her parental guilt had proven too attractive.

"Would you like to see the 1880s collection?" the guide asks. The existence of an 1880s collection implies an 1890s collection and a 1900s collection and who knows what else. Sonia makes an executive decision to take the cultural program back to their hotel room, where the kids take turns pressing the remote's buttons until they land on a channel playing *A Very Brady Sequel*. This is where they pause and as each kid takes on that dazed child-in-front-of-a-television look, Sonia lets out a sigh. They have this on videotape at home, a tape that is miraculously still working despite her daughter reverently feeding it into the maw of their VCR player pretty much every day from 1997 to 1998. That was over six hundred opportunities for Sonia to consider what it was exactly that had her daughter entranced. True, it had Tim Matheson as a father figure, an abundance of siblings and an aura of big-family-fun-ness, but Sonia worried sometimes that, without an understanding of sarcasm, Mila was taking its cheesy seventies morality at face value. She had to hide the tape in the end.

She takes a Dr Pepper from the minibar and rolls its cool condensation across her forehead as the Brady family turns into trippy animation due to the psychedelics accidentally cooked into their pasta sauce. She falls into an uneasy sleep disturbed by dreams of Mrs. Flores, Mr. Alvarez and Marcia Brady holding hands and taking mushrooms.

Someone at the Palo Alto Youth Symphony Orchestra mixer had thought it a good idea to have everyone wear name tags, but instead of writing their names, have them instead put the instrument they played. Which is how Cecily ends up speaking to people as Hi, My Name Is Pianino; Mr. Alvarez as Hi, My Name Is Tuba; and one particularly witty child as Hi, My Name Is Slim Shady, which, despite its zeitgeistiness, does not win him any points with this crowd. Sonia is glad to see that Mila as Violin is met with a degree of respect (unlike one unfortunate Megan, who, as Maracas, is shunned even by her fellow percussionists), although there are too many of Mila's kind to maintain delusions of individualism.

"Maybe I should have tried the viola," Mila says upon discovering the very same problem, but then Sonia and Mila both spot Mrs. Flores in her favourite pinafore dress introducing herself as Mrs. Tambourine Woman with a tinkling laugh and they decide that individualism is not so desirable after all. In fact Sonia finds it oddly comforting to see her daughter with (or at least in the vicinity of) her peers, nothing in that moment differentiating the children, the only hierarchy being whether one can play a vibrato or one's degree of familiarity with Chopin. Here Mila holds her own, and her direct gaze and sombre face speak of confidence and competence rather than oddity.

Sonia and her charges arrived half an hour late, and she had some trouble convincing Mrs. Flores that the extra time was spent discovering the "exclusive collection" of the Historic Button Museum. Although Mrs. Flores's interest is momentarily piqued by the word *exclusive*, she knows a dog-ate-my-homework excuse when she hears one and is distracted from reprimanding Sonia only when she finds a better target in Slim Shady.

The room is abuzz with anticipation of the performance in two days—or the "big game," as Dave continually refers to it, his inability to let go of sports terminology making it clear to all that his son will most likely grow up to resent him. Children from different schools have been invited here for the purpose of performing together; they have been given music to learn, with just two evenings to get to know one another and two days of rehearsals to prepare for the performance. Ostensibly this is an opportunity for cross-school collegiality, for "cultural exchange," as Mrs. Flores had termed it, although what culture schools from Fresno, Bakersfield and Mount Washington could impart to one another is unclear. But the more canny among them know that the Palo Alto Youth Symphony Orchestra in fact organised the special event this year for the purpose of recruitment to their summer program, which is in turn recruitment for their youth company, which in turn becomes recruitment for another thing and another thing until they all die, but at least they played a lot of Bach along the way.

At least that's how it seems to Sonia when she accidentally stumbles into a conversation with Mother of a French Horn (according to her tag). It transpires that she is actually a cousin of the conductor and so her little French horn player could easily have a spot in the orchestra's summer program; it would take only a call, really.

"But, you know, she's got to earn it on her own, so of course I didn't call in the favour."

This strikes Sonia as a very noble idea and also a very stupid one (the two often overlap). The idea certainly would never have occurred to her, and now that it is presented to her, it still seems appealing only in the abstract. Had she known the conductor of the youth orchestra and had she known that the conductor held power over something desirable to her daughter, she would have happily used whatever sway she had. In fact, while Mother of a French Horn continues enumerating the many ways in which she could (but refuses to) help her daughter succeed, Sonia begins scanning the crowd for this certain conductor.

Hope and assumption mingle and evoke an image of a tall youngish man with windswept hair (in other words, a type who might be swayed by a medium-size youngish mother with sheets of shiny black hair), so when one such specimen appears, she takes the opportunity and launches herself in his direction. She is, however, immediately taught a lesson in stereotyping when he turns out to be the superintendent of the banquet hall. This is discovered only after several minutes of complimenting him on his work ("You've achieved something amazing here," she says, and he nods and thinks he *has*—the banquet hall is booked well into the summer).

"Well that was a bust," she says after she beats a retreat to Mila, who has sat down next to the drinks table.

"What was?"

"I was trying to talk you up to the conductor, but it turns out Alan doesn't even play an instrument."

Mila is used to separating the wheat from the chaff when it comes to her mother's conversation and so only responds to the comprehensible part.

"What do you mean, talk me up?" she asks, a note of apprehension creeping through her cool veneer.

"Well, Mrs. French Fucking Horn was bragging that she could get her daughter a spot in the summer program, and I thought I'd throw in my charm—I can be charming, you know—and see what could be done for you."

"Don't do that," she says, then, for politeness's sake, adds, "Please."

"Well, I didn't, you see, because it was Alan all along." She sighs. "But I'll find this conductor, don't you worry." She pats her silky hair and adjusts her curtain bangs.

"I don't want you to, though."

Sonia stops scanning the crowd and looks at her daughter. "Why not, Milosh?"

Mila considers the question and finally says, "If I get a spot in the summer program, I want to know I earned it."

"Dear Lord, apparently 'earning things' is a theme tonight," Sonia responds. But looking down at her earnest ten-year-old violin player, she is a little pleased to find that her own brand of Eastern European hustle hasn't rubbed off on her daughter. That she believes she can work hard and practise and earn her seat in the Palo Alto Youth Symphony Orchestra.

Los Angeles, 1990

WHEN SZONJA CALLED WHEELER'S WHEELY GOOD DRIVING School to double-check that she had met all the requirements for the driving test, it was Mr. Chajit himself who picked up the phone.

"One more class, a lesson, a little practice round—we'll drive around the DMV before the test," he said. Szonja protested that she didn't have any more money for further lessons, but Mr. Chajit assured her that it was part of the original package.

Szonja didn't actually have a car yet, so she had to take two buses to get there, as though she needed any more incentive to get her licence. While waiting for her second bus by a car wash, she went inside the little convenience store attached to it, where people could while away the time purchasing shrink-wrapped muffins and their kids could get plastic toys from little gumball machines to litter their freshly cleaned car with. Szonja stared over the distended dome of her stomach at one such child, kneeling down and plying the machine with a quarter to extract some sort of neon-coloured slime against his mother's wishes. Szonja was making one of those parental assertions that precede experience of actual children—she would let her kid have all the slime in the world, never mind the mess—when she heard someone say, "Rina?" And although it was not her name, she turned instinctively towards the speaker, but the man had turned away already, saying, "Oh, never mind, my mistake," and was briskly getting into his shiny lemon-scented car.

Szonja shielded her eyes against the sun, watching the car drive away. As it rounded the corner, the light shifted to reveal a distinctly familiar blue Subaru.

As she approached the DMV, she could see Mr. Chajit was there in the parking lot beside his red Mazda. Having waited for the bus another twenty minutes, she arrived just half an hour before her road test was to take place, sweating and rattled. Szonja was pretty sure it had been her brother-in-law at the car wash—but did he recognise her too? Did Aron even know she was in Los Angeles? She had called her father after turning back from the airport to let him know she was staying with her friend Tatiana and she dutifully gave him Auntie's name and phone number as though she were still a little girl, going over to her friend's for the night. But he had seemed so closed off, so remote in his grief, that she hadn't even tried to explain the rest of her situation—she couldn't stand the thought of her child being another in a string of disappointments.

She wasn't sure if her father was speaking to Rina still (or again); they never talked about her during their infrequent calls, each minute of silence on their long-distance line counting away scarce dollars. Szonja had put off calling her sister for so long that it had become a ridiculous idea—presenting herself, seven months pregnant, still bopping around the city she was supposed to have left half a year ago. But now that she had run into Aron—and she was sure he would realise it had been her, even if he didn't in the moment—surely her sister would call her. The three of them—

Szonja, Rina and their father—had let this go on long enough now; someone would soon realise how ridiculous they were all being. Her sister—who was always on time wherever she went and never left a book unfinished, who would stop mid-sentence to correct herself if her phrasing hadn't been precise enough—she wouldn't like all these loose ends. Rina would ask their father where Szonja was staying, and then she would call. And this thought, helpfully, given she was about to get behind the wheel, stilled her shaking hand.

Mr. Chajit made no comment about the fact that Szonja was quite visibly pregnant now; he simply opened the driver's door for her and nodded. She drove around the DMV, practising her parking and going onto the freeway briefly, and Mr. Chajit's calm instruction gradually brought Szonja's heart rate down to a comfortable level.

When they arrived back at the DMV and it was time for Szonja to take her driving test, Mr. Chajit shook her hand and said, "Now, remember, during the exam, don't forget to check your blind spots." Szonja waited for him to say more, but it seemed there weren't any synonyms for *blind spot*; the sentence was complete. The finality of it made her a little sad.

Even after Szonja had her driver's permit, Tatiana was unwilling to let her friend take the wheel, so Szonja was obliged to ride shotgun as they drove to the mall in Glendale to pick up some bird feed for her great-aunt's parakeet.

"I feel like I should get her a present or something," Szonja said as Tatiana merged erratically onto the freeway.

"The parakeet?"

"Your aunt."

"Oh, okay, good. We shouldn't indulge the parakeet; it has a better life than either of us." Tatiana was preoccupied with driving as close as possible to the Dodge in front of her, but then, recalled to their conversation, she said, "No, you don't need to get Auntie anything."

"I feel like I should, though. It's so generous of her to let me stay and everything."

"Oh, she loves having someone else to talk at. I should be thanking you for giving me a break from all the nodding and smiling and pretending to show interest in the stories of her time camping with the Yugoslavian Socialist Youth Movement."

"I've always wanted to hear more about the exploits of the Yugoslavian Socialist Youth Movement," Szonja deadpanned. "And you know, she seems very relaxed about the whole baby thing."

Tatiana clicked her indicator on and turned towards their exit. "Oh, well, she won't actually meet the baby, so I guess it doesn't matter to her. I don't know what Auntie would make of a newborn child." Tatiana laughed to herself.

"What do you mean?"

"Szonja, have you met my great-aunt? She's never had children or been around them or probably even had sex." She shuddered a little at the thought. "You would think all that camping with strapping young Yugoslav lads, but no, my mother swears Auntie Jadranka has never even seen a man naked."

"No, I mean why wouldn't she meet the baby?"

"Oh, well, I'll be back in Yugoslavia next month, so I figured you would . . ."

"Move out."

"Well?" Tatiana raised her shoulder a little.

Szonja tried to replay some of their conversations since she'd moved into the Antic household. Had Szonja really never mentioned the fact that she had nowhere else to go? At least not anywhere she wanted to be.

They fell into silence. They arrived at the mall, and the car wound its way around the parking lot and rolled into a dark spot near the sliding doors that led to the brightly lit mall, like a portal to another world.

"I thought . . ." She looked out at the steady stream of shoppers going through the door, which never had quite enough respite from them to fully close. "Well, I don't know what I thought."

Szonja felt the hot prickle of foolishness at the back of her neck as she realised what Tatiana had meant when she invited her to stay with them: that her time there had an expiration date rapidly approaching. Tatiana had seemed so confident, so sure of Szonja's next steps when Szonja told her she was staying, but not in her sister's household; when she'd told her that she wanted an abortion and then that she didn't after all, she had forgotten that Tatiana was exactly her own age. That Tatiana had never been through anything like this. That she was here temporarily, at the mercy of her great-aunt, just as Szonja had been here at the mercy of Rina and Aron. And she couldn't resent her friend, not after all she'd done for her.

"I'll figure something out," Szonja said finally to spare her friend having to offer her more than she already had. She thought briefly of the phone call she was still waiting for, the latent hope of being rescued from her own decisions. But the call stubbornly continued its absence, life arranging itself in the negative space around it.

"Exactly," Tatiana said with the same confidence that had convinced Szonja she would be just fine in Los Angeles without her sister. When she told Tatiana that she planned to keep the baby after all and stay in Los Angeles, her friend had revealed an almost terrifying arsenal of resources to make it happen. She told her to use her sister's name and Social Security number, never to be late on a bill payment, to pay cash where she could and pay taxes as soon as she could. She told her she could use basic health care but also that it was best not to get sick. Szonja didn't ask how she knew all this; she'd never even asked how Tatiana had been permitted to stay for as long as she did or, in fact, how Auntie Jadranka had managed to remain permanently. The tips and workarounds were up for grabs, but the personal specifics were implicitly off-limits.

As it turned out, Auntie Jadranka didn't mind her staying on for longer—or at least, Szonja took her silence on the topic as a form of assent. As Tatiana packed up her belongings in their shared room, Szonja made herself useful: She cleaned the apartment, she picked up Auntie's prescriptions and did her shopping and, most important, she stayed put and looked interested whenever Auntie sat down in the evening to have a bit of slivovitz and gossip about the neighbours.

Tatiana's room in her great-aunt's apartment was completely nondescript. The daybed, the bottom drawer of which pulled out to reveal a second, equally uncomfortable single, was of a blond wood that looked like plastic painted to look like wood, the kind of superfluous decorative effort that only makes a person sad. The walls were peach-coloured, and Tatiana had been allowed exactly one poster (she'd chosen Van Halen, for reasons beyond our scope) but it was so small against the rest of the bare walls that not even all that hair could assert its dominance over the popcorn coral. That poster would hang over Mila's early childhood like an icon, Eddie Van Halen offering his benediction every night.

PORCUPINES

Auntie Jadranka's apartment complex, an afterthought of a building in Eagle Rock, was peopled mostly by men and women like Auntie Jadranka herself: thick accents, murky backgrounds, an aura of loneliness.

There was Mrs. Wojnarowicz, a Polish lady who wore the same exact clothes every day, or perhaps she had many of the same, but Szonja thought that was rather unlikely, given the circumstances they both found themselves living in. She wore a cardigan in a shade of plum that somehow called to Szonja's mind the taste of cough medicine. Or maybe it was that she coughed a lot, a relentless, phlegmy cough that reverberated through their shared walls. The only respite from it was when the vacuum cleaner overwhelmed its sound—Szonja took on some cleaning work for her too.

On their other side lived Larry, their landlord, and their upstairs neighbour was a Romanian woman who had twin boys and who looked like she would cry from relief when Szonja offered to babysit.

Then there was Mr. Szalai, an old Hungarian man who paid for her lunch and quietly slid over a ten-dollar-bill if she went out to the deli with him—the easiest job of all. Szonja would ask him a question, then take big bites of her sandwich, knowing her active participation wouldn't be required for some time.

"Are they running some sort of Eastern European old people's home here?" she asked Tatiana, who had also come through with a work opportunity for Szonja before she went back to Yugoslavia. She took her to downtown LA, where a friend of her mother's worked in a studio that made dresses for a studio that pretended to make dresses for movies. They were looking to hire more seamstresses, and Tatiana assured Szonja that having used a sewing machine before was qualification enough. The woman who led them around was Serbian, and when Tatiana told her where Szonja was from, she said, "There are other Hungarians here," with such perfectly bored placidity on her face that it was impossible to tell whether this was a good thing or whether Szonja made it exactly one too many Hungarians for her liking. But when they emerged from the warehouse squinting like naked mole rats in the midday sun, Tatiana seemed to think it had gone well.

"She'll pay you enough—even with the cut rate, they get a decent chunk of the Hollywood money," she said as they wound through the concrete maze of cars, a man trailing after them with a little trolley hawking pirated videotapes of *Look Who's Talking*. "And she knows about the baby."

If Szonja had had any protests—and several of them had indeed formulated in her mind as they walked through the musty-smelling warehouse—this last comment nipped that in the bud.

At home Szonja was familiar with the back channels and the black market; she always "knew a guy"—an adolescence spent under half-hearted socialism had prepared her well. She was what would someday be called "entrepreneurial" but for now she was just getting by. Life settled into a rhythm, time no longer bookended by the prospect of a call from her sister and a change in circumstances—it just kept unspooling.

At eight months pregnant, she received an envelope, the first piece of mail addressed to her, weighed down by the little plastic card she'd been waiting for. And there she was, looking out of the photo a little defiantly. Beside it, she noticed, in solemn block letters, they had misspelled her name.

Sonia looked at her car dubiously: There was a dent on the left side, one window was stuck open just a sliver and there was a scratch in the shape of a bean on the driver's-side door. And that was just the outside. There was nothing for it, however; the contractions had started and she would have to drive herself to the hospital.

The 1980 Buick station wagon had been purchased under somewhat unusual circumstances.

After Tatiana left, Sonia quickly realised the necessity of having her own car. Their neighbour Larry owned both his apartment and the one Auntie Jadranka was living in, and he had laughed when Sonia said she would be using public transport to get around Los Angeles until she could save up for a car. But he also offered to drive her to work—Sonia had taken the sewing job downtown—so she decided to ignore his condescension in the end.

It was the absence of Mrs. Wojnarowicz's usual noise that, although at first comforting, alerted Sonia to the possibility of a problem. Perhaps sensing that she did not want to know what had caused the miraculous ceasefire of phlegm, she went to Larry's apartment.

"Larry, I've got to go to an appointment, but would you go check on Mrs. Wojnarowicz, please—I have a bad feeling."

"What am I supposed to do about that," he answered, but Sonia could feel his interest was piqued—he did not own Mrs. Wojnarowicz's flat, but he liked to think of himself as landlord to all, owning as he did a majority share in the building's apartments.

"Just go and check on her, would you?"

By the time Sonia was back, the ambulance and the police were packing it in, and packing Mrs. Wojnarowicz away too. Sonia took a walk around the block until she was sure they'd cleared out.

The next week, a piece of white paper was taped to the windshield of Mrs. Wojnarowicz's station wagon with a number and the words *For Sale*. When Sonia rang the number later that day, she heard the phone ring from her neighbour's apartment—but the sound came from Larry's side, by the kitchen.

"Hello?" he said as though irritated to be called on this number he had plastered on a public space.

"Larry?"

"Yes?"

"I'm calling about the car. This is Sonia, from next door."

"Ah, so you want your own car, then?"

Sonia would have felt bad for abandoning Larry to his lonely commute, but a couple of weeks earlier she had found a stepladder propped open in their living room, so she was pretty sure that Larry liked to let himself into Auntie Jadranka's apartment to do his maintenance work when they weren't there, and some boundaries would do both of them good.

"It'll be easier this way."

"If you say so."

"I've got a thousand I can give you in cash."

"Give me nine hundred now and I'll add another five hundred onto your rent."

Sonia had been rather hoping to keep it under a thousand dollars; parting with even that much was painful under their current circumstances.

"How come you're selling Mrs. Wojnarowicz's car anyway?"

"Ah, well . . . she and I had an understanding."

Sonia was pretty sure they'd had no such understanding, and she was also pretty sure Larry knew she knew they'd had no such understanding.

"Give me a thousand by next week and you can take the hunk of junk. Don't say Larry doesn't treat you neighbourly."

PORCUPINES

The station wagon, improbable as it seemed, smelled just as Mrs. Wojnarowicz looked, which was to say, like plum-flavoured cough medicine. But it was the first piece of Los Angeles that Sonia had ever owned, and she loved every inch of it.

Now, getting in the car, Sonia was aware of the waves of pain coming over her, but a feral determination had also materialised, and it carried her all the way to the hospital, to the reception desk and on to the delivery room without so much as a whimper.

When they handed Sonia her daughter, she heard through the haze of recent pain and euphoria one of the nurses asking what the little girl's name would be. A few months ago she had found an old secondhand book of names in a hospital waiting room, and she had felt the weight of this decision so keenly that the little out-of-date secondhand volume went with her everywhere for weeks. She kept it in her hands as often as possible, thumbing through it absent-mindedly at times and at others with an academic rigour she had never applied to her actual studies. It was important to tether this as yet unborn girl to something tangible when she would go out into the world with a last name that would likely mean little to her and an ancestry that was far away but not exotic enough to warrant mentioning. Flipping through the battered paperback, she found among the Annies and Emmas promising elegant little girls with good manners one that felt right, a Russian-sounding name that matched her own (although no one in the family was actually Russian, as far as she knew). And so it was that the two of them came to be a little family of two: Sonia and Mila.

PART III

Los Angeles, 1990–1996

Time passes.

Shirts become bigger, songs become louder. Sonia tries a mango for the first time.

At night, nursing Mila in bed, eyes staring up at her, great gleaming orbs in the dark, little body warm against hers. But then Mila cries—she takes a few seconds, a few too many, perhaps, just looking this little creature in the face, mouth wide, tongue suspended in effort, eyes darting helplessly. She has brought pain into the world and need, ceaseless and all-consuming.

Watching the news of the Balkans with Auntie Jadranka. No word from Tatiana for weeks, months, years. Auntie becomes quieter, less prone to nostalgic monologues.

Rare phone calls to her father become shorter and shorter as they struggle for topics that steer clear of sisters and daughters, then those stop as well.

A recurring dream of him: They sit on the terrace of a Budapest café in spring; her father has ordered a tea, she a glass-bottled Coca-Cola. They sit in silence until, out of nowhere, her father takes her bottle of Coke and pours some of it into his tea. For a moment they both look at the results, perplexed. Then, with trembling hands, he puts the bottle back in front of her and explains angrily that he did it on purpose. Because the Coke will cool down his too-hot tea. He takes a defiant drink from the jumble of brown liquid, and Sonia wakes up each time with his obstinate eyes staring at her from above the rim of his porcelain cup.

But eventually those dreams stop too.

Going to the bank, going to work. The thrill of effort and overcoming. The world becomes bigger for a while. Then it becomes smaller.

Mila rolls and crawls and walks—Sonia claps and laughs and adores. Occasionally she is bored. One banana, two banana, three banana, four. All the songs for Mila are new. Except sometimes, when she's tired, an old folk song about a man falling off his horse by the Danube.

PART IV

San Francisco, 2001

WHATEVER PROBLEMS THE STUDENTS, THE TEACHERS, THE chaperones may have had the day before is put severely into perspective as they step onto Alcatraz Island. Even the weather has, obligingly, become ominous just in time for their visit to the infamous prison.

"Only in America would they make a monument to incarceration," Sonia mutters to herself as they alight from the boat that has transported them from the relative safety of the mainland. Mrs. Flores looks at her like she wants to say, *You had every opportunity to make suggestions for the trip, Ms. Imre!* And then, after some contemplation, she does say that: "You had every opportunity to make suggestions for the trip, Ms. Imre!" But her voice comes out much squeakier than her expression (as it were), and neither of them is left with the impression that this was ever a likely scenario.

Several faces have a green tinge—whether from the rocky boat ride or the thought of entering the prison is difficult to tell. But Mila, despite her grandiose plans for the rest of the day, is awestruck and consumed by their field trip destination—she has, like many children, a morbidity that stems more from innocence than an inherently diabolical nature. (The diabolical nature of children is usually revealed elsewhere, like in the way they roll their eyes anytime you ask them how their day was between the ages of twelve and seventeen or the way they beg and beg for a puppy for two whole years and then leave it in the care of a parent with dog-biting trauma in the past or the way they—well, anyway, the point is children are monsters, but for other reasons.) Sonia does wish, though, that her daughter was just a little less obviously excited.

They enter the complex and are led down a row of cells as the tour guide—a lanky man with hollow cheeks, clearly hired just to amplify the place's eeriness—explains who the most famous inmates were.

"Our most famous inmate was, of course, Machine Gun Kelly—the notorious kidnapper, murderer, gangster and *boot*legger." The way he emphasises the first syllable of the last word, drawing out the *oo* in *boot*, makes it seem like that's the worst of Kelly's crimes, disseminating alcohol. Or, possibly, the man isn't entirely sure what the word *bootlegger* means. The kids dutifully peer inside the cell as the man continues.

"And now let's take a look inside a cell that one of the inmates would have been locked in," the man says, jangling the collection of keys attached to his belt with a thrust of his hips before opening the cell door so they can all peer inside. Sonia brings up the rear of the group, and when she arrives at the cell, she wanders in to take a look and is, for a moment, blissfully alone. The room has been staged to look like it did decades ago, and one small cross-barred window lets in a shaft of weak light from the overcast sky outside. Her relief in her solitude lasts only so long. Once they are separated by brick and iron, the group's noise diminishes from excited chatter to a little mumbling to an occasional cough and then nothing. Sonia ambles out of the cell and realises the group has left her behind. She walks in the direction they were heading, but there are too many turns, all equally uncanny in their abandonment. As much as the clatter of the children grated on her, their high-pitched voices and high-contrast outfits managed to make this desolate old building feel somehow less like a prison. As she winds down one path after another, she feels the familiar quickening of her heartbeat, the coldness down her spine, and her mind leaps like a jittery animal straight into conjuring the faceless men in suits who sometimes come for her in her dreams. Of course this place engenders guilt—who among these men would have served his sentence and, by the end, believed in his own innocence? Sonia stops, leans against a cold wall, puts her head in her hands and presses on her temples as though it might squeeze the racehorse track of thoughts right out of it.

"Ms. Imre, do try and keep up," she hears Mrs. Flores call out, and no one has ever been this pleased to be reprimanded by a fifth-grade teacher. Sonia looks up to see the snake's tail of the group turning another corner ahead, and she starts walking again, quickening her steps to join them.

When she catches up, their tour guide sidles over and says, cryptically, "Not the first one to make a run for it, miss."

And perhaps Sonia takes a second too long to respond, because he puts a reassuring hand on her shoulder and says, "Machine Gun Kelly was actually a model prisoner for the rest of his life, you know. He wrote lots of letters, worked in the laundry, never caused a stir." It is unclear how these bits of information are intended to make Sonia feel better—the man seems to be answering a question no one has asked—but it does jolt Sonia out of her morbid reverie, and she smiles a little at him as he turns back to their group.

When they arrive back at the entrance of the prison, everyone comes shuffling out, all just as subdued as Sonia herself, and she wonders for a moment: What crimes did each of their minds convince them of while they were in there?

As they walk back out towards the boat, Megan H approaches Sonia and asks her where she wandered off to and was she scared and what did she spend her time doing and where did she get her leather jacket and so on and so forth with little breath wasted on, well, breathing. Sonia looks at this child—by all accounts a lovely girl, if a little loquacious—and thinks how strange it is that she can love one child so much but be so unenthusiastic about the genre as a whole. It's as if she said she liked the song "Territorial Pissings" by Nirvana but generally thought that grunge was just a little too noisy.

On the boat ride back, all the adults look like they've recently had a bout of stomach flu, but the children all talk in excited clusters about the notorious men they've just learned about, how they would escape the island if they were imprisoned here. Even Mila is eagerly discussing what they've just seen with Sergio and Kathy, which is a relief to Sonia, as she was beginning to think that Mila had made up her friendship with the two of them to allay her own concerns. She's not the only one to notice; when they disembark from the boat, they are split into groups, one chaperone to four kids, and Linda passes Kathy into Sonia's care with a hesitant smile. So she takes Mila, Kathy, Sergio and Megan (after a little tug-of-war with Riley, who was allocated to Mrs. Flores's group), and they go in search of some lunch on the pier.

And this is when the excitement of the morning's activity drains away into panic for Mila. She looks at the watch her mother gifted her and realises she told this man Anthony that they would meet at Pier 39 at 12:30, and it is now 12:36 (it is actually 12:46, but she has never been good at reading analogue under pressure).

Mila has not accounted for the fact that she has no idea what Anthony looks like; she has vaguely been imagining the bespectacled man on the cover of her book, but of course she knows that he might look completely different, might look like anything. As far as plans made by ten-year-olds go, it's rather a minor error, but now she realises she will have to rely on her mother accidentally noticing him, and this is more difficult than she would have thought. She has never realised before how much her mother's attention flits in every which direction—the ground, the sky, Mila's hair (where she finds a speck of lint), her own hair (which she spots in a shopwindow and immediately begins adjusting)—and around it goes, landing on objects and vistas and ignoring the faces of the people passing by completely.

"Mila, honey, can you stop yanking me around?" she asks as Mila pushes her in the direction of another man (who is about twice Sonia's age but might as well be a contemporary in the eyes of a child). The other children slalom after them like little drunken ducklings, but they are used to being dragged around and assume it's just part of the process of finding lunch.

And then, just as they are about to order from the funnel-cake stand (it's what Sergio asked for, and Sonia does not care enough to dissuade him from having sugary fried dough for lunch), a voice calls out.

"Sonia?"

And then the man attached to the voice is right there, looming over them, not unknown after all. Mila has met him before.

Los Angeles, 1996

When a person looks back on their childhood, they are sure to find, among the little episodes and memories strung together like the many beads of a friendship bracelet, several instances of being dragged along on errands with their parents. To the laundromat, the post office, workplaces, family visits, coffees with ancient-looking friends who remark on how *big* you've grown and then wish you weren't there so they could indulge their narcissism more comfortably—it seems an excessive amount of time is spent trailing after adults. And Mila did not know this yet, but as the daughter of a single parent, she was destined to spend twice as much time as other children learning to occupy herself while her mother did whatever it was that adults did.

Today, Mila has brought with her a miniature skateboard that her two fingers rode, their joints bending like knees. The skateboard whizzed along the table, over the salt and pepper shakers, across the plastic-cased menu of Canter's Deli and landed unceremoniously in the depths of her mother's black coffee.

Unfazed, Sonia plucked the plastic piece out of her coffee, wrapped it in a napkin and said, "Honey, why don't you go see if the lady at the counter finds this entertaining."

Mila took no offence—her grasp of sarcasm was still years and years away—and left her mother to talk to the tall man they'd come here to meet. She had gotten bored of answering the man's questions about her favourite foods and favourite colours anyhow.

Once her daughter was out of earshot, Sonia said, "Sorry about that—it's a phase. The thing is attached to her fingers day and night." This was true; Sonia had to pry it from Mila's sweaty little hands each time she went to sleep. The toy had suffered worse drownings than today's, and yet it always came back, wearier but still rolling along. Which was rather how Sonia herself felt these days.

"Oh, I don't mind," Anthony said. "She's sweet." He looked over at Mila with the reserved fondness of someone who likes children but doesn't know how to act around them. He glanced at Sonia and his hand twitched, as though, without his consent, it was considering whether to hold hers. "It's good to see you, Sonia," he said instead.

"Is it?" she asked slowly, with a half-hearted laugh.

"Of course it is. I've missed you."

Sonia nodded as if to acknowledge the possibility of his statement. Emboldened, she decided to just come right out with the reason she'd asked to meet: "I need your help."

Anthony let out a laugh—but not the cruel, cynical kind of laugh that Sonia had expected when she imagined how this conversation might go, just a surprised huff of air.

"I'm sorry," he said. "I don't know why I did that." He ran his hand through his hair.

"No, it's fine—I know it's a little ridiculous. I'm aware." She looked over at Mila, who had built an obstacle course out of ketchup bottles and was happily riding her little skateboard around it. "If it weren't for Mila, I wouldn't—I mean, it's not that I'm not happy to see you." She grabbed his hand and gave it a brief squeeze. "It is, it's good to see you. You've grown your hair out!"

"Ah, yeah . . . part of the look, you know." He rumpled his hair again—part of the look was also, apparently, to create the appearance that a gust of wind had just blown through it.

"Looks good on you." Sonia smiled and thought, *It's true*. Five years had made Anthony more handsome—the serious expression had never suited the younger man, but he was less boyish now; it was somehow more plausible that the world weighed on him the way his sloped shoulders had always seemed to suggest.

"So . . . I mean, you got in touch after four years—"

"Five," she said. "But yes, it's been a while."

"Five," he said, smiling. "So are you going to tell me what you need help with or do we need to engage in a few more rounds of compliments?"

Sonia took a breath and blew it out on her cold coffee, making the dark liquid ripple. "Mila is starting first grade."

Anthony nodded as though to say he was just about to suggest she do just that. "You need help with tuition?"

"No, no. I'm not asking for money. Mila's starting first grade and it's made me think . . . things need to be more *permanent*. For both of us."

If Sonia had been inclined to reflect on her life over the past six years, perhaps she would have come to the conclusion that her decisions at eighteen were, to put it mildly, a little hasty. Back then, she had not had the least idea what she wanted; what she *didn't* want, on the other hand, had been a starkly lit stage in a one-woman show. But who among us has made her best decisions at the age of eighteen? In the very diner where Sonia sat, there were people who had made choices just as questionable as hers, or worse, at that age. At eighteen, the man in the baseball hat ordering black-and-white cookies at the counter had crashed his first car into a row of shopping carts in the parking lot of a supermarket and gotten one of their employees fired to cover his shame; the woman two booths away, the one who had ordered her usual and overtipped the waitress just to be liked for the briefest moment, had slept with her best friend's boyfriend and in the resulting wreckage of the relationship had passed on the opportunity to go to college; the overtipped waitress herself had done something so unbearable at that age that it had been pushed deep into the darkest recesses of her mind where she could not even regret it. So here was Sonia, some years after making her own rash decision of youth, and now, with her head just a little bit more firmly on her shoulders, trying to make the most of it.

"Part of me has always thought I'll go back home and then this will all be just an interesting thing that happened to me once. But then, for Mila, this is it, this has been her whole life so far. And she's going to start living her life here properly, you know, starting school, making friends, so we should put down roots of some sort." She didn't mention the newspaper articles about a proposed new immigration law that lingered in her mind and swam in front of her eyes every time she went to bed and how unnervingly easy it had been to eke out a quiet life illegally the past six years but how frightening it was waiting for the other shoe to drop.

"Okay . . ." Anthony's eyebrows knitted together the way they used to in their Hebrew classes when he couldn't immediately figure out the answer to the teacher's questions.

"I was wondering if you could help—"

"Of course," he said. "I wanted to help six years ago, it was just—"

"No, I know. This is a different sort of help, though," she said. "I'm really fumbling with this proposal."

PORCUPINES

He shook a packet of Sweet'n Low until a little corner of it tore and let loose a stream of white powder. "Oh, I see." He looked at her with apology in his eyes. "Sonia, Emily and I are moving to San Francisco next month, I've got a job at a record company lined up there and—"

"Emily? Oh, Emily!" Sonia's voice didn't seem to be able to decide whether it was excited or sad, exclaiming or questioning. She sounded like an actor on one of the children's TV shows Mila used to like when she was younger, the amorphous characters performing the different emotions with manic exaggeration.

"Yes, you might remember her, she was my sister's friend. Julie's friend."

Oh, Sonia remembered Emily. She smiled to herself, thinking, *It took the poor girl six years, but here it is, her patience has finally paid off.* She'd flattered and wriggled her way right into the middle of the Greene family, right into the soft centre of it where Sonia herself had once thought she might be happy.

Anthony looked slightly befuddled by her reaction, which recalled Sonia to her original purpose.

"Of course I remember. Good for you guys. No, really." She gave his hand another squeeze, though it lacked the enthusiasm of the one before. "But I didn't mean that it should . . . that *we* should. I only meant something on paper, if you think you'd be willing?"

"No, sure," he said, a little too quickly. "I just mean that . . . that's something to take into account. But I want to help, of course I do."

"I can talk to Emily, if you'd like."

He smiled a little and said, "Do you want to be the one to explain to her why she and I won't be getting married anytime soon?"

"Was that . . . Is that on the table?" she couldn't help asking.

"Only in the way that it is for any two people who have been together, who live together, move to a new city together . . ."

Sonia nodded but didn't offer anything that might ease things between them—Emily did not seem real to her in the way that someone standing in front of her might, so she made no further effort to fathom her feelings.

"The rabbi would be proud," Anthony said.

Sonia laughed, surprising her daughter at the counter—drawn by her mother's good humour, she came and joined them at the table. "Well, you know how deeply I always wanted to please Rabbi Raskin, against all reason."

"I think it was something about the beard."

"And the crinkly eyes . . . his eyes always seemed to smile."

"Yes, well, you couldn't see the actual smile under the beard." Anthony looked over at Mila a little uncertainly. "It would make a good story, you know."

"Hmm?"

"Two young students meet at a Hebrew class, six years later they . . ." He waved his hand around as though *marriage* were a profanity he didn't want a six-year-old to hear.

"Yeah . . . I guess it would."

"What I mean is that we won't have to sell it too much."

San Francisco, 2001

"Sonia?"

Sonia blinks and then, with surprising swiftness, recovers herself and throws her arms Hollywood-wide. "Dovid!"

Mila watches in confusion as her mother hugs the man.

"I wasn't sure you'd show up," he says.

Sonia doesn't miss a beat, glides so easily into the situation presented to her that Mila, despite being the one who put her in this position, worries momentarily whether she's gone a little mad. Sonia laughs and says, "Well, here I am. And here *you* are. At this pier. In San Francisco. Just as we're getting a funnel cake."

Sergio perks up at these words, but the conversation only briefly swerves tantalisingly in that direction, and he throws an agitated look towards the funnel-cake stand.

"Here I am," Anthony says, his small uncertain smile becoming a fraction smaller, more uncertain. He looks around them, the pier a whirligig of activity, the children gathered around Sonia, shifting from one foot to the other.

"Here you are . . . indeed." She is aware that the conversation has now looped over itself several times, but she is still waiting for Anthony to explain himself, and she is particularly conscious of her daughter's presence beside her. There are few words that feel safe to say in front of both.

"I guess it's as good a place as any," he says gamely.

"Yes, it's a . . . nice enough place," she answers, adding Anthony's well-being to her list of worries. It's been a while since she's seen him, but she doesn't remember him being quite so addle-brained.

"Although we could, if you wanted to . . . go somewhere quieter, to talk?"

"Yes, let's sit down," she says, but Sergio lets out a despondent groan just as his stomach lets out a loud rumble, so she adds, "At a restaurant perhaps."

The only place in their vicinity with proper seating is the kind of all-American diner engineered to provoke nostalgia in tourists for a fifties they never experienced, so this is where Sonia steers the children. Once they are wedged into a booth on taut, bursting balloons of leather and the children are given menus so big they can barely hold them, she finally takes a good look at Anthony.

"So," she says.

"So," he answers. "I'm so glad to see you. I'd sort of thought that you were angry with me, and—" As he speaks, Anthony keeps glancing at Kathy seated beside Sonia. Finally, he says, in a whisper so only she can hear him, "Sonia, have you kidnapped that child?"

"What?"

"She seems to be blinking some sort of Morse code distress call at me."

She looks down at Kathy, who has finished perusing her menu and is indeed blinking unnervingly at the two of them.

"Oh, no, that's just—she has dry eyes, don't worry about it." She gives Kathy the packet of crayons and paper mercifully left at the table. Kathy turns the packet in her hands uncertainly—it's been a few years since she's been urged to do colouring, but she's an obliging girl and goes with it. Sonia looks at Mila then, but her own daughter has, thankfully, propped up the menu in front of her like a privacy screen, giving Sonia a little more time to consider ways to explain Anthony's existence to her. For now, she explains the existence of Mila's companions to Anthony instead. "We're on a field trip—hence the kids."

"I did wonder if you'd gone on an adoption spree since we last spoke."

"God, no," she says a little too quickly, and reflexively she pats Mila's arm as though to say, *I still love you, kid, just not the rest of them.*

As the children order their food, Sonia steers the conversation to safe territory, enquiring about Anthony's mother, his sisters, his job, and once she's gotten him on the track of steady conversation, she retreats into her mind to wonder at the coincidence of running into Anthony at the pier. She wasn't thinking of him when she agreed to this trip—after all, what were the chances of running into the one person you know in a city? She can only hope that the memory of Alcatraz and the prospect of funnel cake distract the children enough from her personal life, which has suddenly sprung long legs and sprouted dishevelled hair and is very much on display.

Meanwhile, as the others around her tuck into overpriced grilled cheese sandwiches, Mila watches the adults beside her. Her mother's hands twitch, which they do when she's trying hard not to adjust her hair, but her smile is warm the way it is only with people she knows well. The man, Anthony, however, is reluctant to smile, although the corners of his mouth can't seem to help themselves sometimes. There is something familiar about his expression. The two adults are pleased to see each other but not excited, friendly but wary—their expressions are rudely enigmatic, and Mila can make no sense of it at all.

When they have exhausted their polite exchange of information, Sonia and Anthony lapse into silence for a while, the lull punctured only by the occasional request for ketchup or water from the children.

"So I think we're all set with the paperwork," Anthony says eventually. "Is there anything else you needed on my front?" He seems to be continuing a different conversation than the one they were just stumbling through. "You've found your copy of the marriage certificate—"

Sonia stands up from the table forcefully, like she's Howard Beale and she's had enough. Anthony and the children look up at her with surprise. A few crayons have landed in Kathy's clam chowder, and Megan's grilled cheese is slightly waterlogged from a spilled cup.

"I—need to go to the bathroom," she says, forgoing dignity in order to stop Anthony from finishing his sentence.

While her mother is gone, Mila looks once again at Anthony, suspicion solidifying into knowledge. She's always known that *some* father existed out there—such is the way of things, even if details on the way of things are as yet hazy—but now that she is presented with the man himself, she is a little unsure what to do about it.

She decides to draw inspiration from her mental catalogue of father figures. In her immediate vicinity is Dave, father of a boy also named Dave who plays the clarinet and wears a near-constant expression of fretfulness, like his stomach is always hurting and at any moment he might be raising his hand to request to go to the bathroom. He never does; it just looks like he might. His father also seems perpetually agitated—he is especially preoccupied with his son's eating. More than once just on this trip, Mila has overheard him offering Dave Jr. a Clif Bar and saying, "You gotta keep your strength up, son," like they were at a relay race or a swim meet. From this example, not much of relevance can be concluded, except perhaps that Mila ought to accept any and all Clif Bars (and probably other snacks as well) from Anthony, should he offer.

There is the fourth-grade teacher Mr. Zapata, who besides being known as a teacher is also known as a father because he has twin boys in Mrs. Flores's fifth-grade class. The crossing of the divide between parent and teacher makes everyone involved a little uncomfortable and from this Mila can only conclude that it is advisable to keep interactions with her newly discovered father as much outside of school as possible.

Then there is Megan H's father, who joined an ashram and said mean things about Megan's mother—Mila doesn't know what an ashram is, but it clearly hasn't been a positive influence on Megan's father, so she makes a mental note to enquire after Anthony's views on ashrams.

Mila knows her mother must have had a father too, though she talks about him very little, and once when asked about him she muttered, "He's probably dead," which didn't imply that there was or has been much of a relationship at all and the topic of it made her mother distracted and gloomy. This provides no template for interaction between Mila and her own father but does rather point to the importance of the undertaking, her mother's failings having likely been a result of a lack of fatherly contact.

"I play the violin," she says to Anthony finally, the first words she's spoken to him. His face takes on a polite *That's nice* expression. "We're having a concert and you're invited." Before he can decline, Mila adds that her mother said so and gives him all the details. She takes a blue crayon from the remains of Kathy's clam chowder and writes down the address on the paper placemat beneath her tuna sandwich.

When Sonia returns to the table, Sergio, still harbouring dreams of funnel cake, politely reminds her that they were supposed to meet the rest of the group after lunch. She looks at her watch and says, "Shit," at which point the children begin to giggle. "Anthony, it was so good bumping into you," she says, throwing some cash on the table and leaning down to give him a kiss on the cheek.

"Oh, well, yeah—and I guess I'll see you soon," he says, looking at Mila for reassurance.

"Absolutely, soon," Sonia says, the words *absolutely* and *soon* taking on their polite non-meaning.

Sonia hustles the children out to the pier, where the sun bursts through the cloud cover sharply over hot-dog vendors snapping their tongs, like lobsters with their pincers selling out their landbound brothers.

It happened something like this: While riding the cable cars past Russian Hill, Megan H breathlessly told Riley about Mila's mother and the strange man. Well, perhaps *breathlessly* isn't the right word, since her hot breath blew right into Riley's ear as they bumped and swayed and attempted to stay standing, whispering above the noise of the vehicle. Then, as the trolley jerked to a halt near the Tenderloin (an elderly woman refusing to acknowledge the great hurry of other passengers as she crossed the street in front of them), Riley told Megan A some approximation of what she had heard—the diner became a "real restaurant" and the tall man became "like a basketball player or something." Finally, when they were walking back up the steps to the hotel, men in suits fresh from their conferences streaming past them, Megan A tugged at Cecily's arm and informed her mother that Ms. Imre had taken her group to see a famous basketball player at San Francisco's fanciest restaurant for lunch, and why had they only gotten a hot dog on a stick? To which Cecily's first response was an exasperated reminder that Megan in fact loved hot dogs on sticks, in fact had begged for one, and only a minute later did she think to say, "Ms. Imre did what?" (Actually, the chain did not end there, as Dave Sr. had overheard snippets of the conversation between Cecily and her daughter—something about going to see a famous hot dog? Which the perplexed concierge at the hotel seemed completely uninformed about.)

Later, in the hotel room questioning her daughter, Cecily tried to weed through the superfluous points of the story, but the salient details had been different for each conduit along the way and were different for Cecily herself, so it was difficult to gain certain knowledge with which she could confront Sonia. Beyond the issue of taking the children off to a restaurant when they were clearly told to arrange for a quick lunch on the pier, beyond the inappropriateness of going to meet a strange man in the middle of a field trip, what particularly caught Cecily's attention was a throwaway comment about how, apparently, the two adults had been overheard discussing a certain "marriage certificate" ("surficate," in Megan's rendering, but Cecily was able to work back to its meaning).

This detail got Cecily Auerbach's brain turning like a spit roast at a Sunday barbecue. Incidentally, in the hotel room next to her, Dave was daydreaming about a spit roast at a Sunday barbecue. (The idea of a famous hot dog on a stick had clearly led him on a winding road of meat-based reveries.) Here, finally, was the information Cecily was most curious about. Here, clearly, was Mila's father, Sonia's husband—so why the secrecy?

Cecily decided to use her considerable skills of perception at the evening's orchestra mixer and watch Sonia for signs of difference. Did she have that lovelorn look about her, like she'd just seen the long-lost man of her dreams? Did she have a slight twitch in her eye, the way women who'd just met their ex-husbands do? The woman was exasperatingly secretive—their kids had been in the same classes for years, and Cecily deserved to know more.

Sonia tries to find some respite from Dave. Half an hour ago he caught her contemplating the giant vat of jelly beans placed on one of the tables in the conference hall, apparently a game devised for the children and their families in which they had to guess the number of jelly beans inside. What jelly beans and probability had to do with orchestral music was anyone's guess (much like the number of jelly beans), but there the jar stood, proudly encasing its colourful beans of sugar. Sonia was idly staring at it, lost in thought about the day's odd events.

"So you think you've figured it out?" Dave asked.

"I'm not sure," she said, thinking that she had not figured it out in the least. In her haste to relieve the awkwardness of their encounter with Anthony, she had not bothered to ask him what he had been doing on Pier 39 at the exact time she happened to be there.

"It's a head-scratcher, this one."

"You're not wrong there," she said, shaking her head a little.

"But at the end of the day, it's your basic physics and mathematics," he said, and Sonia looked up at him, wondering how math came into the equation, as it were.

"Oh, the jelly beans."

"Oh, sure, throw me off the scent." Dave seemed to have whipped himself into some agitation as they spoke, and he would not leave her alone until she finally gave in and put her guess of the number of jelly beans into the little box beside the jar, as though he thought if she did it out of his sight, she was sure to cheat her way to whatever fantastic prize was in store for the winner.

But now she has finally escaped him and found peace on one of the benches outside the conference hall. It is suddenly quiet here; only a sliver of the cacophony inside escapes every time someone comes through the doors in search of a bathroom. She has barely had a moment alone since she came on this trip, which was her precise fear when Mila signed them up, so she is reluctant to admit that a part of her doesn't mind all the company, even the dull ones, the competitive ones, the annoying and nosy ones—in fact, she doesn't admit it, but there it is, lingering somewhere in the pockets of her mind.

However, this new warm feeling towards her companions is tested when a group of children spill out of the hall, shepherded by Mr. Alvarez. He instructs them to form a line outside the bathroom down the hall, then spots Sonia seated nearby and makes a move to join her but is beat to the punch by Megan H, whose bladder is forgotten in the face of an opportunity to speak with her new idol.

"Hi, Ms. Imre, what are you doing out here? Are you tired of everyone in there?" Thankfully, Megan's self-confidence prevents her from even imagining that she herself might be tiring—self-awareness at her age could truly be ruinous. She also doesn't necessarily need responses to her interrogation; if mother is anything like daughter, her father's move to the quiet of an ashram becomes a little more understandable. She ploughs on: "Are you excited for the concert? What are you going to be wearing? Can I borrow some of your clothes? Is your husband really coming too?"

It takes some time for this train of thought to arrive in Sonia's mind—she usually just waits for Megan to answer her own enquiries anyway, but when that last question makes its slow roll into Sonia's consciousness, her eyes widen and she instinctively looks up at Mr. Alvarez, hoping he hasn't been paying attention. He is, however, looking straight at her.

"Ooh, my turn," Megan says, bounding over to the bathroom line, which has almost cleared up. "Wait for me, Ms. Imre," she throws over her shoulder, like Sonia is just another fifth-grade girl with whom entering and exiting rooms simultaneously is the height of friendship.

Mr. Alvarez approaches the seat beside Sonia with a gentle smile, and for someone so polite and circuitous, he gets right to the point.

"So . . . your husband will be joining us?" he asks. "Would he be . . . Might he be the one from Vegas?"

The vanity Sonia has is tilted towards her sense of humour and a little towards her looks, not towards her intellect, which she has intellect enough to know is just average. But in this moment, she despairs of the shortcomings of her own mind, as she looks dumbfoundedly at Mr. Alvarez and tries to piece together how the man she recently made out with, the vice principal of her daughter's school, could possibly know anything about husbands and Las Vegas.

Mr. Alvarez has already moved on to apologising for the intrusion into her privacy by the time she comes to her senses.

"I'm sorry, but what are you talking about?"

"Oh, I just mean that it's inappropriate of me to enquire about your personal life, it just seemed that others had mentioned it, and the two of us the other night, well—"

"No, I mean about Vegas—what did you mean about Vegas?"

It is Mr. Alvarez's turn to be confused—for a couple of intelligent adults, they do not in this moment give an impression of having a collectively high IQ. "Well, you said the other night, in Lost Hills, I believe, that the . . . um . . . last time you got, well, inebriated . . . that you got married. In Vegas."

Sonia looks at Mr. Alvarez then, right into his deep-set brown eyes under the melancholy slope of eyebrows, and tries to remember some of their conversation that night. But all she can recall now is his face lit by the blue glow of the vending machine beside them moving slowly towards hers and the way the fingers on his right hand had found the fingers on her left hand just before he kissed her.

"And this is why I shouldn't drink," she says. Mr. Alvarez looks like he is about to protest any problems with Sonia's alcohol consumption, but just then Megan comes skipping out of the bathroom.

"I'm ready!" she declares and holds her hand out to Sonia, who takes it hesitantly and is dragged behind the young girl back into the conference hall, wondering what else she has said to these strangers all around her in the few hours she allowed herself to let her guard down.

Las Vegas, 1996

SONIA AND ANTHONY GOT MARRIED IN LAS VEGAS ON THURSday because Anthony was going back to San Francisco, and his girlfriend, on Sunday.

His sister Marnie was looking after Mila—her own two kids now being sullen teenagers, she seemed glad to do it. "Oh, we'll have a grand time—we'll get Anna's old Barbies out and bake some cookies; Mila won't even notice you're gone."

Sonia, not wanting Marnie to change her mind, did not reveal that Mila was unlikely to be entertained by dolls and cookies. She'd never left Mila in anyone's care overnight. Auntie Jadranka had often stayed with her while Sonia had been working, and sometimes the great-niece of her former neighbour the late Mrs. Wojnarowicz (a woman who was also, somewhat confusingly, called Mrs. Wojnarowicz) babysat for Mila. She had moved into the apartment next to theirs, the one formerly owned by the former Mrs. Wojnarowicz, not long after her great-aunt's death but long enough after her death not to know that the car Sonia was now driving should likely have passed to her or some other relative. Sonia would have felt bad about this, except she didn't. Feeling bad about things was not very prominent in her emotional vocabulary in those days.

In any case, the only thing less appealing than leaving behind her daughter for two nights was trying to explain to her daughter why a sweaty man in white polyester would be telling a tall stranger that he was allowed to kiss her mother now. So she'd stayed with Marnie.

"Did you explain the . . . whole situation to Marnie?" Sonia asked as they were on their way to Vegas. She was driving the Buick, even though Anthony had been reluctant to get in, given its dubious mechanical history. She gripped the leather steering wheel with white knuckles, like she might float out of the car if she didn't.

"I told her a version of it," he said as he rifled through her meagre CD collection in the glove compartment. He kept shaking his head at what he found, not comfortable enough in her company yet to voice his opinions. They had been polite and solicitous throughout the planning of this trip and all that it entailed, their friendship rusty from disuse. After the fifth CD assessed and discarded, Sonia pulled over at a gas station and marched Anthony to the swivelling display by the checkout counter and told him to pick something.

"Hardly Sam Goody's," he muttered to himself, but he came back to the car with three CDs, a pack of Skittles and a small smile.

Sonia had booked a room in a hotel called Treasure Island.

"Fan of Robert Louis Stevenson, are you?" Anthony had asked when she called to let him know.

"Fan of daily pirate shows and themed cocktails," she said.

But, really, it was cheap, available and the first place she'd tried, having recalled it from a made-for-TV movie about a boy who goes hunting for treasure in the hotel. All the hotels she'd found sounded delightfully garish, the themed ones especially appealing.

"Appalling," Anthony said as they walked through the hotel's doors. Sonia rolled her eyes but didn't say anything. They were hit by the metal clink of dozens of slot machines mingling with the noise of a hundred excitable children.

They had booked a single room, neither of them having much money to spare at the time. Anthony was still trying to make it work with his band, King Amber, having graduated from nightclub basements to an EP and a brief state tour without any discernible difference in income, and he had only recently started working at a record label. Sonia was still working any job that required little paperwork but was friendly to children on the premises, mainly dressmaking but also cleaning and, for a couple of glorious months, running a bus tour of celebrity mansions in Pasadena (a couple of months was how long it took for someone to realise she was just pointing at random houses and making up facts). They figured the single room would also do well in creating the impression that their intention to marry was earnest.

"Behold the walls of Jericho!" Sonia said, standing in the narrow space between the two twin beds.

"Don't expect me to strip for you or anything."

"If anyone's Clark Gable in this room, it's me," she said, looking around the room with barely concealed excitement. She opened the blinds, expecting to be met with the blaze of the pirate ship in Buccaneer Bay, but she let out a soft "Oh" at finding that they overlooked the motel next door instead.

After she'd washed her face in the bathroom, Anthony said, "Grab your stuff, Clark."

"Why?"

"We're moving rooms," he said, shrugging. "They gave us the wrong key."

A beleaguered bellman was waiting for them outside and showed them to the other room, going in ahead of them and opening the curtains for them with a somewhat aggressive tug. And there, sure enough, seven floors below them, was Buccaneer Bay, the pirate ship quiet in that moment, in between sinkings.

After the bellman left, Sonia did a little skip to the window.

"Did you just squeal?"

"Shut up." She peered down at her toes, right up against the floor-to-ceiling windows, and looking as though they were about to snap off the mast of the pirate ship. "Maybe."

Something in the sheer excess of Las Vegas, the intoxicating, gaudy exuberance of it all, appealed to Sonia in a fundamental way, so the purpose of their visit was all but forgotten for the evening. Here was a hotel outside of which an entire pirate ship sank into the water every two hours; here was a whole building modelled after an Egyptian pyramid, the windows of each room slanting obligingly to fit the form; and here was a new hotel under construction that collected all of the elements of New York's cityscape and condensed them into an eighteen-acre plot of land in the desert. Here was human ingenuity and effort spectacularly channelled into pure silliness. Sonia had never wanted to belong more. All the while, Anthony's face bore a look of barely concealed disgust that alternated with a strained smile whenever Sonia caught him frowning.

She'd booked a table at the Buccaneer Bay Club, the restaurant overlooking the pirate bay and the show.

"Is it not enough to see it from upstairs?"

Sonia sighed and with a weary tone explained that she wanted to see the faces of the pirates up close when they lost the battle.

"It's hardly going to be Laurence Olivier up there."

"We'll see," she said, and Anthony looked like he wanted to argue further but also like he'd had this very same discussion about the merits of pirate-show actors a million times before and couldn't be bothered to voice the same contentions yet again.

The restaurant was less swashbuckling than its name and the rest of their surroundings had implied, and after opening the leather-encased menu, Sonia let out another small "Oh" at finding that none of the menu items had thematic names.

"Your steak frites will taste just as good," Anthony said, correctly interpreting her look.

"Will it, though?"

The food was good, however. It was an indulgence they could hardly afford, but Sonia found herself caught up in the relative glamour of their surroundings. They made their way through appetisers—prawn cocktail, the opportunity for a sea-themed name truly wasted—and talked about the few people they both knew, circling around from the least interesting (the drummer in Anthony's former band) to the more important ones (Anthony's mother) and were just about to reach the nexus of their spiral to each other when the Battle of Buccaneer Bay began with a bang.

Sonia was immediately consumed by the theatre below them. A similar hush came over the crowd gathered on the street out front as two pirates paddled in a dinghy across the dark water. Sonia's fork hovered in midair as the sneering Englishmen bore down on the pirate ship, the fork's cargo flung across the table when the first cannon hit the hull. At the end of the performance, she was genuinely surprised at the outcome—the English ship sank into the shallow man-made harbour, and the captain stood proud and unflinching as the water inched its way up from his feet to his body to his face until he disappeared completely.

"Wow," she said, turning back to their table. "How is he able to do that?"

"Well, he does it about six times a day, so I'd say practice."

"And when did you become such a cynic?"

"I think around the time Woody Allen started dating his daughter."

"Well, I think it's amazing," she said, and then, to clarify, "The captain. That man goes out there and acts his heart out six times a day to an audience with mouths full of corn on the cob."

"Quite an image."

Sonia sighed and told him he didn't understand.

"I do, actually," he said. "But what I'm curious to know is, if you're so full of admiration for theatrics of all kinds and you happen to live in a city dedicated to performance, have you ever considered—?"

"No, no, no," she said just as the waiter leaned down to clear some plates. He hesitated a little—it was odd, but some diners did want to finish off the whole plate, including garnish. "Apart from the complete impracticality of it, I just think"—Sonia handed the fretful waiter her plate—"you can love something without being consumed by it, without wanting to *be* it."

They both paused then, letting the implications of the words settle between them, like a feather descending slowly on a current. Of course it was Anthony who wanted to be consumed by what he loved—he'd been trying to make it in music for over a decade.

"I don't mean that—" she started.

"Don't worry, I'm not offended," he said, although he'd let the silence go on long enough to put this in question. "And anyway, I've learned my lesson on that front."

"The job in San Francisco?"

"It's still music, you know," he said, and it sounded like something he'd told himself several times before. "Anyway, so you won't be an actress, you won't, you know, play Long John Silver at a Las Vegas resort. But surely there's something else?"

Sonia laughed. "Anthony Greene, are you asking me what I want to be when I grow up?" But he didn't let her play it off and continued to look at her questioningly. "I guess I just want my daughter to be able to answer that question."

Just then the waiter brought over a banana split, the three scoops of ice cream topped with little pirate flags instead of maraschino cherries, the whole thing doused in dark chocolate, a sparkler to match the pyrotechnics going on outside their window perched at its banana mast. The waiter looked at Anthony uncertainly before putting it down in front of Sonia. "A Scallywag Split for the lady?"

Their booking at the chapel was not until ten p.m.—even this appointment was grudgingly given on such short notice—so they had the whole of the next day to while away.

Walking through the casino turned out to be the first hurdle. Anytime Sonia stepped off the green-carpeted pathway that wound its way between the card tables and slot machines, a suited security guard appeared out of nowhere and reminded her to "step out of the casino, ma'am," since she looked underage.

"I've grown a whole human inside of me, you'd think I could be trusted with a glimpse of the craps table."

As it turned out, she could not. By afternoon, Sonia had discovered the wonders of gambling and she was slightly tipsy from the free cocktails that appeared miraculously by her side every time she took a stab at a calculated move. Anthony had gone to the hotel's gym and was likely on his way to some other equally wholesome activity when he spotted her leaning conspiratorially right into the personal space of the middle-aged man beside her.

"So . . . you got a glimpse of the craps table."

She swivelled around at his voice, her piña colada swerving dangerously with her. "They said I couldn't, but look at me now!" The last four words rushed up against one another like a concertina so it sounded more like "lookerminnau."

"Yeah, you showed them," Anthony said, sniffing the drink in her hand. "And how did we do?" He addressed the box man, as Sonia was now sipping her drink with a dreamy expression.

"She's been out for a few rounds now."

"It was mostly the drinks I was after anyway," she told the man with a haughty sniff. "Didn't really need the dice and the ships . . . the ships . . . the *chips*, and all that."

The man nodded sympathetically, a paragon of placidity surrounded by the fraught emotions of some two hundred sinners.

Anthony helped her off her seat and suggested they order room service and sleep it off—Sonia seemed to agree to this, being halfway to sleep already.

"I haven't been drunk since . . . since . . . since I was a baby!" she told him in a stage whisper as they were riding up the elevator.

"No kidding. Is it common for babies to drink back home?"

"Oh, yes, very common . . . and why not give a newborn some pálinka?" This last bit was shouted into the ear of the woman in front of her, vocal modulation having gone out the window.

In the hotel room, Sonia got into bed with her clothes still on. When the bellman brought up the food, she had two fries and then fell asleep to the faint, soothing *click-click-click* of the slot machines, still cradling the plate and mumbling something about yo-ho-ho and a bottle of rum.

At ten to nine they sat on a bench outside the Love-Drunk Chapel smoking, the oppressive heat of the desert making them sluggish. Sonia had woken up a few hours earlier, confused and still a little drunk. Through the smudged glass of sleep and the soft reflected light of the bathroom, Sonia had seen Anthony getting dressed. She had watched him painstakingly roll up the cuffs of a maroon button-down and run wet hands through his hair. For a moment she'd thought, *Is this what it feels like to have a husband?* It was almost comforting, having someone benignly padding about while you woke up. But the thought passed through her mind, leaving as swiftly as it had arrived, having not found fertile ground in which to take root.

Now a silence lay thickly between them, one that was different from the hopeful, hesitant one that had accompanied them on their way to Las Vegas and different also from the comfortable one they still remembered from their early friendship six years ago.

"You look nice," Anthony said without looking at her. She wore a blue spaghetti-strap minidress that Marnie's teenage daughter had lent her.

Sonia glanced down at herself. "I look like a child bride."

Anthony had become nervous as the minutes dragged them towards the chapel—not because of their impending marriage or the questionable morality, legality even, of their endeavour but because it was unlike Sonia, as far as he knew her, to be so introspective. She sat outside the chapel quietly with an unfamiliar expression on her face. There was some fundamental imbalance to them now, so he felt the need to tilt from his own habitual moroseness towards her usual exuberance, to fill the void of her reticence with his words.

"Are you nervous?" he asked.

"Not really," she said without considering it.

"It would be understandable."

"Hmm?"

"To be nervous."

She smiled wanly, as though she hadn't really heard him.

After a while he tried again. "Is it—do you miss Mila?"

This question finally did pierce through her reverie—she tensed up and put out her cigarette as though the thought of her daughter compelled her to be better. She told Anthony that she did miss her daughter, and it should have been true; she was doing this for Mila, after all. But as she had said it, she realised that for the past two days, she had not missed Mila, and the thought made her cheeks hot with shame.

Just then, the man who had booked them in for the ceremony walked out and said, "We're ready for you lovebirds," ploughing right through their contemplative mood with his booming voice of strained jubilance.

Anthony looked at her uncertainly, but Sonia put on a smile, stood up and reached for his hand. "Ready to get married, Anthony Greene?"

He stood up as well and stamped on the dying embers of his cigarette stub. Walking towards the chapel, he asked, "Why do you always do that?"

"What?"

"Use my full name."

"Oh, I don't know. Anthony Greene—nothing bad can happen to an Anthony Greene."

PORCUPINES

* * *

They were offered champagne after the ceremony, but Sonia took one look at it and turned slightly green. The officiant and his assistant stood with rigid grins, the undrunk flutes still in their hands, confused, clearly never having faced this sort of situation at the Love-Drunk Chapel.

"Are you feeling better?" Anthony asked after they'd finished grilled cheese sandwiches at the 24/7 Denny's down the road.

For a moment she thought he meant was she feeling better now that they were married—now that she had made the first step to stay here permanently. She looked out the window of the diner—the shine of Las Vegas had worn away here, a mere couple of streets from the Strip, the lights more garish than ebullient, the revellers more desperate than carefree. It gave her a queasy feeling, like she was about to—

"Nope," she said, and rushed past the stick-thin waitress on her way to introduce four piña coladas, two fries, a grilled cheese and a cup of coffee to some unsuspecting white ceramic.

She came back to the table with as much composure as she could muster. "I'm sorry, I don't know what happened," she said, planting her hands on the table to steady herself.

"Well, you got drunk at two p.m. in a pirate-themed casino."

He said it so plainly, so matter-of-factly, as though she had simply shown up for an appointment arranged a long time ago. In another life this might have been a common occurrence—she was only twenty-five, after all, but age was a clock reset for Mila; her own didn't often cross her mind. It had never occurred to her to mourn her youth—adulthood, in the form of motherhood, had claimed it with such swift finality.

"I got drunk at two p.m. in a pirate-themed casino," she said and started to laugh.

Sonia might have been offended at the way Anthony hustled her past the craps table, past the slot machines and past the blackjack when they arrived back at the hotel, but she had learned her lesson on that front. She did, however, offer to buy him a drink at the Yo-Ho-Ho Bar to compensate for having celebrated their nuptials with Denny's and vomit.

Unlike the hotel restaurant, this bar had taken the theme and run a marathon with it: The bar itself was fashioned as the bisected hull of a ship, and its tenders wore the clothes pirates might wear if those pirates weren't very partial to clothes.

"Why do you like this stuff so much?" Anthony asked as he took apart the various accoutrements of his cocktail—pirate flag, neon stirrer, pineapple slice, a whole floral arrangement.

"It's fun?" Sonia answered. "Does that really require explanation?"

"*Fun* is a relative term. I don't find this"—he gestured at the pile of plastic he'd removed from his drink—"fun. It's Disneyland; it's America at its worst."

"You don't know how to appreciate your own country."

"You're going to tell me that you couldn't have a pirate-themed bar in your sad Soviet home?"

"I'm going to ignore that," she answered, taking a hesitant drink from his cocktail—it was, after all, a little hazardous to the health of her eyes to drink her own with all its decorative elements still intact. After it seemed like they'd dropped the topic, she said,

"You think that because I like to be entertained, I'm somehow more vacuous than you are."

"I didn't say that." He took back his drink from her. "But it's true that you . . . you get easily caught up in this stuff."

"Because I got drunk for the second time in this decade?"

"No, it's not the drinking—it's the . . . this . . . the pirates." He was struggling for words now. "You just don't seem to take yourself very seriously."

"And you take yourself too seriously," she said, laughing. "None of us are perfect creatures. Except perhaps him." She nodded her head sideways at their bartender, whose exposed chest looked like the site of a recent oil spill.

"Case in point."

"What?"

"I can't talk to you seriously for one second," he said, idly puncturing a piece of pineapple with a pirate flag.

"Anthony, I am twenty-five years old, and I have a six-year-old daughter at home—I take my kicks where I can get them. My whole life is serious; I don't need to pretend like I have problems."

He looked up from the wreckage of his drink. "Well, maybe my life isn't as difficult, but you make things harder than they need to be."

"Do I, now?"

"You know you do. You could have stayed with your sister, you could have stayed with me. Or you could have . . ."

"What? Go on. I could have . . . not had Mila?"

"No, God, no, that's not what—" Anthony sighed. "I'm just saying, you could have more . . . more of a life. You could call your sister, for God's sake. You could—"

"Enough, Anthony." Her face had no traces of its former mirth. "I didn't ask for your opinion on my choices."

"No, right, you only asked me to commit a felony with you."

Sonia looked down at her drink and stirred it slowly. "I'm sorry to sully your perfect American name," she said, and even though the words seemed barbed, the way she said them was only resigned. "I really am."

It was true that Sonia had been careful in the past six years since she'd decided to stay in America, but she had not been ashamed. Just being somewhere didn't feel innately like wrongdoing. And she had never found herself uncomfortable in the grey areas of life. But something about pulling Anthony along with her got her dormant conscience going.

"I'm sorry, I didn't mean to be so harsh—I did agree to this," he said, reaching for her hands across the table.

"It's fine, you're right." Looking down at her fingers, held lightly by his, Sonia realised that Anthony, with all his freedom of choice, had chosen to help her in this moment. But it wasn't just a night in Vegas—she would need him to show up to interviews, to take pictures, to send letters; she would need him to fill out forms and share an address with her. She would need him for several more years.

San Francisco, 2001

"Some of the woodwinds are coming too early on bar one twenty," the conductor bellows at the children assembled before her, many of whom may well have been present on this planet as a result of woodwinds coming too early. At least, that is the sort of childish association Sonia's mind would normally conjure if it were not otherwise occupied.

"Do you think Cecily's acting weird?" she asks Linda.

"Weirder than usual?"

"No, I guess not. She just keeps glancing at me like she's . . . *constipated* and somehow I'm to blame."

Linda laughs, but Sonia is not even joking. These are the kinds of thoughts that go round and round in her head since talking to Mr. Alvarez yesterday—she continues to try and replay in her mind what exactly it is that she revealed to him about her marriage to Anthony, wonders who else Mr. Alvarez might have told in the intervening couple of days and why on earth they had to run into the very man now, when she feels so many eyes on her, when she has been so careful to keep the details of her life quietly tucked away from the rest of the world. She has found herself casting suspicious glances at the children she chaperoned the previous day—each one of them possessed of infinite tattling potential. But Sonia's jangling nerves are nothing of note that morning as the young musicians and their parents prepare for the big orchestra event the following day.

The parents have been encouraged to sit in on their rehearsal and bear witness to several dozen children attempting to learn new pieces of music and play them with complete strangers—it is unclear exactly whose torture this has been devised as. The children wear frightened expressions as they stumble over each bar. The one time so far that the conductor complimented them, half the children had already lost their place and stopped playing; what she was complimenting was, in fact, their silence.

The children from the other schools play a large variety of instruments. There is a bucktoothed young girl presiding over a glockenspiel and another sitting behind a set of four cavernous timpani, poised to strike with cotton-ball mallets in her hand. One young boy grapples with a contrabassoon, which makes a sound that can only be described as *musical* with a generous spirit.

In addition to being awed by these exotic instruments, the children from Mount Washington are particularly flustered as they adjust to a new hierarchy they've never experienced before. Their small public-school orchestra, with its bake-sale funding and its penchant for playing popular film scores, seems suddenly amateurish as the staff from the youth orchestra chop and divide their players according to abilities, imposing the strict structure of the real deal.

The conductor goes around assessing each student's talent for chair placement, and when one of the parents asks why they have to "line them up like racing dogs," she responds levelly that the purpose is to maintain "sonic balance."

Accordingly, the violins have been paired up into "desks," sharing a music stand with one player turning the sheet music so that the better violinist can continue playing. The conductor doesn't use the words *better violinist* but a purse of her lips makes it clear. After struggling to get comfortable on her chair with her sprained ankle throbbing, Mila stumbles through her scales and is humbled into her secondary position in a desk with Megan H.

Mila looks around her at the children of varying aptitude she will be playing with—she is reliant on them to make this performance a success in front of her father, and things are not looking up. Megan smiles at her a little. She has decorated her violin case with stickers with various band names and logos, and Mila hesitates for a moment, but then, because Riley is all the way on the other side of the room with the woodwinds (who are still being reprimanded by the conductor), she braves an overture.

"I like your stickers," she says. Many an adolescent friendship has been struck up in such a way, thanks to sticky pieces of paper.

"Thanks!" Megan says, her smile broadening at the compliment.

As they begin to play, Mila glances at Megan, thinking it is not so bad after all that they have been paired together. And Megan, looking back at her, smiles and confirms this by holding her gaze. It seems in this moment of contact that they are confirming something—a decision, finally, to become friends.

"Could you?" Megan says, indicating the music stand between them.

And Mila is thankful after all for the task at hand, which hides the redness of her face—she removes her violin from her shoulder and turns the page.

Although the morning proves to be as tedious as expected, it does give Sonia an opportunity to observe her daughter. Of course she is aware that playing music is important to Mila—she would not be spending her spare time shuttling a teenage violin prodigy around Los Angeles otherwise—but looking at her among her peers now, most of whom show a good level of dedication to their music, she notices something almost relentless about Mila's concentration.

"So, how big a deal is this Youth Symphony summer bonanza anyway?" she asks Linda as they avail themselves of the biscuits and coffee set out for bored parents.

"Well, Kathy told me she will *die* if she doesn't get in, but she also told me the other day that she will *die* if *Roswell* doesn't come back for another season, so I take that with a grain of salt."

"You know, I find that show kind of creepy."

"Me too—I mean, I know they're meant to be aliens, but still."

Sonia realises she has sidetracked the conversation, and reins it back in. "So, the summer program, not that big a deal?"

"Oh, no, it's a big deal if you're serious about music—it's fully funded, room and board, the whole summer with the best music educators. Have you seen these kids, though? I'm not holding my breath." Linda takes a sip of her coffee, then with a slight tilt of her head says, "Mila seems very committed, though—does she get her musicality from you?"

"Oh, God, no—I'm completely tone-deaf."

"Must be her father, then," Linda says—it's not framed as a question and yet it hangs there tensely between them as Sonia struggles for something to say to this. She looks at Linda, benignly sipping her coffee and waving at Kathy as the kids stop playing just long enough for the conductor to find out which of them is producing a flat note. Linda is unaware that, for this moment, she is suspended between a threat and a friend.

PORCUPINES

"Linda," Sonia says, and when she's got her attention, she pauses for a second, giddy with the idea that she could just tell this woman everything, unburden herself over tepid coffee while fifty terrified children play music. "I—" Linda looks at her with her eyebrows raised. "I don't think I can take any more of this music."

Los Angeles, 1997

IT'S HARD TO KNOW WHO REALLY DERIVES PLEASURE FROM CHILdren's birthday parties. Not the child's parents, who do all the planning, prepping, entertaining and cleaning. Not even the birthday boy or girl, given the sudden surge of attention that drags in its wake the pressure to please guests and outdo other birthday parties. The young guests might have fun, at least the few of them who are actually friends. The rest, however, will stand to the side awkwardly, wondering if they've been invited at the behest of their parents or in an attempt at blanket inclusivity. They will hand over their Bath & Body Works grapefruit shower set, their Jamba Juice gift cards and novelty cups like a tepid offering to some severe deity—as insurance rather than from any warm feeling towards their host. Certainly the parents dropping off their children will leave in a smug glow of satisfaction, having handed off their child for a few hours of free childcare—but come pickup time, they receive back cranky sugared-out junkies tumbling down from a high instead of the Sunday-best-dressed, slicked-back-haired polite children they left.

And yet, it has to be done, as Sonia discovered after her daughter's first school year. She had happily dropped off Mila at eight birthday parties in nine months—at bowling alleys, at the community pool, in front of the Build-a-Bear workshop at the mall.

It was an unforeseen perk of Mila's young school career, this occasional stretch of hours to herself over a weekend, and yet it had never occurred to Sonia that when the time came, she would have to reciprocate.

That is, until Mila proclaimed from the back of the car, like a queen on her booster-seat throne, "My birthday party is next week."

"Your birthday party?"

"My birthday is on Tuesday so my party is on Saturday," she said, without question. She had observed the pattern of birthday celebrations—the weekdays on which her classmates had their birthdays, their moms brought doughnuts or pizza or root beer floats to school, and the following Saturday, everyone went and gave them gifts in return. Seeing the alarmed expression on her mother's face in the rearview mirror, Mila proceeded to explain further details of birthday protocol to her.

Of course Sonia had not forgotten her daughter's birthday—eighteen hours of labour etched the date pretty well into her brain. But her plans for celebration had involved a trip to the mall food court followed by half-baked Toll House cookies in bed.

"Have you . . . invited your friends yet?" she ventured hesitantly; hopefully, there was still time to pull the brakes here.

"No, *you* have to print the invites," Mila said in a *Don't you know anything* kind of voice, and Sonia realised that, clearly, she did not.

At home, Sonia sat in their living room, looking around and evaluating the situation. There wasn't much furniture yet. Sonia had been so in awe of their good luck in finding this place within their price range, within the right school district, with beautiful floor-to-ceiling windows overlooking Northeast Los Angeles that she hadn't wanted to spoil it with the kind of second-rate furnishings she could currently afford. "Minimalism," she told Mila as they sat watching TV in the living room with a couch made out of pillows propped against the wall. "That's what it's all about these days."

When they came to view the place, she had told Mila not to get her hopes up, even though the six-year-old was more likely to have hopes attached to spotting a Jack in the Box sign than to real estate, which meant not much to her at this age. She was perfectly happy in that apartment complex in Eagle Rock, first in Auntie Jadranka's spare room and later in their own place down the hall, where she shared a bed with her mother, so even the prospect of having her own room was of little interest.

They had been greeted at the door by the owner, a woman named Dawn, who was somewhere in her fifties but dressed like a clean, well-to-do Woodstock attendee. She spoke in a low, steady voice, like a yoga teacher, and never moved the long hair out of the periphery of her face, even when it must have clearly impeded her vision. She made them chamomile tea in the little galley kitchen that connected the foyer and the living room and showed them around the small, two-bedroom bungalow, pointing out different parts of the house and how they corresponded to her various life events. There was the corner where she had sat rocking her dying cat gently to Valhalla, and there was the patch of wall that she had leaned on for support when her brother announced that he was going into dentistry. Sonia didn't dare ask about such mundane things as utility costs or appliances—it would have clearly ruined the mood Dawn was setting.

It was the first place they looked at, and although Sonia was ready to move right in, she went to see two other places just for due diligence: two cramped little apartments for twice the price of the first one, a fact that reluctantly, against her better judgement, roused her suspicions into action. She called Dawn.

"Look, I hope this doesn't sound ungrateful, but . . . I just need to know if everything about this place is, you know, on the up-and-up." This was a phrase she had learned from her soon-to-be former landlord, Larry, who mostly used it as reassurance when things were almost certainly on the down-and-down. "Because it just seems—"

"Cheap?"

"Well, yeah . . . below market value, perhaps. Not that I'm complaining! It's just that I'd be moving here with my daughter and—"

"I understand," she said in her soothing, husky monotone. "I'll admit it is significantly below the normal price for the area. The thing is, that's on purpose. I wanted to attract a certain type of tenant. I thought if I advertised it at a lower price it would encourage the—"

"Delusional?"

"No . . ."

"The desperate?"

"The dreamers. I wanted no sceptics or cynics in my house; it would ruin the aura permanently. And then how would I ever sell it? So, you see, it was a financial decision too, in the end," she said, laughing.

The woman had clearly lost a few marbles around the time when little Furry Garcia had departed this realm, but Sonia thought all in all, she would still make a better landlord than Larry.

So within a few weeks they moved in—their paltry belongings

dwarfed by the newly plentiful square meters they found themselves in.

Now, with a potential party to host, Sonia finally had to view their home from the perspective of an outsider. She doubted that the floor-to-ceiling vistas would impress a bunch of grade-schoolers—her pantry looked like a ransacked supermarket shelf and she wondered whether the children could be entertained solely by the television. In the end there was only one thing for it—a trip to Costco.

As arbiters of taste go, the Costco discount CD bins were perhaps not the most sophisticated. However, they were a reliable source for "best of" albums by one-hit wonders and soundtracks to obscure early-'80s movies and unintentionally lent Sonia and Mila's music taste the kind of eclecticism that some people strive for through careful curation. The CD bin was their first stop, and they searched for music that might be enjoyed by twenty-odd six- and seven-year-olds and landed on the soundtrack to *Labyrinth* and Eddie Murphy's *How Could It Be* for its lead single, "Party All the Time," which seemed promising (more so than his musical career in general). Then it was on to the snack section, where they purchased industrial-size bags of Pixy Stix, Warheads and Push-Pops. In the games section they found multipacks of board games, a remote-control disco light and an inflatable ball pit with a thousand glow-in-the-dark balls to fill it. By the time Sonia and Mila emerged from the store, Sonia was at once exhausted, dizzy and excited (although she could not identify it, this was the feeling of having wasted a good amount of money on objects and foods that never should have been invented in the first place). She had never hosted a birthday party before—her own young birthdays had been celebrated more sedately, with close family—and as much as she'd resisted the idea in the beginning, she was now determined to make this the best party these kids had ever experienced in their short lives. She'd even found a recipe for the trifle her mother used to make for her own birthdays—three layers of different sponge, pastry cream, raisins, walnuts and a delicious rum sauce. She had never baked one by herself, but it felt right to attempt it now, at this landmark moment of Mila's young life in America.

They rolled their cart full of lurid products to the food court and had a hot dog each to decompress—there were only four days left until the party.

Before her guests arrived, Mila's mother reminded her for the thousandth time that if she was asked where she was from, she should just say California; and if she was asked what her mother did for a living, she should just say she works in an office. Her mother referred to this as the party line, though Mila didn't find it in any way fun; it seemed quite different in fact from all the other things she associated with parties: piñatas, bouncy castles, goody bags. But she nodded in agreement—she was satisfied that they had met the requirements for hosting a party. Invites had been printed, balloons had been blown up and some sort of cake had been baked (although it looked suspiciously un-cakelike to Mila, she'd decided to cut her mother some slack here). Sonia had even had the idea to hand out live goldfish to the guests instead of goody bags. The tiny orange fish now swam together in a big tank, but they had prepared plastic bags for each of them to take two goldfish home in at the end of the party.

PORCUPINES

When the doorbell rang for the first time, Mila ran to greet the guests herself.

Gifts had been given, cake had been eaten and the children had been set up to watch *Pocahontas* in the living room armed with all the sugary snacks and popcorn their hearts could desire, so Sonia went out on her little patio for a smoke. She had been out there for only five minutes when one of the kids, Serena, came outside and sat down next to her. "Mrs. Imre, where's your husband?"

"I don't have one," she said while trying to manoeuvre her cigarette smoke away from the little girl, eventually giving up on it altogether with a sigh.

"How comes?"

"Didn't want one."

"I want to be a bride when I grow up."

Now, Sonia had many opinions, and she took considerable pleasure in expressing them, but as there were very few people in her life to share them with, her bon mots and theories landed mostly on the ears of Mila, or the occasional stranger who struck up a conversation (and then quickly regretted it), and, on this day, poor little bride-to-be Serena.

"Save yourself the trouble, honey. It's all just a trick of language. You see, first you propose, then at the wedding, someone proposes a toast, but if someone propositions a third person, then the other one can propose they split up. No wonder divorce statistics are up in America—we need fewer weddings and a wider vocabulary." She adjusted her sunglasses, feeling pleased with this little speech.

However, Serena's lower lip trembled threateningly, so Sonia quickly switched gears and asked one of the other children who had ventured out onto the patio what he wanted to be when he grew up, and, *Pocahontas* forgotten, this question was then taken up by every single child at the party with enthusiasm, revealing future biologists, firemen, "computer people" and one unfortunate girl's desire to be "something creative," an answer that rather pre-determined her failure in the venture.

This spontaneous but somewhat paltry party game alerted Sonia to the fact that perhaps the kids needed some more entertainment than what was currently provided. So she went inside, turned the disco lights on, launched Eddie's plaintive demand to "party all the time" and, taking hold of Mila's hands, led the dance party by example.

When the kids departed, they were each handed their two goldfish on the way out, and their tired, smiling faces as they crossed the threshold into the arms of their parents assured Sonia that they had done well. One of the mothers, a woman named Cecily, even came back to ask for Sonia's cake recipe, as her little one, Megan, was in the back seat despondent that she couldn't have more. As Sonia and Mila sat on the living-room floor numbing their tongues with leftover Pixy Stix and surveying the wreckage around them, they felt content.

It took a few days for the calls to start coming in.

Serena's mother called to ask what Sonia had said about marriage because her daughter had found their wedding album and placed it in the bin, apparently on her advice.

Sergio's mom called to say that Sergio was upset because one of his goldfish died on the way home and the second one didn't seem to be moving, and what were they supposed to do with the fish anyway?

Morton's father called to say that little Morton might have taken his fish back into the ball pit for a dip before they left and they should have a look at the bottom for the little guys.

Lucy's father called to say that smoking around children was extremely irresponsible.

Aiden's mother called to say that leaving young children unattended for any amount of time was extremely irresponsible.

And finally, Megan's mother called, and Sonia let out a sigh of relief because this call was surely to thank her for the trifle recipe, but instead it was a five-minute diatribe on putting booze in a cake for children.

As reparation for some of the damage caused, Sonia and Mila spent the next weekend driving around Mount Washington collecting what remained of their jolly band of goldfish. They stopped at the strip-mall pet store in Eagle Rock and purchased a proper home and food for them and, abashed, took the advice of the store manager on appropriate goldfish care. Back at the house, Mila contemplated the watery home of their newest family members, Olga, Maria and Irina, while Sonia stared up at the ceiling, splayed out on the floor of their living room. "Well, I think that's the last time we host a party, isn't it, Milosh?"

Mila nodded, her finger trailing along the thick glass of the fish tank, her favourite goldfish, Irina, following along on the other side.

San Francisco, 2001

FOR ALL THEIR SHARED DNA AND ALL OF THEIR TIME SPENT soaking up each other's habits, there is a fundamental difference between mother and daughter: Sonia is alive to the joys of life, perhaps naturally inclined to indulge in them too much, and is forever repressing her exuberance to suit her circumstances; Mila views what little of the world she's seen with scepticism and her own place in it with uncertainty, but for the sake of fitting in, she rouses herself into some form of sociability, however inept. And yet today, it seems they have exchanged dispositions.

All morning Sonia has felt like her lungs are compressed, doling out miserly breaths to the rest of her body. She keeps tugging at her clothes; if only they could give an inch more, perhaps she could get some of the oxygen to her head. First Anthony's appearance at the pier and then Linda's questions the previous day—it has begun to feel like her life is an overstuffed suitcase and she's trying to close it with the weight of her whole body.

Mila, on the other hand, is genuinely excited—the signs of it are all over her: Her mouth quirks up at the corners into an occasional nervous smile, she rubs her palms on her jeans, suddenly alive to the realisation that arms just hang there, and she looks at her watch continually without taking in the meaning of the numbers and hands. She has tuned her violin to perfection—she might have even buffed it with some polish while her fellow players weren't looking—and she's plaited her hair into two neat, no-nonsense braids. She is ready.

At breakfast everyone wears ashen expressions and looks queasily at their cereals, their orange juices, their shoes, before they go off for another morning of rehearsals. In the afternoon they arrive at the concert hall just before a downpour that has been threatening all day releases from the sky. The hall is a gleaming globe inside with a large stage that seems to dwarf the audience seats fanning out in gently sloping semicircles below it. Upon seeing the sheer number of children who will be performing in various groups, those parents less dedicated to their children's successful musical careers make mental calculations of just how many hours of amateur music they have to get through before they get to see their own precious child's moment in the spotlight. Sonia is one such parent, and she quickly seizes a seat near the exit from which she can sneak out for cigarette breaks.

"Good thinking," Linda says, and she plops her handbag in the seat on Sonia's other side. There is a moment of awkwardness as Sonia assesses whether it's wise to give an opportunity for the previous day's conversation to continue. "Or not?" Linda says with a quirk of her eyebrow and a half-lift of her handbag from the seat.

"No, of course, of course," Sonia says, taking Linda's bag and putting it back on the seat. "Do you want to get a drink?" she asks, then adds quickly, "A soft drink."

"Yes, please."

A bar has been set up outside the concert hall, where there will be a reception after the concert, and there are some rumblings among the parents that the students accepted for the summer program will be revealed then too. Apparently, the results of the all-important jelly-bean count competition will also be announced, or so Sonia is told when they run into Dave outside the concert hall.

"Oh, right, well" is all that Sonia manages to respond.

"Playing it cool. I see, I see," Dave says, nodding appreciatively. Sonia decides not to try and argue with this and instead asks him if he's seen a bartender around.

"The bar won't be open until *after* the concert, Ms. Imre, Ms. Park ... and Mr. Ross," says Mrs. Flores in her cautionary teacher voice, looking especially let down by Dave. "Don't look too disappointed."

Before she can explain to Mrs. Flores that she wasn't trying to source booze at two in the afternoon, Sonia hears her name called from the entrance. Her eyes go a little wide and her arms go rigid. Anthony is there, soaked through from the rain that started a few minutes ago. Sonia excuses herself from the group and goes to meet him, aware that the eyes of the parents and teachers behind her must be making their way to the strange man along with her.

"God love you, Anthony Greene, but you seem to have the worst habit of showing up in places you shouldn't," she says, forcing a smile and holding out her hand to take his wet coat, then hustling him out of view. "Let's get you dry."

Despite the fact that she has no idea why he's shown up and that he has done so at the most inopportune moment, Sonia is somehow comforted by Anthony's presence here among all these strangers, in this foreign city. She sits on the bathroom counter while he attempts to dry off bits of his clothes under the hand dryer and thinks, *Here is one of my oldest friends. One of my only friends.*

"Why do I feel like a lover who's been shoved in the closet?" he says as he pulls a lukewarm sock back on his foot, holding on to the hand dryer for balance. "You don't seem all that happy to see me."

Sonia laughs, then sees his questioning look. "I just wasn't expecting you."

"Well, Mila said..." He takes out a crumpled and soaked piece of paper with the location of the concert in now barely legible crayon. "Then again, this should have given me a clue."

"Oh God," Sonia says, a hand covering her eyes. "My daughter invited you to this thing."

Anthony, now fully clothed and somewhat dry, sits up on the counter with her. "She gave the impression that you wanted me to come too," he says, laying the little piece of paper out on the counter beside him. "And seeing as we never got around to talking much at the pier like you wanted to..."

"It wasn't the best moment for catching up with old friends, to be honest."

"Hey, you suggested it in your email," he says, putting up his hands defensively. "'Pier Thirty-Nine, twelve thirty, be there or be square.'"

They look at each other from either side of the sink—understanding dawns on them both at the same time and they let out a synchronous laugh.

"I *knew* I should never have installed AOL."

"I think you might have bigger problems than the internet," he says. "She sounded just like you. Well, minus a few spelling mistakes."

"'Be there or be square'? Really?" she says. "And you thought I wanted to meet you in the middle of a busy pier in San Francisco?"

"Sonia, it sounded like the exact sort of spectacle you enjoy," he says, and these words make Sonia want to cry a little. He is right—the pier was tacky and garish and fun, and she completely forgot to enjoy it. She's forgotten to enjoy any of it. "So, not that it isn't delightful sitting with you in a girls' bathroom, but any idea why your daughter invited me here?" he asks. "I'm honoured, don't get me wrong."

"I honestly don't know. I suppose maybe she's taken a liking to you?"

"Well, don't look so surprised," he says, nudging her shoulder with his. "Does she know about—?"

"No, no—I haven't told her." She looks down at her hands, uncharacteristically bashful. "The thing about Mila is, she doesn't even like it when I talk my way out of a speeding ticket. She's got this look sometimes—her mouth gets all tight and she looks straight at me." Sonia laughs a little, then says, "She wears her socks all the way up to her shins—I asked her once why she always pulls them up so high and she said, 'Why do socks have to be a secret?'"

Anthony smiles. "Why indeed."

"Anyway, that's Mila," Sonia says with a little sigh. "So, no, she doesn't know."

Anthony puts his hand on her shoulder. "We'll be divorced in no time, we only need a few more years, right?"

"Anthony Greene, you know just what to say to a girl," she says, but the thought does calm her—Sonia, like many people who think their problems are unique and unsolvable, has forgotten that just talking to another person can go a long way to assuage one's fears.

"I was actually in LA a couple of weeks ago," he says. "I'm sorry I didn't call. There was barely enough time to see my mother."

"Oh, I'm not offended, Anthony Greene," she says. "My dance card was full anyway."

"Next time," he says. "I mean it. But guess who I ran into while I was there?" He pauses, but Sonia shakes her head to say she doesn't have a guess. "Your sister! And one of her kids, the boy who's around Mila's age."

"Rina?"

"Unless you have another sister I don't know about," he says. "She didn't recognise me. I guess I've aged a bit." He ruffles his hair, redistributing the few grey hairs that have sprouted among the black.

"Rina has girls—two girls. Hannah and Abby." Their names feel strange in Sonia's mouth and she can't remember the last time she said them out loud. "So it probably wasn't her."

They lapse into silence then, and finally Anthony says, "Sonia, don't tell me you haven't seen her since?"

But before Sonia can answer, the bathroom door swings open, scattering the moment like a gunshot in a tree full of birds, and Riley marches in in its wake. She looks at the two adults for only a second before bellowing, "There's a boy in the girls' bathroom!" making both Sonia and Anthony scramble off the counter and demonstrating the power of a fifth-grade tattletale.

"All right, sweetie, Mr. Greene here was doing some plumbing," she says, but she catches Anthony's eye and lets out a giggle. "Some . . . um . . . maintenance. He's leaving now, no harm done." Turning to Anthony, she says, "Do you want to go see a bunch of shit-scared children play classical music?"

"I thought you'd never ask."

They wait for the lights to go dark in the auditorium, then stumble into their seats just in time for the first piece to start, panting a little and still stifling their laughter. Linda is already there in her seat and she looks pointedly at the two of them but doesn't say anything. The lights go even lower, and for a moment Sonia forgets the disquiet of the past few days, her worry of what everyone here thinks—she is just an audience member in a dark seat, watching someone else's drama play out on a stage.

For all her scepticism, Sonia finds herself enjoying almost all of the performances. She sees other Milas out there—determination writ on their faces, concentration skills beyond what should be available to a child—and for a moment her feelings for her own daughter extend to all of them.

Sonia spots Mila among her classmates at the side of the stage as they prepare to go on for their performance. She looks stoic as she tunes her violin, engrossed in the minute adjustments of its pegs, but when she sees her mother and her gaze takes in Anthony beside her, a smile breaks across her face, at once embarrassed and gratified.

Mila finally walks onto the stage and settles in her chair with her violin, Megan H on one side and Austin, the boy who makes the word *rascal* seem quaint and insufficient, on the other. Even he is collected and composed now as they launch into their take on Shostakovich. Halfway through the piece, Anthony's cell phone buzzes between them and he scrambles out of his seat to take a call, but Sonia barely notices. This ragtag group of children has suddenly come together to create fifteen minutes of something delightful, and Mila's playing is confident and poised and—as it turns out—perfectly average.

There is a brief intermission, during which Sonia fully intends to find Anthony and escape to the bar, forgoing the rest of the program, but as the youth orchestra takes the stage, she is drawn back towards the auditorium. Although she has had enough of children and classical music and children playing classical music, when they begin, Sonia can't help but stop in the doorway to satisfy her curiosity. These kids can only be a few years older than Mila and her classmates, and yet there is a beautiful chasm between the two groups: the variety of instruments is greater, their playing is more finessed. Their conductor seems to be adrift in the music, convulsing to an unknown rhythm, his body communicating something to the players arranged in a semicircle before him. They are in the middle of the heavy symphony, which, in their more accomplished rendering, feels familiar in an almost grating way. Sonia is about to turn away from its intensity when the violins slowly die down until the bows are barely vibrating over the strings, and a single oboe comes in with a hopeful note, soon replaced by a trip down to a more sombre sound. The solo is brief, less than a minute, but the girl behind the oboe plays with straight-backed solemnity, and her peers follow each note like she's handing them the secrets of the universe. Sonia holds out for wisdom as well, but all too soon the sound is swallowed up by the return of the other instruments, and she is left strangely bereft.

Budapest, 1983

AFTER A LONG AND BORING POSTING IN SWEDEN, THE IMRE family was back in their hometown, a wintry Budapest redolent with the promise and enthusiasm of the '70s they had left behind. Szonja was installed back in her old school, where everything looked just the same as it had before (linoleum, mostly); the family were back in the same apartment, where everything smelled just the same as it had before (cabbages, mostly). But unbeknownst to them, even as the temperature of the Cold War turned colder (or hotter, depending on one's preferred allegorical framework), the country and its residents had begun to slowly shift and morph into something entirely unfamiliar to the Imres.

Soon the city would shed its Lenin Boulevard, its Mayakovsky Street, its Gorky Alley, its Marx Square and its Engels Square too. (But not, for some reason, Moscow Square, which lingered like a tattered garment purloined from a former lover.) In a mere six years, its inhabitants would find a renewed city where shifts in ideology affected not just their government, their economy and their education but also their ability to turn a corner and know where they were. As one century lumbered on to the next, the citizens of this city would begin to turn their television sets on in unison each night for a slack-jawed, awestruck hour of *Dallas*, airing in their country over ten years after the original but losing none of its potent tanned-skin, oil-rigged capitalist masculinity.

But for now, Szonja navigated the familiar routes of her home as she walked from school to the library to meet her sister, turning onto Rosenberg Couple Street (an actual street name) with not a thought for family feuds and cattle ranches.

Her mind that day was focused on an economic venture of a somewhat smaller scale.

The previous week, she had sat in front of the television in the living room—Rina was in her room and their parents were out for the night, so Szonja had the luxury of the evening's program to herself. She waited for the suited anchorman to drone through the day's news—"US forces continue to occupy Grenada," "Metro Line One declared nuclear bunker" and other cheering thoughts of socialist superiority—and then, finally, the program she'd been waiting for came on. The premise was simple: Each week, the host, with his manic mop of curls, would scour the country, rustle up a suitably worthy young candidate and grant that person one wish, whatever it was. That week it was a mousy-looking boy named Csaba, whose wish was . . . bananas. Actual bananas. Interviewed in front of his garden fence in some small town an hour from the capital, he explained to the host that his mother tried to get them bananas each week, but by the time she found out which store was stocking them, they'd already run out. He hadn't had a banana in months. He didn't seem particularly bothered by this, but the exuberant host squeezed out of him a declaration of his desire for the fruit. Cut to the host and his young ward standing outside the back of a supermarket, waiting for a fresh shipment of bananas.

Meanwhile, some riveting B-roll footage of the line inside the supermarket (all the other people who'd been tipped off about the fruit). A severe-looking woman who was at the front of the line for the remainder of the bananas looked like she would buy one only grudgingly, despite having stood there for forty minutes. Later, her face promised, she would go home and joylessly consume the exotic fruit.

The boy received a five-kilo bag of bananas, as promised (minus the one banana sacrificed to the host's demonstration of just how fresh and real they were), and dutifully thanked everyone for it.

After the show wound down, the host looking pleased with himself at having granted another impossible wish, Szonja sat contemplatively through the commercials and the beginning of a soap opera and thought: *What an idiot.* The boy was about her age—judging from her own appetite, he could have maybe two bananas in a day. What joy would he get from the rest of the sackful? How many could he eat before they all went off? Little Csaba, when asked what he wanted more than anything in the world, had chosen this.

But this was Hungary. A country that was not part of that great union of the Soviets but was still beholden to their leaders. A country that did not have the nerve to start a war but had been on the losing end of all the ones it'd been dragged into. A country that had been the truculent little sibling of the Turkish, the Austrians, the Russians in turn and now had its eyes on America for its latest crack at subjugation (shifting from the outright occupation of the sixteenth century to the purely economic one of the late twentieth, at least). This country had at least three public holidays celebrating failed attempts at self-liberation.

Here, it seemed, bananas constituted excitement.

FRAN FABRICZKI

* * *

The plan was simple.

1. Get onto television show.
2. Ask for lifetime supply of latest Western candy bar.
3. Sell candy bars at school at double the price of Hungarian candy bars and become rich.

The last part had been inspired by a recent encounter at school. Szonja had come back from Sweden with a few select treasures, including Lionel Richie on vinyl, a fresh pair of jeans and two boxes of Swedish liquorice candy. Having changed schools so often, she knew the best course of action was to take these items to school and parade them in front of her classmates. This did not necessarily make her any close friends but it earned her respect and a choice of companions for the year. So on the third day of school, she brought in her liquorice, sat in the back row of the class during break, feet up on the desk, and prepared to eat her candy with an insouciant air. But the crowd that gathered around her gave her a better idea.

"I actually have tons of this at home," she said to the boy close to salivation on her right.

"Maybe you could bring some in to share?" he said hopefully, and Szonja swiftly corrected course.

"Well, not *that* much—this candy is rare, even in Sweden."

The boy leaned back, crestfallen. Szonja turned to her next admirer, a tall athletic girl who looked like she could mean business.

"And it's expensive, but . . . I suppose I could part with some of it at a discount, since we're classmates."

Both boxes sold on the spot, the money stashed away in the back of her notebook. She didn't even like liquorice.

PORCUPINES

So, yes, the plan was simple, but the first step constituted a bit of a hurdle, and Szonja knew whom she could call upon to help—someone with connections and sway across the adult world of Budapest. But Mr. Imre had been in a volatile mood ever since his elder daughter had started flexing her teenage obstinacy in unexpected ways.

Some weeks ago, Szonja had been walking to the market with Rina on an errand for their mother. It was a warm autumn, and they were both lightly dressed for the season with light moods. Rina was teasing Szonja about the boy from her class back in Sweden who had written her a plaintive letter asking when she would return, and her laughter drew the attention of a group of boys idling in the bus stop nearby.

"Such a pretty little Jew," one of them threw at her, the words carrying the menace of young, frustrated sexuality and making both of the girls tense up and look down instinctively.

And how did the boy know that Rina was Jewish? Despite what the Reich's Ministry of Enlightenment once suggested, there isn't one way for a Jew to look (male, hook-nosed, angry). And yet hatred is a finely honed sense even when all the finer senses—the ones that help us find beauty in something inanimate and the ones that connect music with memory—are blunt. So he was not wrong, although neither of the Imre girls had ever heard herself referred to in such a way before. No one had bothered to tell them that they were Jewish, and who would think to ask?

This revelation lingered in the girls' minds quietly, in the place where ideas without context go, either to wither and die or gather the courage to demand for themselves a frame of reference. For Szonja, it did the former; for Rina, the latter.

She began, at first gently, to prod her parents for a little more information about their ancestry. Szonja, for her part, felt she had all she needed on that front. She saw the framed picture of their grandfather on the mantelpiece, a dashing young man leaning out of a train carriage with a shy smile. Mr. Imre didn't speak much about his parents, but when Szonja, handling the picture frame with uncharacteristic care, once asked what he was like, her father had said enigmatically, "A great man. He went to the moon," from which point on she was perpetually in awe of her grandfather. It was actually a picture of Yuri Gagarin, and Mr. Imre was simply stating the factual, but Szonja's imagination remained unfettered for a long time by reality—she bragged about her grandfather the astronaut for years to come.

Rina, however, was looking for something else entirely. When her benign questions about their family yielded no results, she launched into a more straightforward enquiry.

"Why do we celebrate Christmas?" she asked over dinner one night. The family's spoons continued their slow clatter against their bowls of pottage as though no one had heard her.

"What do you mean, sweetheart?" Mrs. Imre asked finally.

"Well, we're Jewish," Rina said, eyes darting from one parent to the other to gauge reactions. "And isn't that a Christian holiday?"

"It's more of a general holiday these days, I think," Mrs. Imre said, at the same time as Mr. Imre responded, "And who said we're Jewish?"

Rina paused, contemplating which of her parents to answer. "Well, are we not?" she said finally—her teenage rebellion was taking a rather mild form, but her boldness was nonetheless unappreciated.

"Don't talk nonsense," Mr. Imre said, redness creeping up his neck, but his voice remained low and steady.

Rina knew she had hit a nerve, which meant she was right, but her father's words still stung—she was not used to being thought of as nonsensical. Some part of Rina was angry at the deception, but respect for her parents superseded anger, so the emotion had to be channelled into an altogether more confusing amalgamation of remorse and determination.

There were many things the Imre family did not talk about. The obvious things to avoid: politics, religion, money, feelings. They never discussed Mr. Imre's job in detail, and they never commented on the ever-rising price of milk. No one complained about any worldly possessions they lacked (although Szonja certainly did in her head).

They also did not talk about the first six years of Mr. Imre's life, which mapped painfully onto the six years of the war and left his once-teeming family tree decimated down to just the one branch that contained himself. They didn't talk about his first memory—of being locked inside a synagogue in the ghetto, the smell of urine mixing with horseflesh and the leather of prayer books. They did not talk about Mrs. Imre's mother, who had just enough life left in her at the end of the war to have her daughter but then ended that life two years later when she found she could not purge the image of a dead woman's shoes marching her out of the liberated camp. Or Mrs. Imre's father, who found his prewar family and fled to the West to rejoin them shortly after. They certainly didn't talk about how it felt to grow up in the lonely aftermath of it all or just how primed they were to be part of something bigger but just how ill-equipped they were for family building.

No, the Imre family had great skill in avoiding a variety of subject matter, to the extent that it would seem they had exhausted *all* possible topics, but as talented as the Imres were at keeping their silence, they were equally adept at filling the empty space by talking about things of little consequence. The day's weather, what happened at school, what Mrs. Imre got at the market—all of these riveting topics were still in play. When even the banal evening conversations were denied her, and her father's cold-shoulder campaign took full force, Rina set aside her burgeoning interests temporarily.

Later, Rina would take the question of faith into her own hands—she would speak to rabbis, join quiet study groups and begin to consider the many seemingly random habits that could cumulatively tie her to her people. In their future, there would be no reconciliation with her parents over shared stories of the past. There would be no frank discussions of intergenerational trauma. There would only be resentment over the yearning for something the other has discarded.

But for now, Rina felt the shame of having upset her father and, through him, her mother, and she did her best to make amends.

Szonja met her sister at the city's central library, a decadent neo-Baroque building that was once the city palace of a minor count but had since been cut into small airless rooms where the linoleum floors and moulded plywood furniture soon made you forget the grand staircase you walked in on. It was not a place Szonja was in the habit of visiting—the hushed voices and the rustle of dusty pages made her fidgety—but her sister had gotten it into her head that a vigorous intellectual preparation for the symphony concert they would be attending in a week was the way to reinstate herself as the keen-witted and obedient daughter she was used to being thought of. Szonja did not see how fetching her sister books from the stacks would smooth out the creased discomfort of their family life, but her sister usually knew better about these things, and she needed her father in a benevolent mood for her own purposes.

Rina paged through book after book: on the history of the Hungarian State Railway Symphony Orchestra, on the composer whose work they were going to see, on the rise in the use of timpani in orchestral music (you never knew what would come up in conversation). Occasionally she read out a passage to Szonja and asked, "Is this interesting?" to which Szonja would give her sister a beleaguered shake of the head: None of this was interesting.

By the time the family arrived at the concert hall, Rina was buoyant and confident in her new knowledge, ready to impress any number of Mr. Imre's colleagues and acquaintances with her subtly penetrating small talk. Mr. Imre was in the running for a posting to DC the following year, and no social interaction was simply for enjoyment—only the most irreproachable party members were chosen for such postings, and every encounter was an opportunity to prove himself. Of course, the more sociable he needed to be, the more of his own taciturn nature he had to overcome—such is the irony of enforced fun.

Gathered in the foyer of the concert hall was an impressive array of party members and their various hangers-on. Even the famed former ideological secretary had come, bringing with him at once a stamp of approval on the proceedings and some unease.

Mr. Imre introduced the very man, along with a couple of other party members, to his family, and here it seemed was Rina's opportunity.

"Mr. Aczél, have you read Volkov's *Testimony*? It has some very enlightening thoughts on the symphony we're about to hear," she said, referencing a book Szonja had found her in the library a few days ago.

"I can't say that I have," the older man said—he was polite and kindly and nothing in his tone had signalled to Rina that she was overstepping in any way, so she continued.

"Well, the book suggests that the symphony, especially the ending, has multiple meanings, some that weren't picked up on at the time it was first performed," she said. Emboldened by the man's continued interest, she added, "And apparently his Eleventh Symphony was inspired by '56."

This simple comment sent a ripple through the assembled adults around her, though to Rina's untrained eye, the mute transfer of energy seemed like interest rather than censure.

Szonja's attention, meanwhile, had been caught by a familiar head of curly hair, and she fidgeted beside her mother, craning to see if it was in fact the man from her TV show. Interrupting the adults' discussion of the book, she tugged at her father's sleeve and said, "Dad, there he is, the man from my show—please will you introduce me?" She was only twelve years old and her voice still lacked modulation—it cut through the conversation around her.

Mr. Imre gave their mother a look that was known to mean *Control your children* (always *your children* when they misbehaved); Mrs. Imre took her cue and dragged Szonja aside with apologies.

As the adults dispersed, and Mrs. Imre gave her a gentle but long-winded scolding about interrupting adults and how appearing on a television show was immodest, Szonja saw her sister pulled aside by their father. Rina hadn't realised that the book she had just been expounding on was considered a contentious reactionary work liable to cause heated debates about whether or not the symphony was supportive of the ideology they were all living under. And then she had mentioned '56—the revolution—the single topic everyone in politics avoided. She had only thought it might be interesting.

Szonja could not hear what Mr. Imre said, but she saw her sister, all the component parts of her, diminishing as she listened to her father with downcast eyes.

Seated for the concert between their parents, both girls listened to the music, a little more subdued. Halfway through the symphony an oboe sounded out a note at once sanguine and mournful, and a few tears cut a salty path down Rina's face. Szonja, looking up at her sister only briefly, squeezed her hand between the ruffles of their dresses.

On their way out, Mr. Imre made sure to mention to several colleagues that his daughter had been moved to tears by the music. Which was true, in a manner. Shostakovich had a way of bringing painful emotions to the fore.

San Francisco, 2001

Mila has seen *The Parent Trap* (both the 1961 and 1998 versions), she's seen *It Takes Two* and at least one other Mary-Kate and Ashley movie where their parents are single and require the assistance of children in their romantic lives. She's also seen *Sleepless in Seattle*, several times, because her mother went through a trying Meg Ryan phase once (it would be many more years before Mila came to appreciate *When Harry Met Sally*...). So she's frustrated to find that things are not going the way they are supposed to go. She is supposed to make a big success of her performance in the final scene, inspiring such pride and recognition in her father that he would have no choice but to reveal himself. He would reconcile with her mother, and along with a knowing and lovable side-character, they would form a contented family unit. But this plan has failed at every hurdle.

First, the performance went just... okay. Mila knows she didn't get into the summer program because she saw the smug look on a few of the kids' faces and also because Austin came right up to her and said, "I got in and you didn't," which kind of gave it away. This is a disappointment, sure, but one she can file away along with the few others she has catalogued over her decade of life (including the fact that real s'mores don't taste as good as s'mores-flavoured Pop-Tarts and that the friendly faces on the Disney Channel grow up to be less-than-appealing adults).

But there is a second, more pressing problem: Anthony left the auditorium in the middle of her performance. If she had had any hope that he could turn a blind eye to the relative failure of their school's performance—and parents around her were constantly doing just that, praising their children beyond any reasonable limit—it was dashed when he got up from his seat with his phone up to his ear, his mind clearly already elsewhere.

Beyond a door to her right, Mila can hear the sound of some hundred adrenaline-spiked kids celebrating, but she cannot bring herself to join them.

On the bench outside the reception hall, Sonia sits beside her daughter, equally dejected. She has felt a strange melancholy pressing down on her since she stumbled out here after the final performance of the day. All her anxieties have given way under the weight of it, and there they sit scattered around her feet: her guilt around the fraud she committed with Anthony; her worries that someone might find out; her worries that *Mila* might find out and not understand; her worries that she has done some unknown, irrevocable damage to her daughter's future; and many other minor faults that cannot even be put into words but have nevertheless persisted and pecked at her conscience. There they sit as a reminder, and she stares at them but is suddenly too tired even to hold them up and care.

But introspection is curbed as she finally emerges from herself to notice Mila beside her. Unaware of the precise layers of disappointment currently roiling beneath her daughter's cool facade, when Sonia becomes conscious of the silence between them, she launches straight into a bolstering oration on what she believes to be the problem.

"Mila, I know you had your heart set on this summer program," she says, stroking one of the neat plaits that frame her little face.

"But let me tell you something, and try to remember this—you don't have to be the best."

"Okay."

"You just have to be better than one or two of your friends."

Mila looks up at her mother doubtfully. "What do you mean?"

"Well, at the concert, was anyone there worse than you?"

"I guess so... Megan dropped her bow once, and Sergio sneezed into his tuba."

"There you go—that's excellent, that's wonderful. Now, when you see Megan or you see Sergio, you can just think, *Well, I'm better than them, at least*—trust me, you will feel better. You don't need to say it out loud or anything, but it will make you feel better inside."

Mila's mouth quirks up a little into the beginnings of a smile but then falters as she considers her mother's advice. "That wouldn't be very nice, though, would it?"

Sonia sighs and for a moment is lost in the consideration of all the "nice" people she's known. "Nice is not something to aspire to, kid. Kind, yes, but nice, no. *Nice* doesn't mean anything at all. You could be the nicest person in the world and all it would mean is that you've learned the right things to say."

Thinking of her futile interaction with Megan the previous day, Mila decides this doesn't sound like such a bad thing, knowing all the right things to say, but Sonia seems satisfied with her own wisdom so Mila just nods, accepting advice to a problem she hadn't been thinking of. They sit in silence for a while, and Sonia is wondering how else she can probe gently into her daughter's feelings when Mila surprises both of them by continuing unprompted.

"I guess I just wanted to show him that I can play music too, that I can play well," she tells the hands folded in her lap.

"Who, honey?"

"Anthony . . . he came to see me play."

"Oh, well, yes, and I'm sure he was very impressed with what he saw," she says. "But to be honest, kid, I'm not sure it matters to Anthony whether you can play well or not."

Mila is usually quite receptive to her mother's blunt honesty, but she looks a little hurt at this. "You said he plays music too—he would have seen that we're alike," she explains.

"And you want to be like Anthony because . . ."

Mila looks up at her mother finally, with an exasperated expression.

"So that he can be sure I'm his daughter."

It's the second time in as many days that Sonia has adopted a look of complete dumbfoundedness, and she is feeling very dumb indeed.

Sonia's first instinct is to ask her daughter why in the world she would think that Anthony is her father, but the wounded expression on her face tells her this might not be the right time. So she just carries on, accepting the reality her daughter has been living with.

"Anthony isn't your father, Milosh—he is an old friend of mine and a lovely person, but not your father." Sonia hesitates, wondering if she should explain that although he is not her father, he is, as it stands, Sonia's husband, that *husband* and *father* are not always the same role, but then, thinking of that stern, unyielding face of integrity Mila sometimes has, her courage wavers, and she decides against it. There will be time for that, and in any case, she knows what the next question on her daughter's roster will be; they've been here before.

"Mila, I know this has been on your mind, and I know I haven't been particularly forthcoming—which is not like us, is it?" She strokes Mila's forehead. "But the thing is, there is no big reveal.

Your father was no one. I mean, I didn't know him—I mean, I knew who he was but we never really got to know each other." Sonia blows out a little horsey breath of frustration. "And maybe he's great, maybe he'd have made a wonderful father, but you have to understand, at the time it was just me—I wanted to live my life, not figure out how to be inside someone else's." She thinks of her mother and a life spent hosting her husband's guests, and of Rina using the force of all her intellect to read the same stories over and over again each year in a synagogue pew. She recalls the moment she realised she would be beholden to Anthony for years to come and the hours and hours of anxiety that single attachment launched in her. "I've seen people fold themselves into other people's lives, and I didn't want that for myself."

"But I'm folded into your life, aren't I?"

And this is the kind of question that is sure to make a mother, even one whose self-confidence is as robust as Sonia's, despise herself, just a little.

On her way back to the party with a slightly shell-shocked Mila by her side, Sonia is suddenly nervous around her own daughter, who seems to have had little reaction to what she has told her. She considers taking Mila back to the hotel to give them both a little more time to process, but as she enters the reception hall, her eyes land immediately on a problem: Anthony, back from taking a business call outside, is talking to Cecily Auerbach. When they spot Sonia, Anthony indicates her to Cecily in a speak-of-the-devil way and Sonia can only hope that the devil has not been characterised as an illegal immigrant with a green-card marriage of four years tethering her desperate body to the mast of this American ship.

"Where have you been?" Dave descends on Sonia with an exasperated sigh.

"Well, Mila and I were—"

"Never mind, they're just about to announce the jelly-bean contest winner."

One of the teachers from the other school has gone up to the podium, two children behind her holding up the jar of jelly beans with their whole bodies, looking like three-headed Cerberus. This game has clearly been devised as a distraction and consolation prize for those children (and those children's overinvested parents) who haven't succeeded in securing places in the orchestra's summer program. The only person this seems to have actually placated, though, is Dave, who is giving Sonia a self-satisfied look in anticipation of his impending win. But Sonia doesn't notice as she scans the room for the familiar mop of dishevelled hair that always rests atop a crowd like a bird's nest in a tree.

Instead, she sees a Banana Republic mannequin come to life and march right in her direction with purpose. Sonia's eyes dart around for an exit but she is fenced in by the crowd that has gathered, Dave on one side, Mila wedged on the other, still holding her hand, and she is too slow to prevent Cecily's voice cutting through the hubbub to say, "Sonia, I've just met your husband?" with the cruel little question mark hovering between them. "Wonderful man."

Sonia looks down at Mila, who has dropped her hand, and she curses herself for not giving her daughter the full explanation while they were alone, while she had control of the story that Cecily has so assiduously poked at. Mila's face—her lovable, impassive face that has calmed even her mother's nerves many times—has gone through so many unfamiliar expressions that her mimicry muscles are likely to be sore the next day. Now, as Mila locks eyes with her mother, her expression cycles through confusion, then betrayal, and then finally lands on anger.

"Mila . . . ," she begins, but her daughter is shoved aside by a blur of blond hair bouncing with the gait of an erratic meerkat.

"Ms. Imre, you won, you won, you won the jelly-bean contest. Can I see your prize? Can I try it? Can we try it together?" Megan says, fidgeting her way between Sonia and Mila.

And then a voice, almost unfamiliar, bellows out from behind her: "That's *my* mom, you idiot!" And with a shove that belies her spaghetti arms, Mila pushes the surprised girl to the floor, where she lands with a sickening crack.

PART V

Los Angeles, 2001

"Awww, sweetheart, how long you been saving up for this?"

Mila blinks at the woman, hair the colour of granite, the texture of straw, light green cardigan draped tidily over a generous figure. It feels wrong to lie to someone so grandmotherly; for a moment, at least.

"Ages... I'm very excited to play with it," she says, looking at the big black box that contains the console she is buying on the day of its release. A line coils behind, made up of kids like her but also nervy teenage boys and excited adult men in this toy store the size of a small stadium. A large sign says ONLY 1 PER CUSTOMER, WHILE SUPPLIES LAST, and everyone's eyes flit to it occasionally, like they're waiting for the last ship out of Pompeii.

"Would it be possible to get one for my friend too?" Mila asks, rounding her eyes and using the line she'd practised with her mother. "She couldn't make it because she's sick."

They had landed on the vague sick friend after striking out with a few other versions, such as claiming the console she'd just bought had been stolen outside or that the second one was for a charity auction.

"Well, aren't you sweet," cardigan grandmother says. "But no, 'fraid not. I bet a lovely girl like you will let your friend play on yours, though."

For a moment Mila forgets that this console is not for her at all, and she thinks perhaps she will share her game with Kathy and Sergio over the weekend. The three of them have spent more time together since returning from San Francisco in the wake of the dramatic end to the orchestra concert.

Violence is not the answer, except, apparently, when it is. The crack they heard upon Megan's impact with the ground had thankfully just been a violin bow, easily replaced. After some initial surprise, Megan herself had recovered quite quickly, and Mila's boldness—counter to everything that teachers, after-school specials and Camy Baker told her—earned her a notoriety and respect among her peers. And yet she felt somehow wrong-footed by her sudden choice of bus-seat partners. There's something to be said for friends who aren't excited by the prospect of your self-implosion, so she retreated to her Ziploc bag of casual buddies.

Cardigan grandmother clears her throat. "That'll be two hundred and ninety-nine dollars," she says a little apologetically, like she's worried Mila might not have anticipated the steep price.

Mila counts out the money in flat, uncreased notes that look like they've yet to participate in the economy, and cardigan grandmother furrows her brow a little but takes the cash and puts the giant black box in a giant plastic bag. "You take care, now."

In the parking lot Mila helps her mother stack the game console onto a large pile of others as a woman walks past scrutinising the scene. It is the middle of a weekday, after all, and there's a ten-year-old hoarding electronics in the back of a Buick.

"Don't mind us," Sonia says, smiling brightly at the woman. "Just living our lives."

Sonia is a big proponent of playing hooky; she will pull Mila out of school on the flimsiest of pretexts and with the unlikeliest of excuses. It isn't that she doesn't care about her daughter's education, but some days watching a movie (something historical, like *Bill & Ted's Excellent Adventure*), spending the day helping Sonia out with a commission (gaining practical skills) or going to the mall (for a critique of consumerism, sure) can be just as educational as sitting in a circle and cutting out paper turkeys (Sonia is clearly a bit fuzzy on what actually goes on at school).

So she has decided today will be one such educational day. It just happens to be a felicitous coincidence that Mila not going back to school this afternoon also means Sonia will not see more of Mr. Alvarez, the person highest on her list of people to avoid since their disciplinary meeting earlier that day.

"I'd say make yourselves comfortable but I haven't managed it in the six years I've worked here, so I would be setting you up for failure," he said when they arrived at his cramped office during Mila's lunch break.

Mr. Alvarez had clearly made some efforts to bring the place in line with the vision of himself as an elite educator—there was an antique globe perched on the windowsill and a few leather-bound books among the filing compartments on his bookshelf, but this gave the impression of a jumble sale rather than a sophisticated office.

"Right," he said after he sat across the desk from Sonia and Mila—he looked from one to the other as if unsure whom to address. "Now that we're all settled back from our trip, I thought it was time to clear the air about the . . . uh . . . incident in San Francisco."

Sonia looked at the door as though expecting Megan's parents to burst in at any minute and demand retribution.

"It'll just be us today," Mr. Alvarez said, correctly reading Sonia's expression. "Mr. Hollings is . . . abroad, I believe, and Mrs. Hollings I spoke to on the phone briefly."

Sonia gave him a prompting look.

"Oh, she's not concerned about Megan's . . . er . . . fall. She did express some . . . consternation over the fact that Megan has been talking about you, Ms. Imre, quite a lot since the trip, but we agreed that this was somewhat outside our scope of concern and probably harmless."

Although when Sonia had helped her up, dusted her off and asked if she was okay, Megan had been immediately placated by the attention, Mila's sudden aggression had not escaped the notice of everyone around them. Sonia still cringed at the hushed silence in the room following her daughter's outburst. Sonia had exclaimed something deranged, like "Someone's had a few too many jelly beans!" and whisked Mila out of the room. Outside, Mila had looked up at her mother and said, "I'm sorry?" with such pitiful confusion on her face, clearly at a loss for an explanation of her own behaviour. Sonia thought she had had enough excitement for one day, so she got them a cab back to the hotel, dropping Anthony off along the way. Anthony was left in the dark about his own part in the dramatic events of that afternoon and wondered benignly, as he got out of the cab, whether his friend's daughter wasn't just a little bit odd.

For the rest of the trip home, Sonia retreated behind her sunglasses, stayed in the motel room, feigned sleep on the bus and generally acted like she had a bad case of narcolepsy. When she was approached by Linda, or Mr. Alvarez, or Cecily, or Megan, or Dave (God, there were an exhausting amount of people on this trip), she sidestepped their advances like a game of "the floor is lava" she'd been training for all her life. She would have been happy to carry on maintaining her distance from the rest of the children and their parents as they dragged themselves closer to the summer holidays, but Mr. Alvarez clearly had other ideas.

"My concern here today is your well-being, Mila," he said.

"Yes, absolutely," Sonia answered—a little off her game. Mr. Alvarez looked at her, gathering his large eyebrows into two slopes.

"I guess I just want to understand what happened," he said, directing his full attention to Mila now. "Why did you push Megan?"

Mila took a second to consider this, then said, "I was under a lot of pressure," solemnly. Sonia had coached her on this answer over toaster strudels that morning. Some alternatives had been going the "Megan pushed me first" route, but there were too many witnesses for that, and inventing a little-known disease that involved involuntary shoving, but keeping up the pretence was not worth the detention or suspension or expulsion coming their way. So Sonia had landed on guilt-tripping, which normally worked very well for her.

"I see . . . under a lot of pressure from the concert?"

"And from school." "From school as well."

Mother and daughter said this in synchrony, which had the unfortunate effect of making it sound completely rehearsed.

"Is there any other reason you can think of, *Mila*?" Mila looked over at her mother for just one second, but it was enough for Mr. Alvarez to understand the situation. "You know what, Mila. How about I talk to your mother for just a few minutes while you wait out in Ms. Shuman's office?"

Alone with Sonia, Mr. Alvarez looked a little more uncertain, reminded as he was of ceding some moral high ground himself during the course of their trip to San Francisco. But he steeled himself—he was an educator, after all, a PhD-accredited educator, no less.

"Look, Ms. Imre, I don't want to be the disciplinarian about this—I don't think it'll do any good for Mila to get suspended and be away from peers more than necessary. But physical violence can't be ignored either. Now, I want to get to the bottom of what happened between Mila and Megan, of what might be behind Mila's actions, if you're willing to help?"

"Of course I want to help—but she said so herself, she was under a lot of pressure. And you've said Mrs. Hollings didn't seem too bothered, Megan certainly seemed fine to me, so . . ."

"Ms. Imre, what I need you to understand is it's not about the results of the behaviour but about the cause."

"Of course it's about the results: 'No harm, no foul,' as they put it," she said, then added for good measure, "'Don't make mountains out of molehills' and . . . and all that . . ." And then she ran out of aphorisms to back her up, so they lapsed into silence.

Mr. Alvarez moved from behind his desk to sit in the chair beside Sonia's—this was usually a friendly gesture, meant to put people at ease, but he regretted immediately bringing them into such proximity and stood right back up again, pacing the small room and settling back behind his desk.

"There are some concerns that Mila might be . . . a little too isolated from her peers," he said finally.

"Oh, are there?" she said, cocking her head and keeping the tone light.

"Yes, some concerns that Mila might not be integrating well, participating, and that—"

"I'm sorry," she said, "sorry to interrupt, but you are aware that Mila takes part in every extracurricular activity on offer at your school?"

"Yes, I am—"

PORCUPINES

"In fact, some that aren't on offer as well—I'm pretty sure she started the chess club herself."

"Yes, Ms. Imre, I'm aware and that's all really wonderful—"

"The after-school history society wasn't exactly Studio 54 either, but she's there every week."

"Yes, and that's all great, but the thing is . . ." Mr. Alvarez paused to consider what the thing was exactly.

"Yes?"

"Well, it doesn't quite amount to much in the way of socialising if she attends meetings and clubs but doesn't . . . talk to anyone."

Sonia considered this, momentarily defeated. "What about the debate team?"

"Ms. Imre—"

"Well, okay, she is a little less chatty when compared to some of the other kids, I'll admit," she said. "When compared to me, I suppose."

"That's just it, though, Ms. Imre," he said, bending a paper clip between his fingers until it catapulted across his desk. "The concern is partly that you yourself are not well integrated into the community."

Sonia paused, startled into considering herself. "Concerns that this single mother, single earner, is not integrating herself into bake sales and fun runs and . . . tailgate parties?"

"We don't do tailga— Never mind. I take your point, but still—children model behaviour after their parents."

"Right, that would be me," she said. "And may I ask where these concerns have materialised from?"

"Excuse me?"

"You said *there are* concerns. Whose concerns? Yours?"

"Yes, mine, certainly—but also some concerns that other parents have brought to my attention."

"I see—so Cecily Auerbach has a bee in her bonnet about me, and therefore my whole family is behaving wrong."

"That's not it at all, and it wasn't— Cecily wasn't the one who raised concerns, not that it matters. The parent, the parents, the people who did, who are concerned, have spoken out because they care."

Sonia laughed. "These people don't know me or care about me or my daughter," she said, but just then it occurred to her that there was one person—someone she'd gotten to know, gotten gradually close to. Someone she thought might care. And the knowledge knocked the fight right out of her.

"Mr. Alvarez, I'm very sorry—for Mila's behaviour, for whatever I've done wrong. We're both very sorry and we promise to do better."

Mr. Alvarez was thrown by this swift about-face and had no time to collect himself before Sonia stood up, gave him a businesslike shake of the hand and left the room.

Outside, Mila was seated on one of the plastic chairs of the school reception, feet skimming the ground as she balanced her biography of Shostakovich in her small hands, all her worries about what was going on inside the vice principal's office momentarily forgotten as she concentrated on the task in front of her in a way Sonia had never quite been able to.

And there was joy to be had in the disparity between herself and her daughter. Mila had hobbies and interests and the perseverance to turn them into skills. Sonia always delighted in taking her to all of the activities she requested—the swim practices, the orchestra events, the poetry readings, the chess clubs. And then there were the buttons made for the student council election, the speech rehearsed for the D.A.R.E. closing ceremony and the paper garlands threaded for the Fourth-Grade Dance Committee—the sheer abundance and randomness of opportunity made her happy, and it made it make sense, keeping their family in this place that provided a ten-year-old with a chance to play a UN delegate and debate the merits of globalisation. But observing her daughter in the past couple of weeks, Sonia began to despair at the way Mila clung to these things. That she seemed to think all of these extracurriculars would somehow give parameters to her social interactions. That she thought a book with rules written by a stranger who knew none of the infuriating and lovable specifics of her would help her make friends.

In this Mila was so frustrating and heartbreaking and single-minded. She was, Sonia realised, so much like Rina.

When Mila finally noticed her mother, she was pulled out of the happier world of her studies, her eyes questioning, and Sonia's flicker of annoyance with her daughter was at once forgotten.

"Don't worry, Milosh," she said. "It'll all be taken care of."

But all the taking care of Sonia has done so far is taking her daughter to buy game consoles for Marek to sell on the Eastern European black market, shaving off the last couple of hours of school with the usual "doctor's appointment" excuse. At their next stop, a small out-of-the-way electronics store, Sonia counts out more cash into Mila's hand for the purchase of another. Mila takes a couple of notes from the top, rumples them up a little, then shuffles them into the pile, which makes it look a little more haphazard, a little more plausible.

Sonia shakes her head, beaming at her daughter. "So proud."

When they are done with their rounds, Sonia suggests they finish off the rest of the afternoon with some frozen yoghurt, but Mila looks at the clock on the dashboard in confusion.

"But when will we pick up Simon?" she asks.

"Oh, I gave Simon the week off, honey, I thought you might want a break," she says, and even as she comes to the end of her sentence, she realises that she's made a classic parenting mistake—thinking with her own brain rather than her daughter's. Sonia thought her daughter might want a break from violin lessons, presuming that she didn't need a reminder of the aftermath of her performance in San Francisco. Mila will skip school, but she will never, never skip swim practice or violin lessons.

"I'll call Simon."

Sonia warms her legs in the June sun, reading a magazine, while Mila and Simon are by the pool, practising a particularly tricky Bach piece. When she looks up from a recap of a new show, *Survivor*, she notices Mila's coach striding towards her, flanked by a gruff-looking older man, and Sonia is sure that they are finally going to kick them out of the club for using the bleachers as a music room. She prepares to deploy her blank foreign expression and heavy accent, but it turns out not to be necessary.

"Ms. Imre, this is Coach Molnar, he'll be taking over for summer practices," Coach Comb-Over says—not his real name, of course, but she has never been able to remember what it is exactly. Something like Coleman or Comack or Compton. The hairstyle, however, perches atop the man's head with certainty. "He just wanted to talk over the schedule with you, figure out how many morning practices you want to sign Mila up for." Coach Comb-Over leaves, and Sonia's mind immediately begins calculations of summer wake-up times, lost sleep and additional swim team dues, so it takes a moment for her to register what she's heard. She looks up at the man, who must be at least sixty years old but has broad swimmer's shoulders that look resistant to the humbling bend of age. He sports a thick Tom Selleck moustache in grey, matching a head of coarse hair in the same shade, and has the general aura of having been dropped here out of the 1980s.

"Molnar?" she asks, and then hesitantly adds, "Hungarian?"

"Romanian," he says, a smile crinkling his weather-beaten face so that it's hard to imagine he ever did look gruff. "There was a Hungarian somewhere up the family tree, though, no doubt. And yourself?"

"Imre," she says, but she pronounces it the right way, *Im-reh*, instead of the way she has for the last ten years, *Imre*, like *Marie*, to smooth things along for the English speakers around her. "It's Hungarian," she says, making sure to refer to the name instead of herself, out of habit.

"Ah, hello, neighbour!" He shakes her hand, laughing like they've both just said the funniest things. "My wife and I are just planning a trip back home and we thought we'd hit up Budapest and Prague and all those good places after Bucharest, if the family lets us leave at all."

"Do you . . . go back often?"

"First time!" he booms. "Defected back during the '76 Montreal games—would have done well for myself there too if Naber hadn't swept all the backstrokes and the relays, damn it." He shook his head, clearly back in that pool twenty-four years ago for the briefest moment. "Anyway, then we snuck on over here after a few years, my wife and I—I went from cold to cold, you know, that's no way for a swimmer to be. Been here ever since. Nice and sunny here, outdoor pools with no heating—that's the life." He opens his palms to indicate their surroundings, like they have landed in a garden of delights rather than the concrete vistas and chlorine fumes of the aquatics centre. Sonia looks around herself with squirrel eyes and instinctively feels like shushing the exuberant man—how can he be talking about defections and crossing borders so casually when she herself has barely mentioned to her own daughter where they're from? In her efforts to wrap up this conversation before he can bring it up again, she agrees to all manner of swim classes for the summer—twice a day and on Sundays—and to chaperoning the monthly open-water swims at Laguna Beach. In that moment she would have agreed to give him her firstborn son, her soul trapped in an oil painting, or a lifetime spent in corporate law if it meant they could part ways sooner.

On the way home, the car begins to make a noise that is not dissimilar to the one its former owner, Mrs. Wojnarowicz, made in her last days. Sonia has no choice but to stop at the car service.

It turns out they will have to leave the car at the service overnight and take the bus home.

"Don't touch the trunk," she tells the mechanic and rubs her hand on her jeans like she's trying to get some dirt off. The man blinks and keeps his head facing so steadily forward, it's clear he wants to be turning it in the direction he's been forbidden.

As they walk down the street towards the bus stop, Mila says, "He's going to think there's a body in there."

"Exactly, Milosh," she says. "Exactly."

By the time they arrive home, Sonia is thoroughly exhausted. She is beginning to feel that the city is rejecting her. People often feel this way, even though cities are really quite indifferent to the humans who inhabit them. Of course, indifference can feel like the cruellest form of rejection—just ask anyone who's ever been in love. It has been nearly ten years since she first landed in Los Angeles, and life has had its ups and downs since then, Sonia has had her fair share of strife, but never has it felt quite as relentless as today. But the universe doesn't wait to take turns, it just doles out its cards in that punishing, uneven pace.

And so even in the comfort of her own home, she isn't safe. When she goes to order a pizza, that monotonous note of possibility, the dial tone, is mysteriously absent. As she brings in the mail from the post box she finds what she is looking for—the phone bill addressed to Auntie Jadranka branded with a censorious overdue stamp.

Years ago, when Sonia saved enough money to move out to another apartment in their building, Auntie had let her set up a phone line in her name. It wasn't clear to what extent she was aware of what was being asked of her (voluntarily participating in identity theft or, as Sonia liked to think of it, "identity lending"). When Sonia brought it up, she had said, "Okay," and then followed up immediately by asking, "Have I told you about the time I spent a month building the Belgrade-Bar railway?" with a staying hand on Sonia's arm that indicated she would be sitting down with the old woman for a couple of hours. And although Auntie had passed away years ago, and now, in their new home, she could have the phone in her own name, she kept it under "Jadranka Antic"—though the name was not hers, it was the first one she could be reached under in America, and so even though it made little sense and revealed a shameful habit of yielding to superstition, she kept it under that name, never late on a payment, never missing a voicemail. It was both a totem of their past and a portal to another future—except that now, on what feels like the longest day of her life, it is just a disconnected phone line.

Sonia cracks a sunflower seed between her teeth as she sits in her car in the school pickup line. In the final weeks of school, Sonia cannot in good conscience let her daughter skip any more classes, so she continues to take Mila to Mount Washington promptly at 7:50 and picks her up promptly at 2:20. Sonia herself avoids the school and everything to do with it as much as possible (only children are ever forced to be mature and responsible—a common misconception about their lifestyles relative to adults). She is as swift at drop-off and pickup as a game of hot potato (Mila in this case being the unfortunate potato), barely coming to a complete stop before Mila clambers in or out of the Buick. But today Mila is late, and here Sonia is now, waiting, the detritus of a hundred sunflower seeds held in her cupholder like they used to be in her father's glass ashtray.

Sonia is quitting smoking. You would be forgiven for believing it a manifestation of guilt—after all, it's a dirty habit and her daughter hates it. But the truth is Sonia quits smoking quite often. (In fact, she's quit smoking twice just today, if you count the mid-morning lapse.) She finds nicotine patches an embarrassing interference with her tan; her preferred method is soothing the oral fixation with sunflower seeds. In her native language there's a word for sunflower seeds, *szotyi*, and there is a verb for the squirrelly way you consume one *szotyi* after another: *szotyizás*. And it is in this undignified activity—which has no name in the English language—that Sonia is most reminded of home.

The longer she spends away from Hungary, the more abstract it has become. Its borders fluctuating over the decades like the contours of a jellyfish, its people defining their culture in accordance with or in opposition to the greater entities who pressed down on them, every element of their cuisine to be found in bordering countries. Sometimes she wonders: Was there ever really a country there?

But then, as her thumb and forefinger move deftly around the tiny shell in the effort to get at the meagre return of a small seed, she thinks there's a whole country where people have given this activity, the very thing she's doing now, a name.

She has time to ponder these things and a multitude of others while she waits for her daughter. Mila is slow to emerge from the building, stopping to talk to her schoolmates, to tie her shoelaces, perhaps to contemplate the mysteries of the grand unified theory, judging from her progress.

Her daughter's leisurely pace leaves just the amount of time needed for another parent to stroll right up to Sonia's car window.

"Hey, stranger," Linda says after Sonia reluctantly rolls the window down. She says hello but continues to look ahead, then at Mila as though they are late for an important meeting, when in fact the only thing waiting for them at home is the three p.m. rerun of *Sister, Sister.*

"I haven't seen you since the trip," she says. "Have you recovered yet? I still wake up at two a.m. in a cold sweat thinking I'm going to have to play some Tchaikovsky."

Sonia smiles stiffly at the dashboard. She looks over at Mila with a sigh, but the girl has chosen this moment to fish something out from the bottom of her backpack.

"Sonia, I . . . I was hoping we could get coffee sometime," she says. "Maybe discuss how Dave is coping with the off-season."

"Sure, maybe, sometime," she says, as though the game-show question were *List the most noncommittal words in the English language.*

"Look, I think I know why you're mad."

Sonia finally looks at Linda, expecting her expression to be rueful or apologetic, but Linda just looks at her plainly.

"It was just an offhand comment to Mr. Alvarez on the way home," she says. "But to be honest, I recognised something in your behaviour, in Mila's behaviour. Occupational hazard, I guess." She puts her hands up and shrugs. "I wanted to help somehow."

"And informing the vice principal is the best way to do that."

Linda takes a moment to consider this. "Mr. Alvarez is not the Man—he has ways of helping—"

"We're fine, thank you, we don't require *help*."

Linda sighs. "Look, Sonia, you're not the first person to have questionable legal status—so, no offence, but you need to get your head out of your ass, if not for yourself, then for your daughter's sake."

Sonia looks Linda in the eye, thinking that each time they talked on the trip, she had been so suave, so sure-footed in her dance around the details of her life.

"I don't know what you're talking about," she says.

"Right . . . well, when you figure it out, I'm here," Linda says, and she squeezes the arm gripping the car window, then leaves.

Sonia is not naturally inclined to dwell on her own faults—life is hard enough already without giving yourself grief—but something has kicked off a first little domino of guilt and introspection, and without anything in the monotony of her suburban life to impede them, the little wooden blocks keep tumbling into each other as she drives from their house to school to the store to school to swim practice to the drive-through to their house again in an endless mind-numbing loop. There is no way to dramatically slam the door when you have to go back for the coat you left in the room. So she sees Mr. Alvarez and Linda and Cecily and Megan (and Megan and Megan) every day, and anger and fear wear down to stiffness and pursed lips, to curt nods and brisk hellos, until finally she arrives at *Oh, who cares.*

By the time the last weekend of the school year comes around and she picks up Kathy at her parents' house to take the two girls to the mall, Sonia can look Linda in the eye and say, "I'll bring them back in a couple of hours or so" without trying to wriggle free from the interaction. She even considers adding a joke, something about getting the girls high on sugar, but the moment passes.

At the mall Kathy and Mila browse the stores and Sonia does some of her own uninterested perusal, holding up a garment here and there, looking around to make sure the girls are still in sight, and very much giving the impression of a shoplifter. They go to the bookstore while Sonia buys a shiny new phone for their new landline and they meet at the food court, where the girls barely touch their meals as they compare their shopping. It is strange, after the last month, to see her daughter so seamlessly fall into this friendship. Kathy turns out to be plainspoken and possessed of many opinions without the need to press them on others, so the sharing of interests between them becomes a joy rather than a contest. And here Mila is, her elbows on the table, hands around a comically large soda, only pausing their discussion for a breathless gulp of Coke, like any other girl.

Mila was late to talk. It was difficult to notice when exactly it became a problem that she wasn't talking, seeing as she had spent nearly two out of the three years of her life in the selfsame state. In the first two years they had had conversations, but they tended to be one-sided and ventriloquistic—the kind that old people with small dogs often have. ("You like belly rubs, don't you? Don't you, now?") Once Mila did speak, it wasn't in the onslaught of words that Sonia had been promised. They were tentative and soft-spoken, but they came with a surprising, fully formed clarity. Her vocabulary was limited in a way Sonia found infinitely endearing, softened at the edges with mispronunciations. Sonia, who had always loved to talk, found herself in the midst of enthusiastic monologues at the littlest prompting from Mila. An enquiry into the contents of a bag of shopping ("What that?") led down a track of tangents so elaborate, she could not recall at the end where it was that they had begun.

Only upon meeting Brady, a ginger-haired boy with remarkable self-possession, at the desolate toddlers' playground in Echo Park did Sonia begin to wonder whether something might be wrong. She didn't realise that Mila had company in the sandpit until Brady's mother told Brady to "leave the nice little girl alone," which prompted Sonia to glance at her daughter. But Mila was just fine—she was moving sand from one bucket to another with the uninterested mechanism of a factory worker, her expression placid, peaceable. The bothering that Brady had been doing, it turned out, was trying to engage her in conversation.

"Want truck?" he said, holding out a small fistful of red plastic. "Good truck. *Big* truck." He went on like this, offering one truck after another like a single-minded car salesman, but Mila only looked at him occasionally, then went back to the important business of her buckets, as if she had a quota to fill.

"She's a little shy, is she?" Brady's mother asked. The first assumption of a mother is never likely to be that someone is simply not interested in her child.

And because Sonia did not yet know of the American convention of highlighting your child's good qualities and hiding her deficiencies, she simply told Brady's mother: "Mila doesn't speak much yet," which, perhaps due to Sonia's surprising candour, was met not with the usual polite "Oh, I see," but with genuine interest.

"How old is she?"

"Just turned three last month."

The woman tried to cover a quick wince with a smile. "Have you been to a speech pathologist with her?"

Sonia looked down at Mila, who looked up at her with what seemed like a slight raise of the eyebrows. She wanted to ask this woman beside her what exactly a speech pathologist did. She wanted to ask whether not knowing meant that it was already too late, whether she should have taken Mila sooner, where else she should have taken her, and many other similar enquiries on the presumption that this woman, who had asked her question with such authority, was an expert in early-childhood development and perhaps could assess all the issues Mila might or might not have. All of these thoughts and feelings she tried to funnel into a single "No," the inflection going up hopefully, questioningly at the end.

The woman hesitated only briefly before she took out a thick leather-bound address book and a notebook and copied out the name and number of a Dr. Marshall and ripped out the page for Sonia like she was the doctor herself, handing Sonia a prescription.

"Sometimes it's to do with neurodevelopmental problems or childhood trauma," she said, but when Sonia took a sharp intake of breath, she added, "Or it could be nothing at all!"

Sonia folded the paper, thanked her and said nothing else because what she really wanted to say was *Stay here and tell me how to do this.*

She kept the folded-up piece of paper in her wallet for years even though she never did take Mila to Dr. Marshall, who turned out to be a private practitioner in Pasadena.

But the fact remained—and with her attention brought to it, it was all too apparent—that Mila did not speak when anyone else was around. Not when Larry came over to fix a plug socket and called her "little lady"; not when they went over to visit with Auntie Jadranka and she sat in the old woman's lap playing with the buttons on her cardigan; not when Sonia took her to work downtown to sit beside her sewing machine among twenty-odd cheek-pinching women; not ever. She spoke only at home, with her.

Sonia could not help but feel the woman's comment wedged uncomfortably where nascent confidence in her mothering had been growing. Something in Mila's brief life—barely more than three years—had distressed her, had made her wary of the world outside their own, and Sonia had failed to protect her from it.

But each year brought new worries to replace the old ones and by the time she reached preschool, Mila was speaking confidently, her vowels rounded, bouncing and American in a way Sonia's never would be.

When they arrive home, Sonia splays out on her living-room floor and begins to set up her new phone. Mila stays nearby with her new books rather than retreating to her room, and Sonia is embarrassingly gratified by her company. But after Mila has gone to bed, Sonia is listless. She looks at the cordless phone as it sits pertly in its docking station, promising long discussions that can be enjoyed in any part of your home. She stares and stares at it, making calculations of time differences and the probability of an answer on the other end until she dials the numbers that spill out as though she uses them every day.

PORCUPINES

"Szia, Apu," she says when the third ring gives way to an answer. "Rég beszéltünk."

And down the line he laughs a little. Yes, it's been a while since they talked.

Mila is ready. She has her diorama in hand, her speech committed to memory and backed up on index cards. She has spent countless hours researching in the library (having voluntarily given up her internet privileges after her misuse of it in the past few months). She knows everything there is to know about the single most influential man in her life. She's ready to tell the world—or at least Mrs. Flores's fifth-grade class—about Dmitry Shostakovich. Mila is aware that an assignment given for the last day of class is generally to be disregarded—if the teachers are finding it hard to drag themselves to the finish line, they can always roll in the TV and VCR and play the class a movie. But when Mrs. Flores reminded all the fifth-graders who had had the privilege of going to San Francisco that they were each to prepare a presentation on a composer of their choice, Mila recognised this as her opportunity for redemption. How this would compensate for having pushed one of her classmates to the floor, caused a scene among her peers and driven her mother to a state of dejection rarely witnessed before in their household was hard to say—but this was the task she was given, and she was determined to rise to it with aplomb.

Standing in front of the class she tells them how Dmitry Shostakovich wanted to be a pianist but they said his style was too dry; she tells them about his opera *Lady Macbeth of Mtsensk* and how dangerous it was that Stalin didn't like it; she tells them how he wrote a piece for as large an orchestra as he could so that by having something to play, the musicians could all earn enough money to afford food. Ending on a bit of a bum note, she tells them about his death in 1975, caused by a combination of motor-neuron disease, lung cancer and heart failure, which she attributes solemnly to his smoking habit. When she's finished, Mrs. Flores leads the stunned class in a short round of polite applause and says, "Thank you, dear, something for us all to ponder over the summer break." Then, because no one else from the trip has bothered to prepare their presentation, Mrs. Flores rolls in the cart.

When the kids are finally let loose, it's like fireworks bursting from their canisters—they spread across the schoolyard, through the front gates and across the parking lot in rushes of summer colours, vibrating with the excitement of nothing to do. Mila spots her mother in her Buick, adjusting her hair in the rearview mirror. When they lock eyes, she gives Mila a quick wink.

When Mila finally packs her schoolbag, lunch box and diorama into the car, Sonia drives on and turns left, the wrong direction for home. Heading off Mila's question, her mother brakes at the stop sign, turns to her and tells her, "Milosh, we're going for a drive. There's someone I want you to meet."

Acknowledgements

THANK YOU TO MY MOTHER—MY FIERCE, FUNNY, ENDLESSLY supportive mother—for everything.

Thanks to my brilliant agents in the UK, Cathryn Summerhayes and Sabhbh Curran, for championing this story from the beginning, and to the wonderful Rebecca Gradinger in the US for all her editorial insight and strategizing. At Curtis Brown, thanks also to Annabel White, Lisa Babalis, and Georgie Mellor, and at UTA thanks to Madison Hernick and Geritza Carasco.

This book would be a mess without my two wonderful editors who worked with me tirelessly. Helen Garnons-Williams: I never thought anyone else could care about the text as much as I do, down to every plot point and word choice, and yet I have long email chains to prove it. Thank you. At Summit, thanks to the fabulous Judy Clain for caring so much about Sonia and Mila. Thank you to Kevwe Okumakube, who provided brilliant notes on the manuscript and held my hand throughout the publishing process. At Summit thanks also to Josefine Kals in publicity and Anna Skrabacz in marketing, as well as Dana Li and Math Monahan for the wonderful cover and Tracy Roe and Kayley Hoffman for saving me from many a malapropism in the copyedit. Thanks also to Rebecca Munro for the proofread and Josh Cohen for the cold read. At Fig Tree, thank you to Olivia Mead and Jane Gentle

ACKNOWLEDGEMENTS

in publicity and Kayla Fuller in marketing, as well as Savreet Virk, and Richard Bravery for the brilliant UK cover.

I don't know if you can teach writing, but I have greatly benefited from the wisdom of people who have undertaken the task. Thank you to Chris Power, who had the dubious honour of reading my first-ever short story, and was kind enough not to dissuade me from trying again. Thanks to KJ Orr and Andrew Michael Hurley at Arvon for their early encouragement. There are many people to thank at UEA: Andrew Cowan and Ashley Hickson-Lovence for the best workshops; Julianne Pachico, for pushing me to answer the difficult questions in the narrative, and for her impeccable book recommendations; Naomi Wood for being an early champion of this project and thereby making its publication a possibility.

English is not my first language, and so English literature is not my primary canon either—I'm very thankful to Toby Scammel and Dr. Michelle Gemelos for their literary instruction; I wish I could have gone on studying with you forever. Thanks also to Dec Munro, comedy teacher extraordinaire. Thanks must also go to all the people (besides my incredibly hardworking mother) who helped me in acquiring my education: László Szalai, Csilla Szalai, István Heinczinger, and Judit Golub.

I was fortunate to have many people offer their time and knowledge as I did research for the novel. Thank you to Liran Morav for his help connecting me to a wider net; Eitan Morav for speaking to me about his experiences; my aunt Dorothy Gaspar, for sharing all her stories about our family; Daphne Orenshein, Linda Abraham, and Rachel Lewis for speaking to me about Orthodox Jewish life in Los Angeles; Slomo Koves, for his insights on Hungarian Jews; Peter Kenez for speaking to me about Hungarian Jews in America; Laszlo Borhi for his insights on Cold War relations

ACKNOWLEDGEMENTS

between the two countries; Hirokazu Yoshikawa for speaking to me about the impacts of illegal immigration on children; and Abbie Davis for providing fascinating details on playing the violin in an orchestra, and making me wish I'd stuck with it.

Thank you to the many people who read fragments, chapters, sections of this work: Anushe Khan Pagnier, Ellen Wiese, Georgia Campbell, Sarah Norek, April Yee, Kimberly Bliss, and Shira Erlichman. Special thanks to Ned Carter Miles, Eimear Arthur, and Lottie Hayes-Clemens for reading the entire manuscript and providing invaluable feedback. Thanks also to Dushi Horti for sitting down to write with me, even if our writing sessions devolved into gossip most of the time. Thanks to both Dushi Horti and Sam Horti for giving their advice throughout the publishing process— no one does a pro/con list better than you guys. Thanks to Sophie Burks for reminding me that there's light at the end of the writing tunnel. Thank you to Matthew Grant for being the first one to say, simply, that I could be a writer.

Thank you to my sister, for being my best friend, my number one fan, and my personal hotline for all Jewish questions.

Thank you to my father, who did not have a chance to read this book and find out exactly how I made use of the hours of knowledge he imparted as I wrote it. I like to imagine my interpretation would have sparked a lively debate between us.

Thank you to my son, for inspiring me to finish this novel before he took over my life; and for making it such a joy for that life to be completely overwhelmed by him when he arrived.

And finally, thank you to Adam. To rephrase Jane Austen a little: If you had given me less, I might be able to talk about it more.